My Heart's Desire

by

Heather Alexander

The Kincaid Brothers, Book Two

Cover Art by *The Wild Rose Press, Inc.*

The Wild Rose Press, Inc.
PO Box 708
Adams Basin, NY 14410-0708
Visit us at www.thewildrosepress.com

Publishing History
First Edition, 2025
Trade Paperback ISBN 978-1-5092-5915-1
Digital ISBN 978-1-5092-5916-8

The Kincaid Brothers, Book Two
Published in the United States of America

Dedication

This book is dedicated to my cousin, Anne. Thank you for your constant support and love.

And for my three fur babies in heaven, Emma, Rascal, and Fergus, always in my heart.

Chapter One

Whisper Creek, Montana—August, Present Day

Amber Harrison strode into the Law Office of Matheson & Kincaid, breezed past the receptionist, and burst through the doors into the oversized corner office. "James, you have to send me back to 1883!"

"What the hell are you talking about? No one's going anywhere, especially you." James shot up from behind his mahogany desk. He was clad in a pressed navy suit, crisp blue shirt, and shined shoes. His blond hair was a disheveled mess as if he'd been running his hands through it. "But if you keep talking crazy, I'm going to send your ass back to New York City."

"C'mon, I'm serious!"

He rounded the desk, taking in her appearance, and pulled long blades of grass from her hair. "Look at you. Your jeans—they're ripped with mud stains. You look like my brother Josh, as a kid, after a fight on the playground. What happened?"

Over the course of the last year, thanks to Emma's one-time reappearance from the nineteenth century, Amber and James became good friends, developing a relationship akin to sister and brother. If her best friend hadn't gone back through the time portal and returned to her time-traveling cowboy husband in 1882, none of this would be happening.

"Not funny. I faceplanted, all right?" The stinging

sensation in her scraped knees and palms was a reminder. She bent her legs and winced. "You're the only one who can help me. I have to go back to Emma. Now!"

He gripped her shoulders. "Slow down. Let's start at the beginning. What's all this about?"

Amber closed her eyes for a quick second, let out a heavy breath, and grabbed her cell phone from her back pocket. She searched for the images she'd taken at the cemetery a half hour ago and handed her phone to James. "Look at these. I got here as fast as I could. Please…"

James scrolled through a dozen pictures. His brows furrowed, and his tanned face lost a bit of color. "What the hell is this?"

"What does it look like? It's Emma and Wyatt's tombstones!"

"Okay, calm down." His voice was soothing with brotherly concern. "Where did you find these?"

"I was on a historic cemetery tour," Amber explained, talking with animated hands. "I thought it would be cool, you know, see the old graves and all that. Idiot me tripped and fell flat right in front of…of their tombstones. Anyway," she said, waving his hands away as he pulled more grass from her hair. "I had my sketch pad with me, as always, because this creative director never leaves home without it." She plopped her handbag on his desk, pulled out the tracings she made of the tombstones, and handed them over. "You know I'm always accidentally deleting my photos, so I wanted backup."

The sketches were even more spine-tinglingly eerie than the photos. They featured two solid objects. Two tombstones. She had *touched* them, *inhaled* their mineral odors, *traced* the lettering with her own trembling hands:

Emma Kincaid 1883
Wyatt Kincaid 1883

Amber missed Emma so much her heart ached. They had known each other since birth. She scarcely owned a childhood memory that did not include her. Over the years, they'd grown to be more than friends. They were family.

Only now, Emma was gone, just like everyone special in her life. If only she could reach her friend in time, Amber might be able to save her.

James ran a hand over his face and cleared his throat. His voice was low and quiet when he spoke. "Did you…did you happen to see a tombstone for my brother, Josh, too? He's with them. And what about the baby? Emma was pregnant when we saw her last year."

She shook her head. "No, just Emma and Wyatt."

He swallowed, and his Adam's apple bobbed up and down. "I'll make copies of these. And please send me all the photos you snapped."

"Sure." She took her phone back and, with shaky fingers, quickly emailed him all the images. "The tombstones…they're both dated 1883. That's one year after Emma went back in time to stay with Wyatt."

"Unfortunately, we don't know the exact date. It could be any month that year."

"True." Amber paced. "All right. Let's think about this." She grabbed a tendril of hair in each of her hands and twirled them into ropes. It was a nervous habit she had since childhood and one she couldn't shake. The motion of her fingers coiling around her hair had a soothing effect. "Maybe Emma and Wyatt got sick and died unexpectedly with some kind of dreaded disease. We've all read and heard about how filthy the nineteenth century could be." She stopped pacing to face him. "Right?"

James ran a hand through his thick hair and shrugged. "It would be hard to fathom that some terrible disease could've taken them down so quickly, but anything is possible. I'd hate to think…" His voice trailed off.

"Or…what if…what if Emma died in childbirth along with her baby, and being so distraught over their deaths, Wyatt killed himself?"

"I know my brother. And for as much grief as he suffered when our parents tragically died together, it would be hard for me to comprehend him taking his own life…no matter how much pain he was in."

She threw up her hands. "What if they were in a horrible accident or if someone, I don't know, hurt them or killed them for some reason? A lot of crazy shit happened in that backward century."

One dark blond brow arched. "Like a gunfight at high noon?"

"C'mon, be serious, James." She bit her bottom lip. "But…isn't it a possibility, considering that's the era they're in? They didn't call it the Wild West for nothing."

"I get your point."

She twirled her hair again. "Ugh, I don't know what I'm saying. I'm just trying to reason through all this."

He walked up to her, pried one of her hands away from her hair twirling, and squeezed it. "Me too. And we will figure it out."

The two of them had spent many hours in this office, discussing the time portal, theories about how it came to be, and getting drunk on James's favorite scotch. Amber never liked single malt before, but she learned to appreciate it, having been to several distilleries after college thanks to a Scottish ex-boyfriend.

"Last year," Amber began, "when Emma told me she would be returning to Wyatt in the nineteenth century, I was gobsmacked. How could my best friend give up *me*, her friends, her business, her life, in this century for your brother who's from here, too, but chose to live in a bygone era? I didn't…couldn't…understand. And I still don't."

"No one gets how you feel more than I do. I lost both my brothers because they, too, chose the Old West instead of returning home. I'm stuck running Wyatt's construction business that I have no mindset for, and I'm handling the firm all by myself." He grunted. "There isn't enough money to pay me to ever go through that damn portal."

She folded her arms across her chest. "Emma better be happy with her decision, because now it may cost her their lives. Your brothers are being complete selfish jerks."

"That they are," he said. "Until they return home from playing cowboys, there's not much I can do."

"Well, if you're not going to go back in time to bring them home, then I will," she said, thrusting her hands on her hips. "Emma's my best friend, and Wyatt and Josh are your brothers. They all belong *here*…that is, if they're still alive, which I hope they are." She swallowed back the rising scream in her throat. "So how do I do it? How do I go through the time portal?"

James stood up and faced her. "I don't think sending you back in time is the best idea, Amber. My whole family is stuck in 1883, as is your best friend, and no one has returned. They could be dead the year you go back to, for all we know. I don't want to risk losing you, too."

"Then I'll go without your help. I know the portal is in the barn on Emma's property. I'll figure it out myself, but I have to try and save them…if it's not too late," she added and turned to go.

James grabbed her arm. "Wait," he said with a sigh. "I'll help you."

She smiled. "You're the best!"

"And woman, that's for certain. Are you sure we're not related?" Releasing her arm, he walked over to the fancy oak bar and poured them each a scotch. "All right, then. To time portals and, hopefully, saving the day."

They clinked glasses.

"I'll drink to that."

****

Yesterday, before Amber left James's office, they both agreed to meet at Emma's place in the morning. While Amber was eager to find her best friend, she was grateful for the extra hours to do a little online research on 1880s Whisper Creek. It would better prepare her for what she was about to encounter. After seeing some old photographs of the town, the false-fronted buildings, and its dirt roads, not to mention the suffocating way the men and women dressed in too many layers of clothes from head to toe, she almost had second thoughts…*almost.* But her best friend's life was at stake.

Amber trudged into the living room, lifting the hem of her skirt. The hideous heels clacked against the wood floor, squishing her feet. "All right, the clothes fit," she admitted, then twirled around. "But how do I look? If you say ridiculous, I'm going to smack you."

"You look great." James grinned. "And once you're

there, I'm sure Emma will have you outfitted in whatever the women are wearing in those days."

"I don't plan to be there long enough to get new clothes." She flexed her hands. "Will it…hurt? I mean, the trip," she said, using air quotes. "Will I get zapped with lightning or see my life flash before my eyes, anything like that?"

James shrugged. "I'm afraid I don't know what the actual passage is like. Based on what Emma said, once you get there, it shouldn't feel like more than a nasty hangover."

"Hangover. Super fun. I can't wait."

Amber didn't have the slightest clue what would happen to her during her trip through the portal or once she arrived. Would she be *floating* or *walking* through the portal? Would she be conscious or unconscious?

One thing was for certain: it would be better to choose comfort over fashion in case she landed hard on her feet. Her workout sneakers were next to the sofa, where she had kicked them off earlier. Those would do.

"All right, the clothes can stay." She unlaced the bothersome shoes. "The heels gotta go. I'm wearing my sneakers, so don't argue with me on this one because you will lose." Tossing the ancient shoes aside, she slipped into her preferred footwear. "Much better." She turned to James; uncertainty tingled in her veins, and reality sank in. "What if…what if I get there but can't get back? Or what if I…I don't make it there? What if I get stuck between time zones or centuries or burn up in a flash that has to do with space-time continuum mumbo jumbo that I clearly know nothing about?"

He shrugged. "There's always that possibility. We don't know much about the portal, how it works, or its origin, which is why I don't think you should go. You're taking a big risk."

She scrunched up her face. "Did you have to put it that way?"

"I'm just reminding you of what you're taking on here."

"I have no choice. Emma is my person. I was mad at her when she chose to go back, but—" She paused. "She's my best friend in the entire world, and she's all I have left. I have to save her and Wyatt…or at least try to. I promise I'll do my best to bring them all back. Josh, too."

He gave her arm a gentle squeeze. "You're brave, Amber. I admire you. And I know how much you love Emma. I love Josh and Wyatt the same." He cleared his throat and said in a scratchy tone, "I wish I was going with you."

"No, you don't," she reminded him. "Besides, it's better that you stay here and protect the portal. I don't know if there's anything you can do on this end to secure our safe return, but just knowing you're here waiting for me, for us, is a big help. Plus, if anyone on your staff found out, they'd think you've gone bonkers and totally lost it. A few fries short of a happy—"

"Point taken." He took her hand and placed one of the photos she had taken at the cemetery in her palm. "Don't forget this."

She stuffed the picture into her skirt pocket. "Got it."

"Now, put this on." He handed her a gold chain bracelet. She'd recognize the designer anywhere. *Emma*.

She lifted her gaze to him. "How'd you get this?"

"Emma left it behind last year. We don't fully

understand how this time portal works. As far as any of us know, to make it through the portal, you need a token from the time you want to go to and return to. This is yours."

"That's fine for going there, but what about the return trip?"

"Your earrings should do, plus your sneakers are back up…I would think."

The mini gold hoop earrings were a gift from Emma. She had made them for Amber's birthday before coming out to Montana last year. Amber never took them off. She put the delicate bracelet on and gazed up at him. "I guess I should go, then."

"I'll wait here for a while. Keep in mind, though, there's nothing I can do if you don't make it—and I wouldn't know that."

"Thanks, that's reassuring."

"Come on," he said, taking her elbow. "I'll walk you to the garage."

They walked toward the structure housing the gateway that would send Amber to another world, another time. She swallowed the rising lump in her throat. The adrenaline coursing through her system operated in overdrive. This was either the bravest decision she ever made…or the dumbest.

"Deep breaths. You'll be all right." James stopped outside the garage and turned to face her. "This is where I leave you, my friend. Wyatt is a neat freak, as you'll see. I haven't moved a thing in the garage. And don't forget the blue chalk outline I drew. That's where the portal should be—"

"Oh, great," she interjected. "I just hope you don't end up with a chalk outline of my body in there, too."

She waved a hand. "Sorry. You were saying…?"

"The portal is on the far wall. When you see the outline, step inside it. Before you know it, you should be reunited with Emma."

"Got it." Amber hated goodbyes. There were too many in her life to count, especially from those whom she loved most. This wasn't goodbye, she reminded herself. She'd be back soon. At least she hoped.

She grabbed James for a quick hug and then turned toward the oversized three-car garage, wondering what her surroundings would look like when—or rather, if—she made it to the nineteenth century. Emma had conveyed what her *personal* trip through the portal was like, and the feelings she had experienced after, but it was hard for Amber to conceive. Hopefully, the trip wouldn't be too bad.

Out of the two of them, Emma had always been the calm one, serene under any type of pressure. Amber, not so much. Right now, she was a wreck, though she tried to keep it together. She wiped her sweaty palms on her skirt and chanted: *stay calm, stay calm, stay calm.* Closing her eyes for a few seconds, she counted backward from ten.

She opened her eyes and glanced over her shoulder at James. He waved at her, and then she turned and walked through the side door of the garage.

James wasn't kidding. Neat freak was an understatement. The garage was impeccable. The floors were painted a soft gray. Who paints their garage floors? The three-car garage was twice the size of her and Emma's first New York City apartment. A family of five could have lived in here and still have room. The entire rear wall consisted of a storage unit with drawers, shelves, and hooks to hang tools. Everything had its own place. The two vehicles belonging to Wyatt remained parked side by side as they had been since he went through the portal over two and a half years ago.

With each tentative step, her pulse raced like a stock car zipping around the speedway at two hundred miles an hour. Her gaze darted everywhere. She waited, expecting something to happen.

The air was cool, and a gentle breeze stirred within the garage. The chalk outline James had mentioned was visible at the rear of the garage. *Shit just got real.* Slowly, she walked toward the outline, stopped for a few seconds, and then stepped inside it.

A small tremor quickly turned into a resounding rumble, shaking the ground as if a freight train whizzed by at warp speed. She glanced around, expecting her surroundings to change. However, nothing appeared different.

Her world suddenly shifted and blurred. Darkness teased her senses, threatening to overtake her, but it was instantaneously replaced with a blue-white light. Everything went dead silent. Fear coiled around her chest, nearly choking the breath from her. She reached out to grab the side mirror on one of Wyatt's cars to get her bearings, but she lost her balance and stumbled toward daylight seeping in through the oversized door.

Once outside, Amber turned and looked behind her. The meticulous three-car garage morphed into a tall wooden barn with its double doors flung wide open. Inside, bales and loose hay lay scattered on the floor. Her stomach clenched, and she swallowed hard to keep the nausea at bay. A golden horse grazed in a small paddock. There was a windmill and tank of some kind behind the barn and chicken coop. Straight ahead was a house. While the house looked the same, nothing else was familiar.

"Did I make it?" Nothing among her surroundings assured her that she had been transported to the correct year. Forcing herself to put one foot in front of the other, she walked toward the house. Her anxiety was on the rise. She sucked in a few deep breaths, but her mind wouldn't shut off. *Shit, what if Emma and Wyatt are already dead, and I'm too late? What if I get stuck here?*

With each step, her legs trembled. She finally reached the back door and raised a shaking hand to knock. "Hello?" Her voice sounded unsteady, even to her own ears. "Emma…? Wyatt…? Are you guys in there?" She pressed her nose up to the glass door, cupping her hands around her eyes to peek inside, but the curtain obstructed her view.

She took a few steps back and assessed the house again. It sure looked like Emma's house in her own time, minus the newer siding, roof, and attractive landscaping. "This has to be right."

Her heart thundered, but that didn't stop her from turning the handle. She opened the door and stepped inside. "Hello…?" she called out again, this time with a little more oomph. "Anybody home?"

The house was silent. The aroma of fresh brewed coffee permeated the air. Someone had to have made that coffee. Where were they? She gripped the edge of the nearest counter to steady herself and her spinning head. Gone were all the modern appliances, furnishings, and décor. Instead, this kitchen consisted of flowery wallpaper, dark stained wood plank floors, and a large wood-burning stove. An array of pots and pans, copper and cast-iron, hung from wooden pegs on the wall.

"I feel like I'm losing my mind."

She had to find out just *where in time* she landed and if, indeed, this was Emma's house. Maybe Emma or Wyatt kept a current newspaper somewhere. If she could get her hands on one, that would at least give her an indication on whether she landed in the right year.

Searching the kitchen, she came up empty. She staggered down the hall, toward the study. The room should be in the same place as the house in the future. Lucky for her, it was, and eerily so. It resembled the room in her own time but with a different desk, this one ornately carved. Everything smelled of fresh wood, like recently cut lumber.

"Don't move," a deep, masculine voice commanded.

Amber froze. The hair on the back of her neck stood up. Waves of fear poured down her spine.

"Hands where I can see them," the voice continued.

Amber thrust her hands straight up into the air. Her stomach burned, fear roiling in its depths. If she didn't have an ulcer when this over, it would be a miracle. She closed her eyes for a second, hoping the voice belonged to Wyatt. Because if it wasn't him, or she was in the wrong year, surely, she was dead. Trespassing was against the law even in this backward time. Great, and she didn't think it was possible for her anxiety level to climb any higher.

"Turn around…slowly."

The initial signs of an oncoming panic attack banged at the door to her senses. Her heart pounded, her chest tightened, and her head spun like she'd just come off the tilt-a-whirl at the amusement park. But she did as she was told and inched herself around, one baby step at a time.

If anything confirmed her trip back in time one hundred and forty years, this was it. The cowboy standing before her was tall, over six feet, and clad in what she expected to see a man from the 1880s to be dressed in. He wore an unbuttoned vest over a linen shirt with the sleeves rolled up to his elbows. His pants were super snug, and his dusty cowboy boots covered his legs from the knees down. The empty holster sat low over his right hip, and the silver spurs at his heels clanked as he moved toward her.

"W-Wyatt?" She swallowed nervously, lowering her hands. "D-don't shoot!"

Dark blond brows shot up when she said his name, but he waved the gun and took another step toward her. "I didn't say you could lower your hands."

Oh, shit!

She thrust her hands up again. "You…you are Wyatt, aren't you? Wyatt Kincaid. Please tell me you are. Otherwise, I'm seriously screwed…in more ways than you could possibly imagine."

Mesmerizing green eyes widened, and then his gaze swept over her from head to toe but remained on her feet. "I'd recognize twenty-first century sneakers anywhere." He tipped his chin toward her footwear, but his gun remained aimed at her.

Relief surged through her, and she sagged a little. This must be Emma's husband. Now she understood what compelled her best friend to return to a previous century. *Emma, you got yourself one fine husband.* Out of all the details Emma revealed about Wyatt last year, Amber didn't recall anything about him having such compelling green eyes. It was difficult to look away, not that she wanted to, she *had* to. This was her best friend's husband. Chalk it up to her time-travel muddled mind.

He took a step toward her and tilted his head to study her. "I'm guessing you're…Amber?"

"Uh-huh. That's right." She nodded, still a little stunned. "Where's Emma? I need to see her."

His scowl quickly turned into a smile, and he holstered his gun. "Wow, the famous Amber Harrison in the flesh."

He recognized her! Inside, she jumped up and down with excitement. "You know me? Wait, I don't know how that's possible. We've never met."

"I recognize you from a photo Emma brought back with her last year…but you're mistaken about who I am."

She retreated a step. "If…if you're not Wyatt Kincaid, then who are you?"

His smile widened, and he extended his hand. "Hi, I'm Josh. Wyatt and James's brother."

Chapter Two

Whisper Creek, Montana—Early August, 1883
Amber did a mental facepalm. She had never met
Wyatt before and assumed the first man she saw on
Emma's property was her best friend's husband. Now
that she'd met Josh, she could see the resemblance
between him and James, but there were differences, too.
Josh's eyes were a more glorious green, a different color
entirely than his brother James's. And Josh's face was
more chiseled and defined with high cheekbones. He had
a few extra laugh lines around his mouth and at the
corners of his eyes. Maybe they were from rough living
in the nineteenth century. But, wow, was he handsome.

"Hi," she said at last, shaking his hand. The
tightness in her chest eased, and she could breathe
normally now. "Oh God, Josh, it never even occurred to
me that you would be here instead of Wyatt. At first, I
thought you were a crazy man about to shoot me for
trespassing."

"I was about to," he admitted, hiding a smile when
she gasped. "That is, until I spotted your fancy
footwear."

"I'm glad you said something before I died of a heart
attack." She pulled her hand away and glanced around
before turning back to Josh. "Wait, what year is this?
Where's Emma? Please tell me it's still 1883!"

"Yes, it's still 1883. Emma is fine, but I think you

need to sit down for a bit. The trip through the portal is unlike anything you've ever experienced before. I know firsthand, so, let's get you somewhere more comfortable."

Without arguing, she followed him into the parlor. He gestured to the sofa while he poured a glass of water from an earthenware pitcher and handed it to her. "Now, why don't you tell me why you came all this way. For you to be here, I'm sure there's a good reason."

"There is." Settling on the sofa, she took a few sips. The water was room-temperature and tasted minerally.

Her gaze went from Josh to her surroundings. Everything seemed eerily familiar…but different. The room resembled the one she had just been in with James, except for the décor, wood beams, and fieldstone fireplace. The wall above the mantle was missing the scenic painting of Glacier National Park with its snow-capped mountains in the distance. The furnishings were nineteenth-century Western though they were new.

"What I'm going to tell you is probably going to come as a shock," she said at last.

"You mean more of a shock than you traveling one hundred and forty years into the past and me finding you in the study?" he teased.

"Yeah, I think so."

His left eyebrow rose a fraction. "Then please, go on."

With shaky fingers, she put the glass on the table. "I came across two tombstones at the old churchyard. They belong to Emma and Wyatt."

"Well, I certainly wouldn't expect they'd be celebrating their one-hundred-and-seventy-something birthday this year. Considering they hadn't made it back to their own time yet, you were bound to find their tombstones." He paused. "Just out of curiosity, what were the dates engraved on them?"

"There were no dates, only their names and the year, this year, 1883."

Josh stiffened and ran a hand over his face. His tanned skin took on a paler hue. "How could this...? I don't..." He didn't finish either thought. Instead, he paced, and then turned to face her, waiting for her to continue.

"It's why I had to come, to warn them and prevent this from happening. That is, if I can and if it's not too late."

"It's not too late. Emma and Wyatt are fine; they're both alive. I heard from Wyatt this morning."

"Heard from...?" Amber closed her eyes. She didn't feel well. The room was spinning. Her mouth was desert dry like enduring a bad cold for a week.

Josh sat down next to her and placed his hand on her arm. "Are you okay? I mean, from the trip here. You look a little shaken."

"Shaken, not stirred?" she joked. "I don't know yet." The feeling, the vibe, in the house, was the same as Emma's house in her own time. How could that be? The entire trip through the centuries was quickly catching up to her.

"I think you're experiencing what we've been calling time travel sickness," he explained. "Wyatt, Emma, and I have all been subject to what you're feeling now."

She rubbed her temples. "James said it would feel like a bad hangover. He was wrong. This is a hangover with the bed spins."

"Ouch, yeah. Maybe you should lay down for a while."

"No, I'll be all right. I just need some aspirin or something."

"I hate to break it to you, but aspirin won't be invented for another decade and a half. And laudanum is way too strong and addictive. Instead, why don't we get you some coffee?"

Amber smiled and stood up. "Sounds like a plan. Whoa." She swayed, and Josh gripped her arms to steady her. "I'm okay, thanks."

"You sure?" When she nodded, he gave her arms a gentle squeeze before letting go. "Come on."

She followed him into the kitchen, he pulled out a chair for her. "Talk about bizarro. This experience would definitely make for a good TV movie. Maybe I should take notes and write my own script, *The Diary of a Time-Traveling City Girl*. This whole thing is surreal."

"That it is," he said, reaching for a blue enamel coffee pot on the stove.

She'd seen pots like that one in cowboy movies. Thankfully, the stove wasn't on. The room was already too warm—or maybe it was just her.

"I made a pot earlier, but I'll need to heat it up outside. Be right back." He was gone barely a few seconds before ambling through the door. "It's too hot to cook inside during the summer, so Wyatt and I made an outdoor grill," he explained. "Coffee should be ready in a few minutes."

"Okay." She nodded. "Now, please tell me where Emma is and when she'll be back. I need to see her."

He ran a hand through the tufts of blond hair, and the locks fell onto his forehead. "They went away for a little while, a mini vacation of sorts."

She squinted, studying his features. "What aren't you telling me?"

He leaned against the counter, crossing his ankles, and folded his arms across his chest. "Someone tried to hurt Wyatt…and Emma. Wyatt was shot at, more than once, and a wheel on Emma's wagon came unhinged while she was riding back from town. Emma got a little freaked out and begged Wyatt to take her away for a while, to get a break from everything."

Thanks to her time-travel-fogged brain, it took a moment for his words to register. "Hang on a sec. Are you telling me someone is out to get Emma and Wyatt?"

He turned to gaze out the window. "Actually, that's a possibility."

"Who would want to hurt either of them?" Her eyes widened. "Oh my God, maybe that's why I found their tombstones! Someone is trying to hurt them, but who?"

Josh turned to her; anger filled his eyes. "The only person I can think of who has a beef with Wyatt is Grey."

She racked her scrambled brain for the source of the familiar name. "Are you talking about the same Grey who started those fires in town after Emma arrived last year? *That* Grey?"

He nodded. "Yep. Griffin Grey. After his trial, he was transferred from the local jail to a prison within the territory. However, with these incidents happening with Wyatt and Emma, we think Grey might have someone working on the outside."

"No wonder Emma wanted to get away. Where did they go?"

"They're staying at a friend's cabin on the outskirts of Montana City. They didn't want to take any chances, especially now that they have Wesley."

"Emma had a boy? Oh, thank God. I've heard nightmare stories about women dying in childbirth." She gushed, thinking of how beautiful and sweet their baby must be. "Aww, I can't wait to meet him. It's hard to believe Emma's a mom. Tell me, what's my honorary nephew like?"

Josh's face went from serious to joy in a split second. "Wesley is a little spitfire, that's for sure. You'll love him. He keeps Emma on her toes. In another year or two, he'll be as troublesome as Wyatt was when he was a kid."

Amber bit her lip, and then said, "I miss Emma, and I so want to meet Wesley. When are they coming back?"

"I'm not sure. Wyatt said before they head home, he'll send me a wire."

"A wire?"

"The telegram is the fastest mode of communication here these days."

"What happened to the Pony Express?"

He chuckled. "They went out of business in 1861. There's been some technological advancements since then."

Amber remembered the photo in her pocket and pulled it out. The sheer image sent her body reeling. She handed it to Josh. "We have to find out what happened—or happens—to them. They could die tomorrow for all we know. They need to come back here sooner than later. I'll feel better once they return."

Josh examined the photo. "I can assure you, right now, Wyatt and his family are safe. The only person we trust in Montana City is our friend, Marshal Kane. They're staying at his cabin."

"And what about this Grey you mentioned?" She was terrified that something bad might happen to Emma and her family, which would bring their names on the tombstones to fruition. "Why does he have it in so bad for Wyatt?"

"A few reasons. One, he thinks Wyatt is the one who got him arrested and thrown in jail. Technically, that would be the both of us, me and Wyatt."

She waited. "And?"

"And…what?"

"You said there were a few reasons. What are the others?"

"Emma," he stated. "Let's just say Grey was…jealous of Wyatt."

She waved a hand. "He's shooting at Wyatt because he married Emma? Oh, puh-leeeeze. That's just the stupidest thing I've ever heard."

"This is the nineteenth century, and I guess he thought the lawmen weren't too swift back then—er, now. When narcissists like Grey are outsmarted, they don't take too well to it. That's when they plan some kind of terror tactic or the like."

"I'm not buying it. There's something more. You know it, and I know it."

Josh nodded. "I agree with you. Maybe it has something to do with me being from the future, too. Maybe Grey wants control of the portal. Unfortunately, I don't know what that other reason is yet, but I plan on finding out."

"At this point, it doesn't really matter. Once Wyatt and Emma get back, we're all leaving this place for good." She was already counting down the minutes.

His green eyes flared with uncertainty. "And how do

you suggest we do that?"

"Through the portal, genius. How else?"

"Shit." He dropped his head back to stare at the ceiling, and then met her gaze. "Houston, we've got a problem, a big one."

"Nothing can be bigger than Emma and Wyatt's names appearing on the tombstones."

"This is a close second," he admitted. "The portal isn't working for us. We've been trying to go back to the twenty-first century for months, since before Wesley was born. Now, we're all stuck in 1883. Me, Emma, Wyatt, Wesley…and now, you."

****

Josh certainly hadn't meant to dump bad news on Amber that way. He should've used a little more finesse. Then again, he hadn't expected his sister-in-law's best friend to show up on his doorstep. Talk about a shock to his system. He and Wyatt had been trying everything humanly possible to return through the portal, but to no avail. And here she comes waltzing right through, falling back in time, like nothing was wrong with it.

Now, she was trapped along with them, and there was no telling for how long.

When he had first walked into the study and found a woman about to raid Wyatt's desk, he thought she was a trespasser, possibly sent by Grey. She turned around, and his heart leapt. Women of his current time wore their hair swept back or up into some sort of fancy coif. Amber's auburn hair was loose and hugging her shoulders. It wasn't until he noticed her footwear that it dawned on him who she was. And for all that Emma had told him about Amber, he never thought she'd be here…and this stunning.

Unfortunately, she had come with some dire news about his family. He had a hard time digesting it. With someone seemingly out to hurt his brother and Emma, now their names on the tombstones made sense. He would do everything in his power to save them in time.

"I'm sorry," Josh told her, his voice low. "I didn't mean to spring the news on you like that, but I also never expected you to venture into the past."

He sat next to her and took her shaking hand in his. Her skin was smooth, like satin; but her palms were clammy, probably from nervousness. Clasping her hand was solid, undeniable proof she was in his current time.

"Me neither," she said. "And I wouldn't have, but I saw their tombstones…I had to come." She squared her shoulders and lifted her chin. "I can't be stuck here, not in this century. What's wrong with the portal?"

"We have no idea. Wyatt and I tried several times to go back to our own time, but we couldn't. All our tokens aren't functioning the way they're supposed to, either. The portal must be broken."

She frowned. "Emma was able to return last year."

"Yes, she was." He nodded. "As her pregnancy advanced, Emma wanted her baby to be born in the twenty-first century. That's why we tried so many times. Personally, I think she was afraid to have the baby at home."

"Maybe it didn't have anything to do with the baby and everything to do with returning to the time she's supposed to be in," Amber insisted.

"I can't argue that. Still, we don't have a user manual for the portal, but we'll figure it out somehow."

"You haven't been able to make it work in all these months," she said slowly. "What makes you so certain you will now?" She pushed herself out of the chair and paced, albeit unsteadily, twirling the ends of her auburn locks. "I had a bad feeling about this trip from the beginning."

He got up from the chair and put his hands on her shoulders, forcing her to stop pacing and face him. If it had been in his power to prevent Amber from making the one-way trip so she wouldn't get stuck there alongside them, he would've.

"I know this may sound silly or naïve, but I believe in my heart there was a reason Wyatt, Emma, and I all ended up in the nineteenth century for an extended stay," he told her, his hands still on her shoulders. "I don't know what that reason is, nor do I understand why we were allowed to make this journey. I am confident that since we found a way here, we'll find a way to return home…for good."

Baby blue eyes fringed with sooty lashes, sparkling with worry, gazed up at him. "And until then…?"

"Until then, all of us need to keep living our lives."

"Super." Amber pulled away from him and sat down. She looked out the window before facing him. "Don't you want to go home, Josh?"

He was taken aback by that. "Of course, I do. Why would you ask me that?"

"It doesn't seem that way, not to James. You and Wyatt have been here longer than he ever thought you'd stay."

"That's because—"

She held up a hand. "When Wyatt first fell through time and landed here, you managed to find a way to go after him. Why didn't you both return then?"

No one in their nineteenth-century world knew from

where he and Wyatt truly came. He couldn't talk about the portal with anyone else outside his family…until now. Amber was almost family, to Emma, anyhow. From what Emma had told him, they'd been best friends since they were born.

"I never thought we'd stay this long," he admitted. "Before I got here, Wyatt had made friends with some of the locals. Our neighbor Sam runs a horse farm, so he ended up giving Wyatt a few horses in exchange for help with wells, upgrades to his barn, and other mechanical contraptions around the ranch. As I'm sure you know, Wyatt has his own construction company in our own time, so he has the experience needed to build and renovate homes. He's got a small woodworking shop in town here, too. This house has his renovation stamp on it."

"I thought he built this house from the foundation up?"

"Nope. The house was abandoned and in need of major restoration, so Wyatt bought the property from the town."

"That would explain why Emma's name was on the deed, too. You know, the one she got last year in our own time with that letter from her nineteenth-century self."

He nodded. "Wyatt added Emma's name after they married. Anyway, when I showed up months after Wyatt first arrived, it was like we had been transported to a fantasy world. At first, it was fun and exciting. Wyatt and I were time travelers in the Old West. We had no responsibilities, no one to answer to, no bills, no memories here, nothing. Before I left my own time, I bought some old currency from this era. I figured we might need it. Plus, I wasn't sure how long we'd be here for. It's a good thing I did, too, because we were able to use that for major purchases. Wyatt and I needed an escape after our parents died," he added quietly.

She tilted her head, her blue eyes assessing him. "Did you ever think about James? He's been trying to keep everything running without you two. Do you think he needed *this*—your disappearance—after your parents died?"

He waved a hand. "James is more than all right. He's always been our guardian, our protector. This gives him a little breather from us, an escape, for a bit."

"Your brother is paying for your irresponsibility. How is that a breather for him?"

He frowned. "What do you mean?"

"Put yourself in his shoes. How do you think James feels, knowing his little brothers deserted him to play cowboys in the Old West without giving a flying fudgesicle as to what he's going through back home? And that's not all. You two have been gone for years now. People are sniffing around, questioning him regarding your whereabouts."

"Before I came back for Wyatt, I spoke to all our friends. James and I made up a story about me meeting up with Wyatt on a long-term survival trip across Africa. Who was asking?"

She rolled her eyes. "Apparently, your ex-girlfriend is getting married and wanted closure."

"Ashley?" He scratched his jaw. "I haven't talked to her in years."

"Clearly, she wanted to talk to you."

Shoveling both hands through his hair, Josh let out a huge breath. Amber was right, of course, though he hadn't seen it that way until now. He and Wyatt did desert James, but not intentionally. Initially, they both assumed their businesses back home would go on with James in charge. Their brother was unflappable. They knew James could weather any storm that came his way. If needed, he would hire the right people to take over Wyatt's business. What would a few months away hurt?

Unfortunately, the months had turned into years. And now…there was no telling if they could return.

"I've only been here for a few hours, and already I hate this century," she grumbled.

"You haven't seen anything of it yet, so don't judge too harshly."

"Too late for that. This is where my best friend chose to be. Instead of living happily ever after in Manhattan, she's here, in this backward century." She flung both arms. "So don't preach to me, cowboy."

Josh admired her brutal honesty, and after hearing his sister-in-law speak so fondly of her best friend, he couldn't believe the woman was here…in the *nineteenth* century. According to Emma, never in a million years would Amber go back in time—for anyone. And now, she came not only with news about Wyatt and Emma's names on tombstones, but also with details about what James was handling on his own. Josh had been too wrapped up in enjoying life in the nineteenth century to even contemplate there would be consequences affecting his brother in their own time. Mentally, he kicked himself.

He glanced out the window to the coffee pot warming on the outdoor stove. Judging by the amount of steam billowing out, it was ready. "Be right back," he said, snagging a small dish towel. Outside, he grabbed the pot, and then returned to the kitchen. "I've got fresh milk from Sam's cow, and plenty of sugar."

"Milk from a cow," she muttered. "This should be interesting. Sure, I'll take both. Thanks."

He added both, gave it a stir, and then handed her the mug with the steaming brew. "Hopefully, this will help defog your mind and ease the headache. Caffeine usually helps with that."

She accepted the mug, took a sip, and spit it out. He handed her a cloth napkin. "Oh…my…God. This is awful! It tastes and smells like burned wood from a thousand firepits ago." Gazing at him, she amended with a cringy face, "Oh, sorry. My bad."

"It's okay," he admitted. "Let me guess, too gritty, extremely strong, and nowhere near as good as back home, right?"

"No chance I can get some foam on this, huh?" she teased.

Josh raised his mug in a cheers gesture. "You're not the only who misses good coffee." He sank into a chair and took a big gulp. While he had grown accustomed to the flavor, right now, it tasted too bitter. Maybe it was the reality of his situation finally sinking in.

"Tell me about James," he said, quietly. "And please, no more lectures. I feel guilty enough. You've got me thinking about everything in a different light now. I hope you know I miss him…a lot."

"He misses you and Wyatt," Amber replied. "Personally, I think James needs a little happiness. And when I say happiness, I mean a girlfriend."

He waved a hand. "Don't let him fool you. James always has a girlfriend."

"Business-suit-and-stuffy-tie James?" She shook her head. "No way. In the entire year I've known him,

I've never once met a girlfriend of his. He's not dating anyone. Besides, I'm like his little sister. He would've said something to me."

"Little sister, eh?" He couldn't explain why, but he found that tidbit of information to be a relief. "How'd that happen?"

"When Emma returned to the nineteenth century last year, James and I spoke every night on the phone. He'd assure me Emma and Wyatt would *someday* return. Then when I started working remotely, I'd come out here to Whisper Creek every few weeks, hoping Emma would've come back because she was homesick. James and I spent many a weekend talking about Emma and Wyatt…and you. I feel like I've gotten to know you and your brother through him."

"Then you would also know that if James hasn't said anything about a girlfriend it's because he's not serious enough to bring one around."

"You're probably right. What about you? Is there a little lady?" She held up a hand, showcasing perfectly manicured nails. "No, it's courting. They call it courting here, in this time. Right?"

"They do call it that, and the answer is no."

"Considering you're living in the nineteenth century, I'm not surprised."

He let that comment go. There was no need to update her on his love life, or lack thereof. Josh was content being the most eligible bachelor in town. Of course, that didn't stop him from discreetly visiting one particular woman at Madame Veronique's. And while many single prim-and-proper young women had hoped to get a marriage proposal out of him by batting their eyelashes and strutting their bustle in front of him, he never gave any of them the time of day. He couldn't. One little romp in the hay, so to speak, would result in a shotgun wedding. And he didn't like any of them enough to want to spend his life with them.

"This is surreal, Josh," Amber said, her gaze sweeping around the kitchen again. "And unsettling, and bizarre. I mean, I just left *this* house and, well, it looks similar but different. Hours ago, I stood in this very kitchen…with your brother, and now…"

"I hear you. I've been there myself."

Amber shifted in the chair, tugging at her long skirt. "Ugh, this outfit bites. I'd give anything for a summer dress or shorts about now."

The frilly blue blouse with the suffocatingly high neckline and long dark skirt looked great on her. The clothes hugged her in all the right places, and the colors suited her creamy complexion, matching her blue eyes. To fit in this century, all she had to do was style her hair in a fancy bun.

"Since it looks like you'll be staying awhile, you'll need more to wear than what you have on. This week, I'll take you into town to get fitted for new clothes," he told her, coming to his feet. "In the meantime, I'll set you up in a guestroom. I'm sorry you came all this way just to get stuck with me."

"It's okay. I mean, thanks for putting me up while Emma's not here."

"My pleasure."

"Plus, it'll give us a chance to get to know each other."

He smiled. "I'd like that. Now, let me show you to your room and give you some temporary attire."

She stood up and rounded the table. "If you're

thinking of Emma's dresses, forget it, pal. She's at least two sizes smaller and three inches shorter."

His gaze traveled up and down her curvy form. "I'm sure you can make do with a pair of my pants and a shirt or two until you meet with the dressmaker."

"That would be super, considering I probably look like a dork in this outfit."

"Nah, just not of the latest fashion."

"Tell James, my twenty-first century stylist, that," she said, laughing.

They were midway down the hall to the wing with the bedrooms when he stopped. If she was anything like Emma, he knew what she would want before changing.

"Thanks to Wyatt's construction expertise back when we were in the future," he began, "we're not that primitive. It'll be a few more decades before rural plumbing comes to these parts, but in the meantime, we constructed our own system." He flung open the door. "Voila," he said, moving aside so she could enter.

He had to admit, he and Wyatt did a good job with the bathroom. The dark wood floor was a stark contrast to the oversized white porcelain bathtub. A pipe led from the tub and disappeared into a floorboard. It took the two of them forever to get that hooked up. Beside the wide sink, stood an old-fashioned toilet with a pull cord hanging from the tank above. A linen cabinet, white wainscoting, and a summery floral wallpaper with dusty pink roses and yellow morning glories that Emma chose completed the small room. Considering the crude construction materials they had to work with, the project turned out much better than they had anticipated.

"The tub is new," he told her, running his hand along the rim. "Wyatt had it shipped from England for Emma.

Porcelain tubs won't be a big deal here for a few more years, but we managed to get one, thanks to a traveling salesman we met last year when we went to Chicago. There's no real plumbing here, but we updated the few pumps under the house and the ones out back, plus the separate wells, and all that. Keep in mind water only runs for a few minutes, so don't take too long. Boiling pots of water will take forever, so this is what you get. It's simple to work." He tapped the floor pump with his foot, then pointed to the spout for the tub and the showerhead above. "In the meantime, I'll throw some dinner together."

She cast him a dubious look. "Whoa, you cook?"

"I do a great many things you will soon come to discover," he replied. "I'll leave some clothes by the door for you."

Josh went to his room to select a pair of bulky denims and a soft linen shirt. It had been a long time since he let a woman borrow his clothes, especially one he hadn't slept with.

Dropping the small bundle on the floor outside the bathroom door, he stopped and smiled. With Wyatt and Emma away, it would be nice to have company, someone to talk to and share his meals with. And who better than his sister-in-law's beautiful best friend from their own time.

Chapter Three

Amber closed the door and leaned against it, embracing the respite. This was the first moment she had to herself since landing in another century. After a few moments of silence, she pumped the water, undressed, and then stepped into the shower. The cool water felt good, therapeutic, but nowhere near as amazing as her shower back home with the recently installed triple showerhead with multi-spray patterns. She had splurged on that last year. Now, *that* was a great shower. Since she bought her apartment a couple of years back, she'd been making changes here and there. Her body sighed. Would she learn to adjust to her temporary accommodations and the lack of modern technology here the way Emma did? Not likely.

Through no fault of her own, her plan to warn Emma and Wyatt about their impending deaths had been put on hold. Now, she had no choice but to stay put until they returned from Montana City. That meant, she would be staying here…with Josh…under the same roof. It was an awkward situation, residing with a complete stranger, even though he was related to her best friend. Good thing he was easy on the eyes—very easy, that is.

She tugged on Josh's jeans. They were baggy. His oversized cream-colored linen shirt was devoid of buttons, so she slipped it over her head. It hung halfway down her thighs. The faint scent of sandalwood and soap clung to his clothes, tickling her nose.

When she returned to the kitchen, Josh was nowhere to be found, but his tenor voice drew her to the open back door. Outside, he was flipping something in a pan at the grill, while singing. The sizzling steaks sounded better than they smelled. She was hungry, but unfortunately, the aroma made her stomach roil. The trip through time left a wave of nausea behind that wouldn't quit.

Clearing her throat, she walked up behind him and peered over his shoulder. "Hey," she said.

Josh turned to her and smiled. "Hey back. You look better. You've got some color in your cheeks. I hope the shower helped a bit."

"A bit."

"Still have a headache?"

She shook her head. "Not so much now."

"Good," he said, returning to his cooking.

"So this is the grill you boys built."

"Yep."

It was a combination of a grill and brick oven with a stove on top.

"Impressive."

He tapped the huge cast iron pan with the fork. "You eat meat, right?"

She shook her head at the thick slice of beef, pulling a serious face. "Dead flesh? No way. Never touch the stuff."

His smile faded. "Please tell me you're kidding."

She burst out laughing and cuffed him on the arm. "Of course I'm kidding. Emma is the pescatarian, not me."

"You're so gonna pay for that, missy," he said, flipping the meat. "Nice to know you're a joker. We'll

35

get along amazingly."

"Why be serious when you can be funny? At least, I try. Sometimes, unsuccessfully, and sometimes successfully without trying."

Amusement flickered in his eyes. "I wasn't expecting company, so there's not much except for these leftovers. I've been mooching off of Sam most nights."

"No worries. I'm not hungry anyway. That trip through the portal made me super queasy." She made a sour face and patted her stomach. "As long as you're not cooking liver, I'll eat just about anything."

"That I'll never cook, so you're in the clear."

"Tell me, what's it like living here with Emma and Wyatt in the Old West?"

"I don't live with them anymore," he admitted. "I figured those two lovebirds didn't need a third wheel around." He jerked a thumb toward the hill. "I moved in with Sam next door. When I'm not staying in town at the marshal's, that is. He's a great guy and has become a good friend. His wife died some years ago in childbirth along with their daughter, so he pretty much keeps to himself, except for me and Wyatt and Emma. But now, I'm back here temporarily while Wyatt and Emma are away. Once they return—"

"We'll be outta here as soon as we get that stupid portal working again," she cut him off, clapping her hands.

Josh was about to say something, but instead, indicated the large plate on the brick counter next to the grill. She handed it to him, and he dumped the meat onto it. "I'm starved," he said. "Let's eat."

He pulled out the chair for her at the picnic table, lit a few lamps, and then dug into his dinner. Amber had no appetite and picked at her food, moving it from one place to another on the plate. While he ate, she filled him in on the current events of their own time and what he had missed while living here.

During their conversation, the cacophony of nocturnal animals and bugs didn't go unnoticed. It was like that whenever she had stayed at Emma's Montana place and unlike the big city with car horns, subways, and buses droning out anything that wasn't within two inches.

"The world sounds like it has become a crazy, busy place," he said. "Maybe it's a good thing I stayed here."

"You were born in the twentieth century. Isn't that reason enough to not want to stay here? I mean, people still ride horses to get anywhere. There's no running water or sewage systems. No telephones or cars, for that matter. It's all so…so backward."

Josh laughed. "It's not as backward as you think. Give it a chance. I hate to remind you, but you may be here awhile—a long while. Try not to judge this century until you've spent some time here. Okay?"

She pressed her lips together and nodded reluctantly. "Okay."

"Good."

"Now," she said, leaning her elbows on the table, "tell me they're all right—Emma and Wyatt. I know you said they took a mini vacation of sorts, but I'm really worried about them. If I hadn't seen their names on those tombstones, I wouldn't have known Emma was in danger."

He got up, rounded the table, and squeezed her shoulder. "I know you're worried, and since you brought that news, I am, too. However, they're safe. I promise you will be reunited with Emma as soon as they get back."

She ran both hands through her hair, lifting her mass of heavy waves off her shoulders, and yawned loudly. "All righty then, cowboy. I guess you're officially stuck with me for now."

A smile spread across his face. "I certainly don't mind. Besides, I have a feeling you're more fun than my little brother and his lovely wife. Don't get me wrong, Wyatt and Emma are great; but they're all over each other every second of the day."

"Like I need to hear this."

He chuckled, then rubbed his hands together. "Okay, so since you're not up for food, how about bed?"

Bed? What? She smacked her lips. Her pulse raced with the sudden vision of them tangled in the sheets. Where had that come from? "I, uh," she mumbled.

"It's been a whirlwind day for you. I'll let you get some rest. You must be exhausted. Time travel knocks the life out of you."

"Got that right." She stood up and collected the dishes.

"Forget those," he told her. "Tonight, you need rest. Tomorrow, you can help me with the chores."

"Yay, chores. I'm here not even a day, and already I'm being put to work," she teased. "Thanks."

Josh chuckled. He led her into the house and down the long hall lined with wood flooring and wainscot walls. "Fresh linens are in there," he said, indicating the tall cabinet at the end of the hall. "I wasn't expecting company, so I didn't bother making the guest bed. Anyway, sleep as late as you want. Holler if you need anything. I'm just down there in the next room. Good night, Amber." He walked away, whistling a familiar tune.

Amber watched him go, then turned to the cabinets and pulled out the sheets. Inside her room, she frowned at the bare mattress. "I've seen way too many Western movies," she mumbled. "This sucks."

She tugged a starchy sheet around the bulky mattress, tucking the extra material in place. The padding was nowhere near as luxurious as the queen size bed with the pillowtop in her apartment. *Nothing is like back home, nor will it ever be like back home. Why torture yourself by comparing*? So true.

Stripping out of her clothing, she washed her bra and panties, hung them over the chair, and then crawled under the sheet and sighed. She was grateful to have a solid bed under her body and a member of Emma's family in the next room. With Josh nearby, she felt safer being in a different century…and out in the middle of nowhere.

The windows were open, letting in the cool night air. No extra blanket was needed. She yawned and stretched. As tired as she was from her journey through time, her mind couldn't stop racing. Closing her eyes, her thoughts went immediately to her best friend.

Emma, I've got to see you and stop your name from appearing on that damn tombstone.

****

Josh stood in the middle of the kitchen. Remnants of dinner were piled neatly on the counter, but he couldn't be bothered with that now. Amber's arrival put a damper on his plans to ride over to Deer Lodge. He couldn't very well leave her alone for any length of time. If anything happened to her, or Grey's minions tried to hurt her while he was away, he would be responsible. Until he knew who was behind the threats on Wyatt and Emma, he wouldn't let his guard down nor would he leave Amber behind. Taking her with him to the prison where Grey was incarcerated wasn't the best option, but it was his only one.

Inside the pantry, he pulled out a small leather trunk from a hidden compartment under the floorboards. The space was big enough for them to hide in if they ever needed to. It was the place where he, Wyatt, and Emma had kept all their twenty-first century clothes, cell phones, and tokens hidden. Removing a parcel tied with string from the trunk, Josh then carried it into the study. It had been months since he rummaged through the bundle. With Amber's arrival, he suddenly felt homesick.

Pouring himself a tall whiskey, he sat behind the wide desk Wyatt hand carved last year. His brother was one talented woodworker, and Wyatt loved creating with his hands. Once they returned to their own time, though, what would happen to everything here? The house was in Wyatt and Emma's names. There would be no kin left behind. Josh would have to talk to Wyatt about leaving a will or a letter of intent…just in case. Then again, Emma received the property deed in the future, which was the impetus for her trip back in time. Time travel was confusing at best.

He loosened the string and pushed the paper aside. One of the items within was a small pouch containing the remainder of the nineteenth-century money Josh had purchased in his own time and brought back with him. The other item was a small envelope containing a handful of newspaper articles featuring Griffin Grey. If

Josh and Wyatt hadn't figured out what he was up to and nailed the bastard, Grey would've continued burning down businesses and homes in Whisper Creek. And now, he was hell-bent on seeking revenge.

A long slow sip of whiskey warmed its way down his throat, settling in his stomach. The second sip tasted better than the first. Never a fan of the booze prior to his trip here, it was something he'd grown accustomed to, like everything else. He didn't know how long he would be in the nineteenth century, so he had to make the best of it.

A sudden gust of wind blew through the open windows. The curtains flapped, an indication that a storm was fast approaching. Without the convenience of a weather app or a cell phone, he never knew what the conditions would be from day to day. Sometimes the clouds and the color of the sky at a particular time of day were indications. Other times, it was a crapshoot.

Rising from the chair, he walked to the window. The breeze was cooler now than it had been earlier. He glanced outside toward the barn. The hair on the back of his neck stood up. A faint, whitish-blue light bordered the space between the barn door and the frame. The only other time he had ever seen that light was when the portal was active.

Josh snuffed the lamps in the study and the ones in the kitchen and grabbed his gun belt off the peg on the wall. He charged out the back door and ran to the barn, but the strange light was gone. Cocking his gun, he slowly pulled the barn door open enough to slip inside. His hearing tuned into the sounds of everything around him. All was silent.

The blueish-white light reappeared in a bright

flash…in the same spot where the portal stood. A sudden coldness hit him to the core. Could another traveler be coming through? He was about to light a lamp but stopped. The portal door *whooshed* open. It sounded like a sliding door on a spaceship in those space travel sci-fi movies. If that wasn't peculiar enough, a section of the barn wall *morphed* into a tall and wide doorway filled with that same harsh light.

Josh cocked his gun with one hand and shielded his eyes with his other. He focused on a shadow within the light, trying to decipher who or what it was. The only person who he could think of was his brother. "James, is that you?"

"I don't have much time," came an unfamiliar voice. It wasn't James.

He hadn't really expected anyone to respond, not even this brother. A shot of adrenaline rushed through his body, and he took a few steps back. "Who the hell are you?" he demanded, raising his gun.

A tall, slender man emerged from the blue light. He was striking with violet-colored eyes. His face looked young, devoid of any wrinkles or lines, even though his short hair was pure white. His jumpsuit was a solid charcoal color, and his boots appeared to be part of his suit. The armband on his left sleeve flashed.

"My name is Malachi, and I'm here as a friend," the man said, his voice low. "You and your family are in grave danger, Josh. I have to help you return to your rightful time before it's too late. Unfortunately, we only have until December thirty-first to make that happen."

"Whoa, what are you talking about?"

"All will be revealed soon enough. I promise." He looked over his shoulder and said quietly, "It's not safe for me now, but I'll be back to help you. I promise…"

"Wait!" Josh cried.

Then…the man and the shining light of the portal vanished.

Chapter Four

Streaks of sunlight flickered through the open bedroom windows, lighting the floor in small pools of warmth. Amber groaned and rolled over. Her mind was fogged, and she couldn't recall why. A gentle, warm breeze forced the curtains to swell in a soothing fashion, encouraging her return to dreamland. Everything was quiet, too quiet, except for the sound of birds chirping. Nature's sounds were soothing, but so different than what she was used to living in the city. Sinking back against the pillows, she closed her eyes and sighed. It felt so good to sleep late. She hadn't done that in ages.

Something gnawed at her brain, and she sprang up, clutching the sheet to her chest. The room looked familiar, yet the furnishings were not what she remembered. The bedroom she had claimed for herself at Emma's place in the future had a queen-size bed with a fancy oak headboard, matching dresser, settee, and several paintings adorning the walls. In this room, however, there was a wide hickory style dresser, small iron-frame bed, and long oval mirror. Sconces adorned the walls covered in a warm, decorative Victorian pattern, and a lone wood chair sat in the opposite corner.

It was a solid minute before the events of the past twenty-four hours came flooding back to her mind in torrents. 1883 was no longer a place Emma chose to return to—Amber was now there to feel it, live it, and hopefully, rescue her friend from it.

She kicked off the sheet, jumped out of bed, and went to the window. The smell of hay and earth wafting in enveloped her senses. The scenery looked different than it had yesterday morning when she was in this very same house…but in her own time. Beautiful rolling hills sat in the distance, colorful wildflowers dotted the earth, and the sounds of horses neighing resonated in the air.

Her stomach swirled, and she swallowed down the lump of anxiety threatening to climb up her throat. Closing her eyes, she did a quick one-minute breathing exercise to get her racing thoughts under control. Traveling back one hundred and forty years into the past did a number on her emotional health, to say the least.

Satisfied with her brief mental workout, she reached for her bra and panties hanging over the chair that she had washed out last night. Borrowing Josh's pants and a shirt was one thing, but she would be totally grossed out if he had offered her a clean pair of ladies' underwear, even if they did belong to Emma. *Did women even wear panties in this century*? Bra and panties in place, she tugged on Josh's jeans and shirt.

She checked herself in the tall oval mirror and cringed. "Day two, and I'm missing the future. Big time."

Padding barefoot down the hall and into the bathroom, she used the old-fashioned toilet with the pull chain flusher. She had seen similar ones back home in museums and old historic homes. Unfortunately, she couldn't locate any toilet paper, so she was forced to wash herself with a small cloth. Yanking the chain, she watched the water dribble out of the bowl, to where, she had no clue. The flush had no noise either, which was odd.

On the counter next to a small jar was a note from Josh with a smiley face. *For your teeth*. She removed the lid and smelled the contents. Ugh. The scent was earthy and stale, like rocks and dirt. There was no toothbrush, so she dipped her finger into the jar and rubbed her teeth with the godawful tasting gravel. It was worse than that natural baking soda crap she once tried back home. After gagging on the vile stuff, she rinsed out her mouth. Having completed her morning routine, she set out in search of Josh.

The aroma of freshly brewed coffee beckoned her to the kitchen. All the mugs were the same size. She grabbed one and poured herself a serving from the enamel pot sitting on the non-burning stove. One sip and she nearly spewed it. How could she have forgotten how bad it tasted? What she wouldn't give for a latte from her favorite café right now.

"Good morning, sunshine." Josh walked through the back door, carrying a small stack of clothes. "I thought you were going to sleep for a century."

"I could've," she admitted, dumping a large portion of sugar into the mug, and stirring. She took a sip, made a face, and added one more teaspoon for good measure. "Traveling through time sure did knock me out. Why didn't you wake me?"

"I figured you could use some extra shuteye. The last twenty-four hours have been stressful for you, to say the least."

"Thanks," she muttered. "Normally, I'm up at the crack of dawn."

He waved a hand and changed the subject. "I see you found the coffee."

She raised the mug and made a face. "Not bad for hours-old brew."

"You lie." Josh chuckled. "And it's not hours old. I made it less than a half hour ago. You were still sleeping when I checked on you, but I thought maybe the aroma might wake you. The coffee's not so bad once you get used to it."

Wait. He watched me while I slept? That was sweet…and a little sexy. She must've been dead tired to not wake at the sound of him entering her room. A heavy sleeper, she was not. "Sorry, you get zero credit," she said at last. "It was the blinding sun seeping through the window that woke me."

"And here I thought it was my expert coffee skills." He walked over to the table, pulled a chair out, and plopped the bundle on it. "These are for you…on loan."

Amber eyed him skeptically and checked out the pile of clothes. Three long skirts, one brown, one dark green, and one blue; three blouses with ruffles on the collar; and a pair of soft brown leather shoes similar to the ones James had provided for her that she refused to wear. She held up the blouse against her chest. They just might fit. "Where'd you get these?"

"Sam," he said, walking over to the counter. "He didn't have the heart to throw out Millie's clothes after she passed. I, uh, told him Emma's best friend from back East was visiting and didn't have anything else to wear, your luggage was stolen, that sort of thing. Anyway, from what he says, you're about Millie's size, so…"

"That's so sad about his wife, but sweet that he's willing to loan them to me." Touched by a stranger's generosity, she gave the blouse a gentle pat, knowing all too well what it took for Sam to share something of his late loved one. "I'll take good care of them. I promise. Please thank him for me."

"You can thank him yourself when you meet him later." He wrapped a biscuit in a checkered napkin and handed it to her. He crooked his finger, motioning for her to follow him. "Come on."

She placed the blouse on top of the pile, and then slipped on her sneakers that she had left by the back door. Josh led her on a narrow path, fringed by tall grass and colorful wildflowers, to the top of the small hill. They gazed down at a beautiful wide lake at the bottom of the basin. No sound rang out from the land surrounding it, except for the birds and soft rustle of the leaves. The mountain air smelled clean and fresh like flowers and the great outdoors. A warm, gentle breeze fanned her. Off in the distance two other homes dotted the land on each side of the lake.

"That's Sam's place." Josh pointed to the nearest spread. It boasted a ranch-style home, wide barn with a paddock that was five times the size of Wyatt's, and a corral. "What do you think?"

Amber turned too fast. They bumped heads and laughed. "It's beautiful here, and so much different than modern-day Montana," she told him. "They're building all those new cookie-cutter developments in record time."

"Yeah, pretty soon it'll start looking like New York."

"*Nothing* compares to New York, buddy," she assured him.

"And nothing compares to Montana." Josh bit off a chunk of biscuit and swallowed it down with a gulp of coffee. "Did you know I lived there for a while? New

York, that is." He sat down on a wooden bench perched under the shade of a tree and gestured for her to sit.

Amber took the spot next to him. "What? No way. When?" Never in a million years would she have ever guessed this sexy country boy could live in a big city.

"It's where I went to college," he explained. "I always wanted to see what all the fuss was about. You know, the city that never sleeps, restaurants open twenty-four-seven, and it being the melting pot of the world. Anyway, I decided to go to college there before heading to law school. I promised myself, no matter what, I would return home to practice in the family firm. It meant a lot to my parents."

"That's wonderful. They'd be very proud of you. It sounds like you were close."

"Thanks, and we were all close, me, my parents, and my brothers."

"There's one thing I still don't get," she said. "You and Wyatt go by Kincaid, but James uses Matheson, mainly for work. I know it's your mom's maiden name, but what's up with that?"

Josh smiled, gazing off into the distance. "Matheson is our middle name—mine, Wyatt's, and James's. I represent—or rather, represented—the Kincaid side of the law firm, while James represents the Matheson side, mom's side." He shrugged. "It's just our way of trying to keep both our parents alive."

"James told me about the avalanche. What a horrible accident…" Suffocating that way had to be one of the worst ways die. She shivered. His loss was a reminder of what she had suffered as well. Her voice softened, and she touched his hand. "I'm so sorry. I know that sounds lame, but there are no words for such an unfathomable loss."

He turned to her and nodded. "Thank you."

Her eyes burned with unshed tears for him, for his loss…and her own. Her hand lingered a moment longer before she pulled away. "So tell me about you now. Why would you choose to stay in a backwards century when you could be enjoying all the modern-day conveniences of the twenty-first century? And this house—" She flung an arm. "—it's lovely, but I just don't understand why Wyatt and you would build a house when you have a life back in the future."

Josh stood up and gazed out at the land. "It's just a house, as Wyatt will tell you when you meet him. As for me, my home is wherever I go."

She frowned. "Don't you miss your own time?"

He hesitated before answering. "I miss my big brother, that's for sure, but I have my little brother here. My parents are dead. No matter where I am, I'd never be able to see them again. By working for the marshal here, I still get to practice law in a way, so I haven't really lost anything by remaining in the nineteenth century." He shrugged. "In terms of modern conveniences and technology, well, there are a few things I do miss."

She raised an eyebrow. "Such as?"

He chuckled. "Don't laugh. I got a sports car when I joined the firm."

She laughed anyway. "Typical. What else?"

"There's not much else to miss, aside from transportation. Not for me, anyway. I didn't leave a wife or children behind. James is running the firm, so…"

Amber stared at the grass beneath her feet. Josh seemed like the type of person who could survive no matter where he lived. Adapting to new surroundings came easy, just as it did for Emma. From what she observed so far, he was at home whether he was chasing outlaws in this century or taking criminals to court in his own time.

But what about her? Could she give up her place in the future to live in a century where women were still fighting for their voting rights and civil rights?

Hard pass.

She studied him, tilting her head. "I think there's more to it. There's another reason you would stay here, if it weren't for the portal malfunction, that is."

"Maybe, maybe not." It was his turn to study her for a moment. "And what about you? Have you ever thought of giving up the twenty-first century for the Old West?"

"Changing the direction of questioning, I see. All right. I came here on a mission. And once I get my best friend and her family back home, I never want to hear about that freakin' portal again. That is, *if* we ever get home." She took a bite of the biscuit, but it had no taste. If they couldn't fix the portal or find out what was wrong with it, they would all be stuck here…indefinitely. She threw up a little.

Josh nudged her. "Are you all right?"

She raised her mug and took a sip, swallowing back the nausea. "Peachy."

"Listen, I need to talk to you about something." He got up, put his mug down on the bench, and then stood in front of her. "I know you just got here, but I have to make a run to Deer Lodge, and I'd like for you to come with me. In fact, I insist."

"What's Deer Lodge?"

"The prison where Grey is being held."

"I'm not going to any prison," she shot back. "This

is the Old West! Anything could happen to me in there."

"I can assure you will not be stepping foot inside the prison. However, I do think it would be best if you accompany me. I'm hesitant to leave you here unprotected for days, just out of precaution. I'll get us a couple rooms at the boarding house in town, and you can wait for me there."

"Cool. My first ride to an Old West prison in the real Old West!" she said, shaking her head. "I can't believe this is my life."

Josh paced, shoveling both hands through his hair. He stopped and faced her. "There's more."

"Of course, there is," she mumbled.

It was a long moment before he spoke. "Last night after you went to bed, I was in the study for a bit. And…shit, this might sound crazy."

"Crazier than all of us traveling back in time to the nineteenth century? Try me."

"Good point. It's about the portal."

Her ears perked up at that. "Did you figure out what's wrong with it?"

"Not quite."

"What are you talking about then?"

"There was a strange light coming from the barn, so I went to investigate. A man appeared out of nowhere…right where the portal is located…through the weird blue-white light. He didn't look like he was from here or even our real time."

"Now, you're freaking me out." A flicker of apprehension pierced her, and she stood up. "Who was he? And what did he say?"

"His name is Malachi. He said he's our friend, he's going to help us return to our rightful time, and that it wasn't safe for him, but he would be back."

"A friend, huh?" Amber plopped back down onto the bench. Alarm swirled in her body at tornado speed. "So does this mean this *friend*, or someone like him, is personally, physically in charge of the portal?"

Josh shrugged. "I don't know for sure."

"I never even considered that. I thought the portal was just there. You know, some unexplainable freak thing, like the pyramids."

"I believe there is an explanation and a reason for everything, including this damn time portal…and the guy who just showed up out of the blue."

"Okay, tell me more," she said eagerly. "What did he look like? Where's he from? And what the hell kind of name is Malachi?"

Josh rubbed his chin. "He was tall and thin with short, pure white hair. He had a gadget of some kind on his arm that kept flashing different colors. There really wasn't time for a conversation. It all happened so quickly, and then he was gone. Oh, and he said we have to get back to our time by December thirty-first."

"He gave you an actual date?" Amber bit her bottom lip, gazing at Josh. "Look, please don't get upset with me for asking this, but do you think maybe…you dozed off and this was some sort of weird dream? Or maybe you're just, I don't know, losing your mind because you've been here too long? I'd understand that."

His mouth twisted wryly. "Definitely not."

"Okay, then," she said. "Why the mystery? Why didn't this guy just tell you what the hell is going on? He told you he'll come back to help, right? Why wouldn't he tell you more?"

He paced again, repeatedly shoveling a hand

through his hair. "The man seemed rushed. He was looking over his shoulder."

"Like he didn't want to get busted talking to you," she suggested.

He stopped and faced her. "Now that you mention it, yeah."

"All right. Let's put all this together," she said, rising to her feet. "There's a guy from whenever and wherever in time who showed up through the portal. He wants to help us get back to our real time, but not yet. He says he'll be back."

"Correct."

She grabbed some of her hair and twirled the ends into a tight rope. "Then maybe we don't have to worry about fixing the portal or figuring out what's wrong it. This guy—or whoever is in charge of the portal, if anyone actually is—will get us through. That's the only thing that makes sense. Even so, I'm still skeptical that this person out of the blue is offering to help."

"Something doesn't add up."

"Hell-o, we're talking time portals here, Josh. *Nothing* adds up," she reminded him. "Wait, if he, or someone is truly in charge of the portal, why is our deadline December thirty-first? That's New Year's Eve."

"Good question."

****

Josh's stomach burned like a five-alarm fire out of control. Where were antacids when he needed them? When he first followed Wyatt through the time portal, they had hoped to be in the nineteenth century only long enough to figure out a way back. Unfortunately, the weeks turned into months and those quickly turned into years.

And now, because of him and Wyatt, they may have jeopardized the future of their entire family.

"Hell-o, Earth to Josh." Amber snapped her fingers in front of his face. "Are you okay?" She watched him while twirling the ends of her auburn waves into long, curly knots. "Is it the idea of being trapped here forever that scares you…or is it that things are possibly out of your control and maybe, just *maybe*, you could've prevented this…if you went back when you should've?"

"Ouch. You got me at the jugular, girl."

"I'm sorry," she said, making that cute, cringy face again. Her eyebrows wrinkled. "I'm just saying it like I see it." She reached for his hands and squeezed them. "It's my turn to reassure you. We *will* find our way through the portal and go home—with or without that portal keeper guy coming back for us. Because there's no way in hell that I will ever spend the rest of my days in this freakin' century. No way. Not happening. Like the proverbial saying goes: if there's a will, there's a way."

He held onto one of her hands. "I like your positivity. You and I are definitely going to get along great, but…portal keeper?"

She shrugged. "What else do you want to call him? Doorman?"

"I like doorman."

Amber rolled her eyes. "Okay, so until the *doorman* shows up again, why don't we just get this show on the road and head to Deer Lodge today?"

He glanced up at the midday sun. Riding during the hottest part of the day wasn't ideal, especially for Amber. He wasn't sure she could take the long hours of sunshine and no sunblock without much of a break. "It's too late now. We'll need to get an early start tomorrow, avoid the bulk of the heat. For today, though, let's get you in a saddle."

"Been there. Done that." She waved a hand and grinned. "You didn't think this city girl could ride, did ya, cowboy? C'mon, admit it."

"You got me there. I admit it." He couldn't hide his chuckle. "You certainly are full of surprises."

"Wait till you get to know me," she shot back with a wink and headed toward the barn.

Josh liked Amber. She was funny, smart, and damn beautiful. He was a sucker for blue eyes, and Christ, she had the bluest he'd ever seen. His mind was already going places he hadn't considered since before he left the twenty-first century. Maybe he'd chalk it up to being single too long...or just being in this century.

He followed her around to the side of the house. She stopped in front of the paddock and leaned against the wood fence. "I don't remember seeing the darker horse before," she said, canting her head. "The gold one, yes."

Two horses grazed in the paddock. His and the reddish-brown mare Amber referred to.

"While you were sleeping in this morning," he began, "I brought Winnie over from Sam's. That's when he gave me the clothes for you to borrow. Since Wyatt and Emma went away, we've been keeping the mare at Sam's. He's got the room and more than enough stable hands. She's the perfect horse for you, gentle and calm."

"Winnie is Emma's horse, right?"

"She is."

Amber laughed. "I can't believe she named her horse that. Emma always loved that silly old bear."

"And his bouncy companion."

"You, too? Don't tell me you named your horse after another character in that book."

"Nope. I named mine after a character, you could say, but from a movie."

"Hmm." She glanced over at the pale horse, running a hand through her thick mane. The scent of the lavender shampoo she must've borrowed from Emma filled his senses. He didn't remember his sister-in-law's hair smelling like that.

He leaned toward her. "I'll give you three guesses."

She tapped a forefinger to her chin. "Considering we're in the Old West, I'll go with…Wyatt Earp? Doc Holliday? No, I've got it! Ike Clanton!"

He chuckled and shook his head. "Not even close. Want to try again?"

She sighed. "You said three guesses is all I get."

"Very well." He sighed dramatically. "His name is…drum roll, please…Delorean."

"You named your horse—" She stopped and tossed her head back, laughing. The sound of her merriment was contagious, and he laughed, too. "Oh, wow. I love that movie! It's one of my favorites."

"Mine too. I couldn't help it. It's perfect. No one here even knows what that refers to."

"You're lucky," she said, elbowing him. "If they did, you'd be the envy of thousands. Everyone clamoring to get to know the mad scientist who discovered how to travel in time." She cast him a sideways glance. "And, of course, you'd have all the ladies in town swooning at your feet."

"They already do," he allowed with a devilish grin.

A wave of red rolled up Amber's neck to her cheeks, and she looked away. Was she blushing? "Yeah, I get that," she said. "I mean, you're a handsome guy. Smart. Charming. Why wouldn't the women around here fall at your feet?"

"Okay, now you're mocking me."

"Maybe a little."

"I didn't mean to sound so arrogant. Things are just different here. And if there's a single man within a hundred miles, well…"

"I get the picture, so you can stop painting it."

His cheeks burned. "Okay, I'm shutting up now."

She met his gaze. "I'm messing with you."

He tore his eyes away at last. "Shall we?" He draped his arm around her shoulder and led her to the barn. "We're going to start at the beginning."

"I've already told you I can ride. It's been a while, though. College days. Emma and I went to a dude ranch in Colorado one summer."

He laughed. "I can't even picture that."

"Yeah, well, it wasn't what we were expecting, that's for sure."

"That I believe," he agreed. "Okay, but before you can get on a horse, you must learn about the saddles—and how to get in one the correct way."

Amber stopped inside the doorway, shaking her head. "No way. This is where the time portal is—and where the doorman appeared. Just because the portal doesn't work for you right now, doesn't mean it won't work for me. Did you think of that? I got here with zero problems. And I don't want to accidentally go back until I see Emma. Emma first; time portal second. Got it?"

He took her by the hand and gestured to the back wall of the barn. "The portal is over in that vicinity. You're not going anywhere. Besides, we renovated the barn with more stalls and rooms down the aisle so we could avoid that particular area altogether."

"Oh."

Josh led her down the aisle toward the end of the barn and into a smaller room, the tack room. Bridles, straps, and other items hung on one wall. In the center, four Western style saddles rested on their respective stands. Two were larger than the others. He pulled one of the smaller saddles off its stand and laid it across a wooden horse before securing the cinches.

He patted the cantle. "Before you ride, you need to understand the saddle, mainly, how to get it on the horse correctly. You don't want it to fall off while you're riding, and you certainly don't want to injure the horse."

Amber folded her arms across her chest. "I know how to saddle a horse. And I know how to ride."

"Great. Show me."

"What, you don't believe me?"

"I would just like to be assured of your skills. That's all."

"Fine," she huffed. The stirrups on the saddle hung closer to the ground than if she were mounting a real horse. Amber put her left foot in the stirrup, then swung her right leg over. "Voila. See! Easy peasy."

He eyed her up and down. "How well can you ride?"

"I can't go galloping off into the sunset, if that's what you're asking."

"How fast do you feel comfortable riding?"

She threw her hands up. "Why? What difference does it make?"

He leaned over her, one hand on the horn in front of her and the other on the cantle behind her butt. Her hair smelled incredible. "Because when you're on a horse, you need to be prepared."

She squirmed in the saddle and tossed her hair over her shoulder. "Josh, I'll be riding along with you into town not chasing down some dirty outlaws. That's your job as deputy."

"I just mean if the horse gets spooked or…" While she might think this was not an important exercise, Josh needed her to be prepared—for anything. He patted her shoulder. "All right, grab the saddle, and I'll introduce you to Winnie."

Josh took his own saddle off the wood brace and headed to the paddock. Amber trudged behind him, lugging the saddle, and blowing loose auburn tendrils off her dewy face. Sweat pearled on her lip, and he suddenly had the urge to wipe it off with a gentle swipe of his thumb.

"I guess you're not going to help me," she grumbled, swinging the saddle over the mare's back with a huff.

"Weren't you the one who bragged you knew how to ride and saddle a horse?" he reminded her, scrutinizing her every move. "It's my job, as teacher, to watch and observe. Besides, you're doing great."

"Gee, thanks."

"Now for the bridle. Watch me first." He placed his arm over the horse's head, between the ears, and then pulled the bridle up, securing the straps. "Think you can do it?"

Clumsily, she repeated his movements and slipped the bridle over Winnie's head. On the second try, she got it. She stood back and gave him a smug look. "How's that?"

"I'm impressed."

She cocked her head to the side, smiling. "Like I

said, wait till you get to know me. I'm full of surprises."

If he gazed into her baby blue orbs for much longer, he would be more than a little distracted. It took a lot of will power to turn away. He cleared his throat and said, "Hey, how about a ride now?"

"Sure. And it's a good thing you didn't make me wear that stupid skirt for this. It's hard enough riding in pants."

"It's not a stupid skirt. You wear it well."

She licked her lips. "Thanks."

Josh hopped into the saddle and waited for her to do the same. Amber wasn't what he had expected. He had a preconceived notion that she was bossy and pampered— but who wasn't a little pampered in the twenty-first century? And of course, she had to be authoritative if she was running a company along with Emma. However, Emma didn't do Amber's description justice. She was stunning, a knockout.

Having this beautiful woman within his sights, day in and day out, well, that could be a problem, especially if they couldn't get the portal to work again…or the doorman didn't show up to help them go back to the future.

Chapter Five

Amber stepped outside into the cool morning air garbed in borrowed clothes from the late Millie. The rising sun looked glorious, casting a warm, golden glow across the horizon. The back door banged against the frame, and she jumped. Being in another century, not to mention how she got there, would take some getting used to. The tall, wooden barn was a sore reminder. Only two days ago, it was a twenty-first century three-car garage.

Josh whistled something melodic, and his horse came trotting out of the paddock to nuzzle against his shoulder. He rubbed the horse's face and then got busy hitching him to the old-fashion wagon. This was the second time she'd seen Josh with a gun holstered around his tapered waist, but it was the first time she'd noticed the tin star pinned on his vest designating him a deputy. She couldn't recall if he was wearing the badge on the day she had arrived. Then again, she was in shock and didn't remember much.

He walked over to her, lifted his hat to wipe the sweat from his brow, and smiled. "Ready?"

"As ready as I'll ever be." She yanked a finger in the direction of the small green shed. "What's in there?"

"Now, it's a shed, like the ones back home filled with tools."

"What was it before?"

"An outhouse."

"That's gross."

"We hardly ever used it, but we covered everything up below it and remodeled the inside. Shall we?"

She spared the wagon a skeptical glance. "We're riding in that?"

"Yes, ma'am."

The wagon had four large, but thin-rimmed wooden wheels, a boxy wooden frame, and a slightly padded bench that was higher than it appeared from a distance. She gave the side panel a good shake, and thankfully, it didn't budge. It seemed secure, but she was no expert in nineteenth-century wagons. "Is it safe enough?"

"Of course, it is. I'd never put you in harm's way. Hop in," he suggested, brushing his hands off on his trousers.

"Uh, sure." Saddling a horse wasn't a problem, but trying to get into this old-fashion wagon was more difficult, especially in a dress. There was a tiny step, if it could be called that, but that was it. How was she going to lift herself—

"Here," Josh interrupted her train of thought, "I'll give you a hand."

There was no time to refuse. Strong hands clamped on her waist and hoisted her up. She fell sideways onto the hard bench, her butt half dangling off. When she collected her skirts and righted herself, she threw Josh a death glare; but the touch of amusement in his eyes softened her anger. "Such chivalry," she teased.

"Getting in and out of the wagon will get easier the more you do it. Now, scoot yourself over so I can get in, please."

She inched over, and Josh climbed in with ease like he'd done so a million times before. He glanced at her feet. "You're lucky Millie's shoes fit, too. Otherwise, you'd be wearing Emma's."

"Emma's a size seven; I'm an eight. There's no way that would've happened."

"I never said they'd be comfortable."

"Wiseass," she mumbled. Thankfully, Millie's shoes fit like they were made for her. The idea of wearing Emma's wouldn't have been any fun, and Amber's twenty-first century footwear would draw attention she didn't want or need. She left those under her bed.

Josh slapped the reins and off they went. The wagon bumped and jostled along the dirt roads. She gripped the side rail to keep from toppling over, but until they got to smoother roads, she was reluctant to let go. The bench was wide enough for the two of them, but there was no way to prevent their thighs from rubbing against each other. Josh's nearness was a bit unsettling. Her body was responding in ways she didn't want to acknowledge. It could lead her down a dangerous road of what-if and vulnerability. That wasn't something she was comfortable with...or ready for.

They rode in silence for a while, enjoying the beautiful weather and the sights, unlike anything Amber would see living in a concrete city with skyscrapers and buildings as far as the eye could see. While she had been visiting Whisper Creek and Helena each month since Emma left, in her own time there was no reason to ride horseback or in a wagon. This was a first, and she could do without the rough, dirt road, though.

A few hours later, Josh asked, "Are you hungry?"

"Is there a café or inn or whatever you call them coming up soon?"

"None of the above. However, I did bring a small

basket of bread, cheese, and hard biscuits. They're a bit stale."

"Sounds super fattening," she remarked, hoping her sarcasm was evident. "I can see I'll be gaining a few pounds on this trip."

"There's nothing wrong with a woman having a little meat on her bones." He leaned forward on his elbows, his gaze fixed on her. "I don't think you have anything to worry about."

"Thanks." A sudden swirly heat erupted in her belly at the compliment. The warm sensation was unfamiliar and new, and she willed it away. Maybe it was just time-travel sickness catching up to her. *Yeah, that's it*. The sun was rising higher in the sky, warming the back of her neck. She couldn't recall how long the ride would be to Deer Lodge. "Um, so how long until we get there?"

"Ah, you're *that* kind of traveler," he said, sitting up straight. "May I remind you this is the nineteenth century? You're not traveling at seventy-miles-per-hour in a car on a highway. You're riding at a slow pace with a horse and wagon. Technically, this trip could take us one day on horseback, but that means either stopping to rest the horses, and we travel during the night: or switching horses along the way. And I won't ride any other horse. Delorean has become too valuable to me."

"Oh. I didn't realize."

He nudged her. "It won't be that bad. Besides, this will give us a chance to get to know each other better. You said so yourself."

"That I did," she agreed, shifting her weight. Damn bench was beyond uncomfortable. By now, she probably had a dozen bruises on her butt.

Josh must've noticed. "Wyatt added some

cushioning to the bench after Emma complained, but I guess it's not comfy enough. Sorry about that."

"It's fine."

She fanned herself with both hands. The sun was almost directly above them now, and the sweat was beading down the side of her face. The back of her neck was dewy, and she had that uncomfortable boob sweat.

He leaned in close. "Maybe I should've brought you a fan."

"It wouldn't be so bad if I wasn't wearing fifty-two layers of heavy clothing."

"That many, eh?" He reached behind the bench and plunked a much-too-big hat on her head. "This should help a bit." He turned his gaze to the road once more, softly whistling a tune she recognized from their own time.

She tied the string into a knot beneath her chin but had to tilt her head way back to see anything. A whiff of sandalwood surrounded her, the same fragrance from Josh's shirt. It must be his soap of choice. Now, every time she smelled sandalwood, she would associate it with him. And that wasn't a bad thing.

"So," Amber began, racking her brain for a conversation starter. "Tell me about Emma, and what's been going on with her."

Josh's body jerked toward her a time or two as he steered the wagon around some serious potholes and rocks in the road that would no doubt end up busting one of the skimpy wheels. Did he travel with a spare like they did in their own time?

"Emma loves being a mom," he told her, casting a glance in her direction. "She and Wyatt are sickeningly adorable together. They love each other…the way my parents loved each other. It's nice to see. Plus, she misses you."

She looked at him, and her heart thudded. "Really?"

"She talks about you all the time. Wesley's been hearing about Auntie Amber since before he came out of the womb."

Tears stung the backs of her eyes, and she blinked them away. "I feel horrible."

"About what?"

"I was so mad at her last year when she returned to our time. I-I couldn't understand why she wanted to go back to the Old West." *And leave me*. She sniffed. "I'll admit, her being gone has been like a death to me. We've been best friends since we were in diapers." She looked down at her hands. "Since Emma left, I talk to her like she's still here, still with me. It's weird, I know, but it helps."

He smiled. "You are definitely two peas in a pod. More than once, I caught her talking to you, too. She would just smile and say, 'I miss my best friend.'"

When Amber decided to make the trip back in time, she hadn't even considered Emma might not be there. She automatically assumed her friend and husband would be home. Where else would they be? It wasn't as if they'd be working at an office somewhere. This was the Old West. All she wanted to do was save Emma and Wyatt from an untimely death. That is, if she could find them before the engraving on their tombstones came to fruition. As luck would have it, they were away. Instead, she found Josh, and meeting him had thrown her off balance.

He nudged her. "Earth to Amber."

She playfully shoved his elbow away. "I'm sorry. I

was just thinking. I didn't hear what you said."

"I said we should stop for a bit so I can give my horse food and water. Plus, it'll be a good time for a…bathroom break."

She looked around, then at him. "Where?"

Josh tugged the reins, and the wagon came to a stop. He jumped out, rounded the wagon, and held up his arms. Amber put her hands on his shoulders. Josh grabbed her hips, and she fell against him. Her body slowly slid down the length of his hard, muscular frame. Warmth filled her. Their eyes met—and locked. Damn him for having the most gorgeous green eyes she had ever seen. She licked her lips, at a loss for words.

"You can use those bushes, if you need to," he said, cocking his head. "I've got to water my horse."

"Okey dokie." She raised the hem on her skirt and trudged into the bushes, looking for a safe spot. Oh, no! She didn't have toilet paper with her. "Josh…?" she shouted.

"Sorry to disappoint you, city girl, but you'll have to make do without toilet paper for now. I'll pick up some sheets from the general store when we get back."

"Super." She rolled her eyes and finished her business, searching for a few extra-large leaves. The idea of wiping herself with anything but toilet paper grossed her out, but she did it anyway. Hopefully, the leaves she pulled off the nearby plant weren't poison ivy. Righting her panties and skirt, she washed her hands in the stream, then marched back to Josh.

"Everything all right?" he asked.

"Peachy." She tried to climb back into the wagon but couldn't quite get herself up on her own. Josh's hands were around her waist again to assist. "Thanks."

He tossed the oat bag into the back of the wagon, then climbed in, and slapped the reins. "A few more hours and then we'll stop for the night."

****

Josh enjoyed riding in companionable silence. Since he and Amber had just met, he wanted to get to know her, the *real* Amber Harrison. Over the course of the past year, Emma talked about her so much that sometimes he wondered if the funny stories were true. One thing was certain. She was brave as all hell. After all, she traveled back in time to save her best friend. Given the choice, not everyone would do that. It meant facing the unknown and forsaking one's own life and routine.

He glanced at her. The sun had colored her cheeks a healthy red, giving her face a warm glow, not that she needed it. She was naturally beautiful. "Tell me, what was Amber Harrison like as a child? Inquiring minds want to know."

She turned her face toward him, tipped her hat back, and smiled. Pearly white teeth peeked out from between full ruby lips. "Oh, you know, the same. I was daring and always pushing others to do crazy stuff…"

"That I believe. After all, you're here…in another century."

She met his gaze. "That I am, cowboy."

"What about your parents? What were they like?"

She looked away, biting down on her lip. "My mom was the best mom ever. We did everything together. She and Emma's mom were super close. I guess that's why Emma and I are more like sisters than best friends. Can't tell you about my dad because he up and left before I was born."

His stomach bottomed out. He was a fool to assume

that because he had an amazing mom who always encouraged her children to do their best, and a father who doted on him and his brothers, that she did, too. "I'm sorry."

"Don't be," she said, waving a hand. "I can't miss what I never had. My mom was my whole world…until she was killed, along with my grandpa. An old man with dementia who had no business driving got behind the wheel and…" She smoothed out her skirt, staring into her lap.

"I'm so sorry." What else was there to say when someone divulged that they, too, lost a loved one, and so tragically, too. He itched to ask a thousand questions, but instead, gave her the time to continue if she wanted to. If she didn't, he wouldn't press her.

"I think I get why you wanted to stay here," she said at last.

"You do?"

"Your parents were never in the nineteenth century, so you don't have any memories of them physically here, though you carry them in your heart."

"Wow, are you sure you're not psychic?" Josh let out a slow, deep breath. "You're right, though. It's easier to stay lost with no physical reminders of the life I once lived with the people I'll always love but will never see again."

"Don't stay lost too long. You still have family at home waiting for you." She shook her head. "Ugh, forgive me. I think the trip through time turned my mind to mush."

"There's nothing to forgive. It's happened to me, too. Don't worry."

He slapped the reins, and the wagon continued its

bouncing journey onward. His heart twisted tight. Losing his parents had been a nightmare he still couldn't wake up from. And the thought of losing either of his brothers to an early death was more than he could fathom. Yet, Amber experienced the untimely loss of the only parent she had ever known along with her beloved grandparent. It would never make any sense to him why the good died young, but thieving, murdering bastards were left to walk this earth. He had the sudden urge to hold her tight and do his best to keep her safe.

They rode in silence for quite some time before Josh announced, "And…here we are." He yanked the reins, and the wagon stopped.

"Where?" Amber asked, eyeing the surroundings.

"The horse needs to rest, and so do we." He got out of the wagon and helped her down before grabbing two saddlebags and blankets. "You can spread these out over there—" He cocked his head toward a small clearing. "There are extra blankets in the wagon we can use for pillows."

Amber frowned, marching over to the clearing. "When you said we'll stop for the night, this isn't exactly what I had in mind," she said.

"I know." He laughed, then unhitched his horse to graze near a small stream. "It'll be fun," he said, returning to her. "Think of it as…an adventure."

She thrust her hands on her hips and made a screwy face at the beginnings of their camp. "I guess staying at a hotel or an inn is out of the question, huh?"

"We'd have to ride too many miles out of the way, so yes, it is. I'm sorry." Snatching the basket out of the wagon, he put it in the middle of the blanket. "I'll make us a fire and see if I can rustle up a critter or two for dinner."

Her eyes widened. "Whoa, hold your horses there, cowboy. I'm okay eating dead flesh after some butcher has made it edible and all that, but don't expect me to eat anything that was just walking around here moments ago. Because if it's cute, I'll be giving it a name."

Josh couldn't stop the burst of laughter that escaped him. "I don't mean to laugh, but the longer you're here, the less you'll be thinking about that. Believe me. Start with this," he said, picking up the basket and handing it to her. "I'll go see what else I can find."

Chuckling to himself, he left the traps inside the wagon and set out for the thicket in search of something else to eat.

Chapter Six

Amber kept glancing at Josh. They were sitting around the small campfire, sharing a loaf of stale bread, a chunk of cheese, and a small mugful of wild huckleberries Josh had gathered. She popped a few of the purplish berries into her mouth. There were some tart ones in the bunch, but overall, they were sweet and now her new favorite berry. A small enamel coffee pot, like the one at the house but smaller, sat to the side, off the blaze of the fire. The fact that he didn't hunt for their dinner didn't go unnoticed or unappreciated. It was like he was going out of his way to make her feel comfortable in an uncomfortable situation. His kind nature warmed her.

The trip through the centuries had to be wreaking havoc on her system, turning her brain to mush. Why else would she even mention her mom and Grandpa to Josh? It wasn't like she divulged all her childhood nightmares. Still, she never talked about their deaths or even her sister to anyone, outside of Emma and her therapist. Josh had made her feel comfortable, safe. Normally, Amber was more guarded, careful never to reveal anything too personal.

"Thanks for not catching dinner," she said. "I don't think I could've enjoyed it if you had."

"And that is exactly why I decided that berries would be best." Josh tossed a huckleberry into the air and successfully caught it in his mouth. "Plus, they're healthier for you, or so they say. They've got antioxidants or something. Emma makes amazing jam out of these and blueberries."

"Yeah, I had noticed the rows of jam jars in the pantry," she said with a nod. "It's hard for me to imagine her as little Miss Frontier Mom. She was always so independent and creative, a true career woman. I guess I never thought she'd get married and settle down to being a happy homemaker."

"And what about you?" He tossed a huckleberry at her. There was a playful glint in his eyes...or maybe that was the glow of the fire. "Do you want those same things—children and marriage and all that comes with it?"

"Me?" That caught her off guard, but she'd give him the same answer whenever someone asked her that very same annoying question. "Oh, I don't think so. Marriage and kids may be good for some people, but not me. Emma is the mom-type. I'm the favorite auntie type." Dating was too much of an effort and always left at least one person with a broken heart. Besides, her time was precious, and most of it over the past year had been spent worrying about Emma living in another century. What guy would put up with that?

Josh watched her for a moment, then squatted down to pour the coffee, balancing two cups, one on each thigh. The fabric of his pants strained against the muscles in his powerful thighs. He did everything with ease, and there wasn't anything he neglected to bring on their trip...except toilet paper.

"Coffee?" He handed her a tin cup.

"Thanks." She took a few sips and decided coffee

wasn't such a great idea. The road trip brew wasn't as good as the one he made back at the house, and she wasn't sure her stomach could handle it.

"I'll stay up for a bit, but if you want to get some shuteye, feel free."

Setting aside the cup, she stood up and walked toward the thicket. "I guess I better find another bush first," she said lightly.

His laughter followed her into the darkness, lit only by the light of the bright moon. Amber took care of business, then went down to the stream to wash out her bra and panties. *Note to self: if I ever travel back in time again, bring extra panties and real soap.* The floral soap Emma had made smelled nice, but it was already too drying on her sensitive skin. Without facial cleansers suited to her skin type, she couldn't wash her face properly. Since she wasn't wearing any makeup, washing with only water should be okay. She hoped. The last thing she wanted was a face full of flaky, dry skin or worse, zits.

A few minutes later, she returned and laid out her underwear to dry on the front bench of the wagon. Josh was reclining comfortably on the blanket, his hat covering his face, most likely asleep.

"I didn't hear any screaming this time," he mumbled from beneath the hat. "I guess all went well?"

"You're such a wiseass."

He pulled the hat off his face, grinning. "It's all part of my charm."

"I can see that."

He placed his hat over his face and entwined his fingers, resting them on his chest. "We should leave at dawn. It won't be a long ride tomorrow."

She settled on the blanket, but it was difficult to get comfortable with a stiff saddlebag under her head for a pillow. The scurrying of unidentifiable critters in the background, the rustling of leaves, and other crunching sounds in the distance pricked at her spine, as did the random thought of Indians lurking in the bushes. This was really how cowboys in the nineteen-hundreds traveled. All the films and TV shows she had seen over the years romanticized the Old West. Not once did they make mention of how they bathed or relieved themselves. Now, she understood why.

"I have to be honest with you, Josh," she announced. "I'm not sure about this camping business. There are all sorts of weird noises that are freaking me out. Plus, I keep picturing us either being scalped by Indians or getting bitten by venomous snakes—or worse. Don't forget, I'm a city girl, and there's only so much bravado I can exhibit."

He removed his hat again to glance at her. "Don't worry. I won't let anything eat you while you sleep."

"Not funny. Now I'll be up all night." Clearly, he was not taking pity on her. It wasn't like there was anything he could do, anyway. After all, they were out in the wild…away from civilization…where no one could hear them if they were set upon by grizzly bears or Indians! Great, now she'd *never* sleep. "How cold will it get tonight?"

"Not too cold, but there will be a chill." He reached behind his head and gave her the blanket he was using for a pillow. "Use mine. I won't need it."

"That's so sweet of you. Thanks." Amber covered herself with the thin blanket that reached to her shins and tucked it below her chin. She closed her eyes and sighed, but sleep evaded her. Something ran through the leaves a few feet away. The symphony of the forest amplified to a crescendo, and a critter of some kind crawled across her hand.

"Get it off me!" Amber slapped at the blanket, and then jumped to her feet, shaking out her skirt.

"I can see this is going to be a long night." Josh got up and checked her hair and clothes for any evidence of the critter. "Why don't we set you up in the wagon tonight? I think you'll be more comfortable in there."

"You'll get no argument from me." She clutched the blanket against her, while Josh moved her makeshift bed to the back of the wagon. He even propped up the saddlebags for pillows.

"My lady," he said, with a sweep of his arm.

"Thank you, kind sir." She climbed into the wagon and got settled, already feeling better. "I'm sorry. You must think I'm such a baby."

"No, I think you're a city girl who has yet to become one with nature," he said with a wink and turned to go.

"Wait! Where are you going?"

For a hot second, he looked confused. He hitched a thumb toward their camp. "I'm sleeping by the fire."

"Um…would you mind…staying here with me? I'd feel better if I knew you were close by."

He eyed the wagon, and then her. "Sure."

Amber released the breath she'd been holding. She lived in New York City—the city that never sleeps, the capital of the world where taxis constantly honked their horns, and crazy people walked around at all hours of the day and night—how could she be afraid of a few nocturnal noises? Maybe because this was the wild, Wild West.

Josh settled himself on the front bench. He tucked his saddlebag under his head for a pillow and plunked his hat over his face. "Nite, Amber."

"Nite." She closed her eyes and drifted off to sleep with a smile.

****

Amber stirred, but she snuggled into the surrounding warmth of her scratchy blanket, enjoying the comfort of dreamland. A cool breeze blew, and she opened her eyes. Josh's piercing emerald gaze met hers. He was leaning over the back of the bench, grinning.

"Good morning," he said, and the soft lines around his eyes crinkled a little.

Clearing her throat, she pulled the blanket over her mouth so he wouldn't smell her morning breath, and said, "Morning."

Josh rested his chin on his arm. The half-sleepy expression on his face curved his mouth into a hint of a smile. He had nice lips. His butternut blond hair fell onto his forehead, and she fought the urge to smooth it back. Wide dark eyebrows shaded deep-set green eyes. The Kincaid brothers sure came from one spectacular gene pool of hotness.

He tugged her blanket playfully. "What's this about?"

"Morning breath."

"Ah." With his free hand, he handed her a small jar. "I brought that great tasting tooth scrub for you."

Aww. "Thank you," she mumbled under the blanket. "You're too good to me. I'll go by the stream and freshen up." Jar in hand, she scooted herself to the end of the wagon before jumping off.

"Don't forget these." He twirled her modern skimpy

lace panties around his forefinger.

How could she have forgotten she had left them on the bench to dry overnight? She covered her face with a hand and laughed. "You really are such a wiseass. I think you need a good whuppin'."

He waggled his eyebrows. "That could be fun."

"*Gah.*" She stammered, unable to think of a proper comeback for that unexpected response. Snatching her panties from his hand, she grabbed her bra off the bench, and then headed for the stream.

Damn man had her system all out of whack. And why was that, by the way? She had never been this affected by anyone before. Well, maybe once after college with her Scottish ex, but not recently. Josh had a way of slowly weaving his way into her head, not to mention getting her blushing like a ninth grader.

Fifteen minutes later, after taking care of morning necessities and forcing herself to think of something other than Josh, she returned to their camp. The horse was hitched up, and Josh was ready to go. He helped her into the wagon and off they went, heading for Deer Lodge. Unlike yesterday, their ride would be much quicker since they had fewer miles to cover.

A little while later, the town came into view as the wagon jounced along the rough roads to Main Street. Buildings were spread out in all directions, and they looked like something out of a nineteenth-century photograph, except in color. Most of the structures were on the shorter side. Some of the two-story buildings lining each side of the road had false fronts. The usual establishments of saloons, general stores, banks, and barbers appeared along the way. In the distance, three church steeples dotted the area, and a large stone building with a high wood fence sat on the south end of the town.

Cowboys rode by wearing stained bandanas, pants, and vests with six-shooters strapped to their waists. Some of the women had bustles, while others wore simple blouses and skirts. No matter what the women wore, they all had a six-inch hem of dirt and mud. What's worse, the smell of horse dung permeated the air. The stench was so bad, Amber nearly gagged.

"Eew, gross," she said, covering her nose. "It smells like poop, and lots of it."

"C'mon, it's not that bad." Josh pulled a handkerchief out of his pocket and handed it to her. "You'll get used to it."

She covered half her face with it. "No chance of that," she choked out. "Where's the inn we're staying at?"

"Just up ahead. It's a boarding house, really. I'll see if I can get us two rooms."

With the cloth covering her face, the smell was tolerable. "Too bad you couldn't call ahead or make a reservation online. How will you know if there are rooms available?"

"I'll find out once we get there, and I ask."

"We're in the Dark Ages," she mumbled, which elicited a chuckle from Josh.

At the far end of town, they stopped in front of a two-story house with a sorry excuse for a porch. The home looked like it had seen better days. A fresh coat of paint, clean windows, and a few repairs to the railing would make it look more inviting.

Josh tossed Amber the reins and got out. "I'll be back in a minute. Wait here."

"Gee, thanks," she mumbled, watching him walk away. She glanced down the street. Except for the occasional passerby, a wagon or two, and tumbleweeds rolling down the street, it was uneventful.

A few minutes later Josh returned. "I've got good news and bad, which would you like first?" he asked.

"Bad news. There's no point in delaying it."

"All right." He looked surprised at her comment. "Mrs. Roth only has one room available. I didn't tell her we'd need two. If I did, there would be too many questions, and this is the only place in town I'll stay. Anyway, one room means you'll have to be my wife on this trip. Is that okay with you, Mrs. Kincaid?"

"Uh, yeah. I guess." She had never been a pretend wife before, except in acting class in high school. "I'm just curious, what was the good news?"

"Mrs. Roth will have supper ready at five. I should be back by then."

"Where are you going?"

"The prison."

Josh lifted his arms and grabbed her waist. Amber put her hands on his shoulders and slid against him until her feet touched the dusty ground. His hands lingered for a moment.

"You're going now?" she asked.

"Yeah, I want to get this out of the way so we can head back tomorrow. I don't want to be away from home for too long."

Josh took her hand and led her inside. The appetizing aroma of food cooking in the kitchen filled the air. They were greeted by an older woman whom she assumed was Mrs. Roth. Her blue eyes sparkled when she saw Josh.

"This must be your lovely wife," the woman said, smiling.

"It is," Josh replied, his face suddenly red. "Mrs. Roth, this is…Mrs. Kincaid."

"It's a pleasure," Mrs. Roth said, reaching for Amber's hands. "Why, the few times the good deputy has stayed here, he made no mention of a wife."

"Um, that's because we're newly married," he told her.

"Oh, that's wonderful news," she said, and then turned back to Amber. "I'm happy to meet you, dear. Your husband is such a good man and doesn't deserve to be alone. Pardon me for just a moment." She walked away, toward the back of the house, talking to herself, then returned with a small tray of biscuits and tea. "For you, Mrs. Kincaid. I know your husband has business to tend to now. We can sit and have a visit while he's away."

"Sounds like fun. And please, call me Amber." Amber turned to Josh, batting her eyes, and playing up her fake wife role. "All right, sweetheart, I guess I'll see you later."

"You will, indeed, sweets." Josh reached for her hands, pulled her close, and gazed down at her. "Mmm, I like calling you that," he whispered. "It suits you, sweets."

Sweets? The world suddenly went still. Her heart did some major thumping against her chest when he planted a soft kiss on her cheek. Her skin tingled…*everywhere*. She mentally shook herself, not knowing what to make of her reaction.

Before she could say anything else, he donned his hat, snatched a biscuit off the tray, and walked out the door.

"You must tell me how you two met," Mrs. Roth said, pouring out two cups of tea.

****

Josh tied his horse to the hitching post inside the prison's tall wooden fence and went inside the building. He had been to Deer Lodge a few times before, and each time, the place made his skin crawl. This time was no different. The inmates were serving time for a wide range of crimes, including horse theft, assault, and murder. At this time of day, most of the prisoners were out of their cells working on chores, gardening, and cutting wood.

He walked up to the main desk inside the entryway. The warden was a tough looking, handlebar-mustached man. "Kincaid," he said, greeting Josh with a nod. "Reed sent over a wire that you want to see Grey."

"Yes, sir," Josh replied.

"Carson!" The warden barked over his shoulder at a guard waiting at the iron-bar door behind the desk.

Carson was a tall, lanky fellow with a scruffy beard and dirt smudges on his uniform and hat. He didn't look like the sharpest tool in the shed. Josh kept an eye on him while the man struggled to unlock the heavy iron door and ushered him down the dark, dank hall currently lit only by the light of the guard's lamp. Most of the inmates were outside, so Josh wasn't subject to any potential heckling, which was the norm when a lawman showed up. Prisoners hated to see deputies and marshals on the premises. It was a reminder of who put them behind bars for their crimes.

Josh counted fourteen cells in the corridor, and Carson stopped at the second to last one. He eyed Josh over his shoulder, unlocked the door, and then went inside. Chains rattled and muffled voices came from within.

Carson returned, walking right up to Josh. They were the same height. He smelled like he hadn't had a bath in a month—or brushed his teeth for a year. "You sure you want to go inside?"

Josh leaned back, pinching his nose. "Out of my way," he demanded.

The guard mumbled something under his breath, and then stepped aside. Josh walked into the cell, and the door slammed shut behind him.

"I'll be right out here," Carson said, showcasing his toothless grin.

The space couldn't have been more than six-by-eight feet. It was small, dark, and clammy, and it smelled like urine and sweat. A small chamber pot sat in the corner, perhaps, the source of the stench. The floor was covered in dirt. A mouse scouted for some crumbs in the far corner. There was no bed, except for a bench with a blanket at the foot of it. On it sat a middle-aged man in handcuffs chained to the wall behind him. From what he heard the warden ran a tight ship. This cell shouldn't look like such a pigsty.

"Well, well," Griffin Grey said, raising his chained hands in greeting. There was dirt around his once perfectly manicured fingernails. "If it isn't my old pal, Deputy Josh Kincaid. I must say, I'm surprised you made the trip to see little ol' me."

Grey had aged years in the few months since Josh last saw him. While the man still had a thick head of hair, it was mostly gray now. His face was etched with deep lines, and purple shadows highlighted his sunken eyes. The man's cold, blue gaze hadn't changed, but his physique had. He was thinner and gaunter looking than his former self, and his prison uniform draped on his body like it was just a mere hanger constructed of bones.

"Let's cut the bullshit." Josh crossed the cell to stand in front of Grey. "I want to know about the portal. More specifically, what do you know about it, and how did you discover it in the future?"

Grey tilted his head to the side, studying Josh. "I don't see you for months, Deputy, and now you come in here demanding information from me. Why should I tell you anything?"

"What's the difference? You're not going anywhere."

Grey stood up slowly, as if age had caught up with him, but his chains kept him bound to the cement wall. They stood eye to eye. The blue of Grey's eyes was like cold steel. Even if the man hadn't been shackled, Josh wouldn't be afraid of him. Grey wasn't the type of man to resort to physical violence. He left that to his minions.

"I found the portal quite by accident." Grey's jaw clenched; his eyes slightly narrowed. "A few years ago, in the future that is, I was looking for a vacation property to purchase. I had a ranch in Butte but liked Whisper Creek better. As I drove by your brother's spread, admiring its view, and not knowing it was his at the time, I liked it immediately. There was a certain…feeling about it, if you will. It wasn't for sale then, and no one seemed to be home, so I took it upon myself to check out the property. I had hoped to make the owner an offer he couldn't refuse."

"Go on," Josh prodded when Grey fell silent.

"There was an odd light coming from the side door of the garage. It was unlike anything I'd ever seen before.

I knocked on the door and called out a greeting, but no one answered. It was unlocked, so I went inside. I didn't see the light again, but one minute I was in the garage and the next minute, after a maze of bright light and total silence, I was in a barn."

Josh wracked his brain, trying to figure out just *when* Grey had been on his brother's property in their own time. It must've been right before Wyatt went through the portal. "Then what?"

"Once I convinced myself that I was not losing my mind, I decided to take a walk and investigate. After walking for miles, I ended up in town, exploring Whisper Creek as it was in the nineteenth century. Hours later, I worried about whether I'd be able to get back, and I returned to the barn. I must've walked around every inch of that building until I went through the portal and back to the exact location I had left from."

"How did you get back to your real time?"

"Back then, I didn't comprehend how, but after giving it much thought, I figured it out. You see, the day that I first traveled back, I had conducted some business in Helena. Tucked in my suit pocket was a legal document I had signed hours earlier in my own time." He shrugged. "It was the only thing that made sense to me, that having something written or a tactile object from a particular time period was required to travel."

Josh studied him for a moment, waiting for more. "But you had nothing on you dated the nineteenth century."

A slow grin curled his lips. "I did. That document, a property deed, was originally from 1880."

Chills skidded down Josh's spine. Curiosity ate at him. "What property?"

Grey shrugged a shoulder. "Let's just say it's property in town that belongs to me."

"Is that when you decided to cheat people out of their hard-earned savings here in this century?"

"Oh, Kincaid," he said, sardonically. "When I realized that what I did here had an impact on my life in the future, well, I couldn't help it. I'm a businessman. I like money. And I saw an opportunity to make some—correction, lots of—money."

"Did you hire someone to threaten or try to kill Emma Kincaid?" Josh charged.

Grey's eyes widened. "That's not my style. Like I said, I like money and making it. I'd rather be doing that than sitting here, rotting away. My health has taken a bit of a hit. It's very damp in the cooler months." He held up his shackled hands. "And as you can see, I'm in no position to harm anyone." He took a step toward Josh, the farthest he could move with shackles. "Don't worry, Kincaid. I wouldn't harm a hair on Emma's pretty, little head. She's a precious gem."

Josh should get a medal for restraining himself from beating the shit out of Grey. Blood rushed to his face in a flash of heat, and he bit down hard, gritting his teeth. He clenched his fists to keep from punching the bastard.

"Oh, come now, Deputy," Grey taunted. "I'm in *here*, prison, thanks to you and your brother. What could I possibly do to your family from behind bars?"

When Josh spoke again, his voice was scratchy like gravel. "Does the date December thirty-first mean anything to you?"

Grey frowned. "No. Should it?"

Josh studied Grey's reaction. He wasn't an expert on body language; but he could read people well enough.

Grey was withholding information. "Even with you behind bars I don't trust you."

"I guess I can't please everyone." A grin appeared on Grey's thin, chapped lips. He tilted his head; his eyes were hard and cold. "I see no reason for you to be here now, Kincaid. After all, you're just one of the deputies who got me arrested. And well, I can't be tried twice for the same crime, or something along those lines."

"That is true, but I came here with a purpose."

"Ah, I knew there had to be a reason. The suspense is killing me."

Josh removed his hat and swept a hand through his hair, damp with sweat. "I sure hope it is, because even if you did serve out your entire sentence here, I want you to know, to understand, that you're never returning home the way you arrived. So you may as well sit back, relax, and enjoy your permanent stay in a nineteenth-century prison with all its wonderful accommodations that the warden has to offer." He turned to leave.

"Wait!" Grey shouted.

Josh stopped and slowly turned around.

Grey leaned forward and lowered his voice. "I can make it worth your while…if you get me an early release."

Josh flexed his jaw. "Bribing an officer of the law? You should know better." He moved within inches of Grey. "Let me be clear so there's no misunderstanding. I came here to assure you that you will never see the light of day or the portal again. Ever. You will never be *allowed* on our property. Ever. My brother and I will make sure of that."

Grey's face turned red, taut with anger. "I am not going to spend another fucking minute longer than I have to in this shithole century."

Josh folded his arms across his chest. "Yeah, it kind of sucks that you got busted and have to sit behind bars to pay for your crimes. I wouldn't be too happy either if I cheated people out of their hard-earned money and expected to get away with it…but didn't." He leaned toward the door and shouted, "Guard!"

Carson returned to unlock the door. Without another glance at Grey, Josh marched out of the stuffy cell.

"Kincaid, wait!" Grey shouted. "Dammit, I said wait!"

Chapter Seven

Amber spent the remainder of the afternoon with Mrs. Roth, listening to her talk about her life with her husband and her plans to live with her sister in California. She liked Mrs. Roth and was amazed at how the woman made an entire meal during their conversation without missing a beat. Amber helped, of course, but her kitchen skills were limited. They were just boiling the potatoes when Josh returned.

"Deputy!" Mrs. Roth beamed, wiping her hands on her apron. "You're just in time. Dinner is ready. The other guests will be down to join us shortly."

"Perfect timing then." Josh walked up to Amber and peered over her shoulder. "You cook?" he whispered in her ear.

"I make better reservations," she replied, nudging him away. His laughter made her smile. If anyone had told her a week ago that she would end up walking through a time portal and landing in 1883, she'd never believe it.

The table was set, and the other boarders came down for dinner. Aside from her and Josh, there was a young married couple and a mother with her toddler daughter. She couldn't imagine what it would be like to raise a child in such a backward century as this one with no electricity in rural areas, no telephones, and no decent healthcare. The people living in this place in time didn't think of it that way. It was only her perspective, of course. And that made her wonder how the families around this table would feel if they had ventured into the future, to Amber's time. Would they be in awe or frightened or curious? If only they knew where Amber and Josh truly came from.

Amber kept quiet through dinner and let Josh do most of the talking, mainly because she didn't want to say anything out of context or inappropriate for this century. Certain expressions and sayings that were well understood in her own time could be misconstrued here, and she didn't want to embarrass herself or Josh. If she started rambling on, she might expose something of the future, and she couldn't allow that to happen.

After dinner, Amber and Josh said goodnight, and then climbed the creaky wooden steps to their room on the second floor.

"All right, the suspense is killing me," she admitted. "I've been wanting to ask you since you got back—how did it go with Grey?"

"As I expected," Josh replied, as they reached the landing, juggling both of their bags. "My mission was to get him to cough up details on how he discovered the portal, which he did. And then I promised him that even if he were ever to get out of jail, Wyatt and I would never let him near the portal. He didn't like that."

"I imagine he wouldn't; but there was another reason you went."

He nodded. "I needed to see his eyes, see if he was up to something. My gut says it's him and his associates that shot at Wyatt. Until I have proof, there's not much I can do. This is us," Josh announced, opening the door at the end of the hall.

Amber hadn't been to their room yet, so she wasn't sure what to expect. A woosh of moist, warm air hit her in the face. The room was small, stuffy, and smelled like old linens that had been stuffed into a box in the attic for too long. One lone window looked out over the street, and the sounds of horses' hooves and wagons clattering outside were close enough to touch. What really grabbed her attention was the teeny, tiny bed against the opposite wall. It was so narrow it could pass for a twin. A washstand with a pitcher and basin, two upholstered parlor chairs, and a chamber pot next to the bed completed the room.

"After you, sweets," Josh said close to her ear, and his warm breath sent goosebumps tingling across her flesh. She rubbed them away and walked into the room.

"It's like a suite at the Ritz," she joked, spreading her arms wide.

He laughed and then dropped their bags on the bed. "I forgot how small the rooms are here. When it's just me, it's no big deal. Sorry."

"It's fine," she assured him. "It comes with the territory of traveling back to the Old West." She grabbed her bag and headed for the door. "So where's the bathroom? I've been holding it all day, and I want to take a bath."

A smile tugged at his lips. "I hate to disappoint you, city girl, but Mrs. Roth doesn't have one."

"No bathroom…at all?"

He pointed. "There's a chamber pot to relieve yourself and an outhouse outside, of course. Guests usually bathe in the big tub in the kitchen."

Amber bit her tongue to keep from voicing her displeasure. She wasn't the type of person who would ever willingly choose to live in this century, not when she had hot showers, spas, and her fancy cappuccino machine at home. Thankfully, this was only temporary…that is, if they could get the damn portal working again. "All righty, then," she said at last. "I'll ask Mrs. Roth about the tub."

"I'm afraid you're going to have a long wait for hot water. There are only so many buckets that can fit in her hearth at one time."

"This just keeps getting better, doesn't it?"

"I think so," he said, gazing down at her. "Listen, I know this isn't what you were expecting, so I will make you a promise. When we return to Whisper Creek, I will draw you the hottest, soapiest, bestest bath you've ever had in your life. Until then, you can enjoy a sponge bath in the privacy of our room. I'll get you some water, and then wait downstairs until you're done. Okay?"

Amber's heart melted. Josh was so considerate and sweet, and here she was acting like a pampered modern girl…which she was. That's not what she wanted him to think, though. She wanted to impress him, make him think she was as adaptable as he was to whatever situation came her way.

"Thank you for such an amazing offer," she said. "I'll take you up on that."

"Excellent," he said, opening the door. "I'll be back in a flash." True to his word, several minutes later, Josh returned with two buckets of warm water. He placed them and a small bar of soap by the washstand. "I'll return in a half hour. In the meantime, have fun."

Amber waited until the sound of his footfalls faded away at the bottom of the steps before she indulged in a sponge bath. The soap Josh left for her was similar in texture and size to the one she used at Emma's. This one, though, smelled summery like verbena and lavender. After washing up, she dressed in Millie's simple shift that would pass for a nightgown. Unfortunately, the material was gauzier than she expected and barely touched her knees. Grabbing her blouse, modern-day bra, and panties, she dunked them all into the second bucket and scrubbed them clean with the small chunk of lye soap she found next to the basin.

No sooner had she finished draping her wet clothes over the backs of the two chairs that there was a knock on the door.

"It's me," Josh whispered loudly.

"Come in."

The door opened, and he stood there, hand on the knob. His gaze roamed over her, lingering on her breasts. "Hey," he said in a low, throaty voice that sounded sexy to her.

"Hey," she replied. Heat rushed to her face, burning her cheeks. The soft fabric of her nightgown did nothing to cover her suddenly perky nipples, and she folded her arms over her chest. "Perfect timing. I'm all done. Thanks again for the privacy."

"You're welcome." He gestured to the two buckets of now dirty water. "I'll take these. I'm going to wash up downstairs." He picked up the buckets and headed out the door.

Amber turned down the cover on the bed and frowned. It was barely big enough for one person, and she wasn't about to sleep on the floor or ask Josh to, either. She sighed, went to the window, and stuck her head out. The crisp night air felt refreshing on her damp skin and about twenty degrees cooler. The evening sky had turned into night, but that didn't stop the hecklers. A few shabby-looking men across the street caught sight of her and whistled, shouting things that translated the same in any century.

"Idiots," she mumbled.

Amber pulled back into the room and gasped. Josh had returned wearing nothing except a too small, thread-bare towel tucked around his tapered hips. Not much was left to her imagination. He took a step, and the towel parted, exposing a perfectly muscular thigh, covered in a light dusting of blond hair. His chest was tanned and smooth. And, oh, those abs—*hell-o, six-pack*! His arms were well chiseled and tight, flexing as he clutched his boots and gun belt in one hand. All those delicious muscles must be from days of hard work around the house. Heat surged southward to her core. Her body was on full alert.

"Hey," he said at last in that same sexy, gravelly voice as before. He dropped his boots and belt by the door. A cloth of some kind was slung over one shoulder.

She swallowed. It had been so long since she'd seen a half-naked man. And one thing was for certain, her body remembered how to respond. "Hey," she returned. She licked her lips and tore her gaze away. "Where…where are your clothes?"

"Mrs. Roth has them. Whenever I stay here, I pay her extra to wash what I rode in on. She's saving up to travel to San Francisco to live with her sister. I figure it's a bit of a help, and I hate wearing sweaty clothes twice— or in this case, three times. If you want your clothes washed, too, just leave them outside the door in the hallway."

"That's all right. I already washed my blouse and

undies. Hopefully, they come out okay."

He spared those items a glance, grabbed the garment off his shoulder, and then slipped the old-fashioned nightshirt over his head.

"What are you wearing?" she asked, covering her mouth to hide her laughter.

"Don't laugh," he said, trying not to laugh either. "This is what men wear to bed in our current time."

The material was so short, it barely touched his thighs. If he bent over, she would catch a glimpse of his butt. Maybe she should drop something on the floor and see if he would bend over! She wouldn't mind stealing a peek. He reached under the nightshirt and yanked off the towel. *He was naked under there*! Her mind was going places...

"Compliments of Mrs. Roth," he continued, tossing the towel on one of the two chairs. "It belonged to her late husband. I told her the long johns would be much too warm for tonight." He glanced down at himself, and then shrugged, chuckling. "I guess he was a lot shorter."

She rolled her eyes and giggled. "You think?"

Josh reached for the extra blanket at the foot of the bed. "I'll sleep on the floor."

"Okay. I mean, no. Wait. There's... enough room for the two of us." She touched his hand, but then pulled away. "I think we can manage. We're both adults. You've been incredibly sweet to me since I arrived. I can't have you sleeping on this ridiculously hard, splintered floor."

He met her gaze, then quirked an eyebrow upward. "Are you sure?"

Be still, beating heart. "Positive."

"All right," he replied after a slight hesitation.

"Thanks." He crawled into bed, scooted to one side, and patted the mattress. "C'mon, let's get some rest. We'll be leaving early."

Her belly erupted like a thousand butterflies had been let loose. Warmth filled her veins, shooting in all directions. The temperature in the room spiked at least by a hundred degrees, if her body was any judge.

"I promise, I won't bite," he assured her when she didn't move. "By the way, I have something fun planned for you tomorrow."

"Oh? I can't wait to hear this."

"On the way back to Whisper Creek, I'm going to teach you how to steer the wagon."

"Will the excitement never cease?" she joked but still didn't make any attempt at moving toward the bed.

"I'm growing gray hair waiting."

And you'd look amazing with gray hair, I'm sure.

Amber reminded herself that she wasn't going to *sleep* with him. They were just going to sleep…together…in the same bed. No big deal. It's not like she was going to make out with him—or even have sex with him!

"I'm coming." She cringed inwardly at the double entendre, and then crawled into bed with her back to Josh. It was too hot in the room to use a sheet. His skimpy nightshirt and her flimsy gown provided the only wall of protection separating their warm bodies.

Closing her eyes, she prayed she would fall asleep quickly instead of having erotic dreams about the man sharing her bed.

****

Something itchy tickled Josh's nose. He opened his eyes, one at a time. The room was dark. Reaching for the small ticking clock next to the bed, he checked the time. It was barely past four. Amber was snuggled up against him, her nightgown hiked up to her thighs. Her hair smelled like the outdoors, though a faint hint of the lavender-scented shampoo she had used the other day lingered. The fragrance drove him crazy. All he wanted was to get closer to her, but he had to keep his distance. With half his body too close to her and one cheek hanging off the mattress, it was next to impossible.

He had stayed at the boarding house before and had no problem with the small space. However, sharing that sorry excuse for a bed with the most beautiful woman he'd ever laid eyes on, well, it took great restraint not to flip her on her back and take her…for starters. Images flashed through his head of what it would be like to kiss her luscious lips, and then run his mouth over her delectable body, tasting every inch of her honeyed flesh.

Christ, he'd never been so tempted in his life before. It wasn't like him to be this infatuated. They'd only known each other for a week, but it felt like a year. Regardless, he needed to keep his feelings under control. His body was wide awake, thinking of what her naked body would look like bathed in warm candlelight as he pleasured her until she cried out his name, her fingers biting into his shoulders, begging for more. Dammit. Lying in bed for hours on end next to the sleeping beauty only meant more torture, so he got up. They'd have to leave soon, anyway. Why torment himself any further? She was intoxicating, to say the least. And if it was up to him…hell, his lack of sleep would be for a different reason.

Slowly, and ever so carefully so as not to wake her, Josh planted both feet on the floor. He gazed over his shoulder at her, longing to run his hands through her long, auburn mane. What the hell was wrong with him? He should be focused on yesterday's meeting with Grey, not to mention Wyatt and his family. Instead, he was lusting after his sister-in-law's best friend.

Josh had been intrigued by her since the moment they met. Amber was a feisty woman who spoke her mind and held nothing back. More importantly, she traveled centuries to save her best friend, and that alone spoke volumes to her character. She had no ulterior motive or a desire to hang around in the Old West. She put her life in her own time on hold. Amber looked out for others, had their best interest at heart. It was easy to see why Emma loved her so much.

He tiptoed to the door, opened it, and checked the hallway. Sure enough, Mrs. Roth had left his washed and dried clothes in a neat, folded pile. He brought them into the room and slipped into his garments before claiming the empty cushioned chair in the corner. There, at least, he could get some shuteye, even if it was just for a couple of hours.

His gaze returned to Amber. Her chest rose and fell in a gentle rhythm with her breathing. She slept so peacefully, like she was having the sweetest dreams. He pondered what would happen once they returned to the future. Would she forget all about him and their time together, no matter how long that would turn out to be, and return to her normal life in New York City? Probably. After all, Amber was a sophisticated city girl. He was a country boy. Even though they were from the same time, they were from two different worlds. She loved her loud city life and everything in it. He loved the vastness and stillness of the outdoors.

Plunking his hat on his lap, he leaned his head against the wall and drifted off to sleep…dreaming of the woman occupying that very small bed, wishing she was in it for another reason.

****

The unsettling feeling of being watched permeated Amber's dream, and she forced herself awake. She blinked at the sudden darkness and sighed with relief. No one else was there. Wait. Where was Josh? The last thing she remembered was going to sleep…with him in the same bed!

Springing up, she clutched at the flimsy excuse for a sheet and gazed around the room. The only light was the moonlight seeping in through the window. It had to be the wee hours of the morning. Everything was eerily quiet. Even from the window there were no sounds of life on the street.

"Josh?" she whispered, squinting.

"I'm here." Josh lit a nearby lamp, and the room glowed. "Mornin', sweets." He was sitting in a corner chair fully dressed, hat in lap, his trusty saddlebags at his feet. His gaze steadily remained on her, and a warmth spread from her belly to her face.

"Why are you up so early?"

He shrugged. "I couldn't sleep."

"Oh. Was it the bed?"

"Yes."

"Oh." Talk about awkward. She could just imagine what she looked like without having had a real shower since leaving her own time, and she probably smelled like it, too. There's only so much she could scrub off in a sponge bath with ancient soap that dried her skin to resemble that of a lizard. To top it off, her hair was an unruly mess of knots, her usual bedhead morning look. No wonder he had to get out of bed! Inwardly, she cringed.

She waited for him to say more, but he didn't. Normally, he was chipper and way too perky in the morning, but not this time. His face was tight with tension, and his eyes were riveted on her. "What time is it?"

"Just after five," he replied, adjusting the hat in his lap. Two deep lines of worry appeared between his eyes.

She wished she could read his mind, but damn, for this time of morning, he looked good, stubble and all. "Is everything all right?"

"Why wouldn't it be?"

"You tell me. Were you watching me sleep? Because that's just…weird." But erotic, in a way. Maybe it wasn't a dream that someone watched her. It was Josh.

He cocked his head to the side. "No, I was waiting in the dark for you to wake up so we could get going."

"Oh," she said again.

Josh tugged his boots on, stood up, and then strapped the gun belt around his hips. This wasn't the first time she'd seen him put on the belt. This morning, though, there was something a little…sexy about the way he buckled the leather strap low around his waist. The weathered holster hugged his tapered hips, and a sudden image flashed in her mind of her thighs wrapped tightly around those same hips. *Oh my God, stop*!

He grabbed his saddlebags, and then walked to the door.

"Where are you going?" Her voice was a little shaky.

"Meet me downstairs in fifteen minutes." With that,

he walked out of the room and quietly closed the door behind him.

Amber flopped back against the bed, her head a mix of emotions—and her body a complete inferno of unfulfilled desire. Last night, she was nervous about sharing a bed with him, and while nothing happened, she wished it had. Maybe that was the problem. As attracted to Josh as she was, she was there on a mission. Once her best friend returned through the portal and was safe, back in their own time, then maybe things could be different. But damn, he was deliciously tempting…and distracting.

After dressing and rubbing that awful scrub on her teeth, she checked herself in the mirror. She winced at her nineteenth-century blouse and skirt, and then went downstairs to meet Josh.

For such an ungodly hour, Mrs. Roth was dressed and wide awake, waiting in the parlor with a basket of food. She saw Amber and smiled. "Did you sleep well?"

Amber couldn't help but smile in return, thinking of how she slept next to Josh in the confines of the teeny, tiny bed they had shared. It was the best night's sleep she'd gotten since arriving in this crazy century. "Very well, thank you, Mrs. Roth. My, er, husband and I thank you for you such warm hospitality."

The older woman took Amber's hands in hers. "I hope you and Deputy Kincaid will visit again. I know he comes to town from time to time on law business and such. Come before next spring. That's when I plan to move to my sister's in California."

Amber didn't have the heart to tell her that she'd never be back this way. In fact, if they could get the portal up and running tomorrow, she would be out of this century in a New York minute. Instead, she said, "As long as Josh's business permits me to accompany him, I'll do so."

"Don't forget this." Mrs. Roth handed Amber the basket and pointed as she explained what was packed within. "There's some fried chicken, a fresh loaf of bread that just came out of the oven, apples, and a chunk of cheese. That should tide you two over until you reach Whisper Creek."

Touched by the woman's thoughtfulness, Amber's throat tightened, and she pulled her into a hug. Maybe this century wasn't as bad as she first thought. The people here seemed genuinely kind and a little more caring than back home. "Thank you again."

Once outside, Josh hopped down from the wagon to help her. He grabbed the basket hanging on her arm, placed it in the wagon, and then stood before her, mere inches away.

"Hey," he said in that sexy voice, and his usual smile was back in place.

"Hey." This was their own little greeting, their own little hello. "Um, so, are we ready to go?"

"Just as soon as you get in."

Josh's strong hands gripped her at the waist and helped her onto the bench. Once she was settled, he climbed in, slapped the reins, and they began their two-day trip back to Whisper Creek. She wondered if Josh would sleep on the bench again on the overnight part of their journey. Not that she wanted him to. Being close to him got her blood pumping and thinking thoughts she wasn't sure she should be thinking.

They rode for several hours before Josh tugged the reins and the wagon stopped.

"What's the matter?" she asked.

"How quickly you forget. I promised to teach you how to steer the wagon."

"What, now?"

He grinned. "No better time than the present."

"I guess it can't be much different from being in the saddle."

"That's where you're wrong, and why I need to show you. You've already seen me harness the horse, so we'll skip that part for now." He handed her the reins. "At all times, you're to keep the reins in your hands. Never let go, no matter what happens. Now, hold the reins between your index and third fingers, like so."

Amber fumbled with the reins until she held them just as he had explained. "Got it…I think."

"You're doing great," he assured her. "Delorean doesn't need verbal commands, so if you flick the reins like this—" He reached over and gave them a gentle tug and click-click with his tongue. "—he'll follow your lead."

The wagon lurched forward, and Amber smiled. "Got it."

"You'll get used to the feel of the horse's mouth down the length of the rein. It's different than riding horseback."

Amber wasn't sure what she preferred, riding horseback or the ouchy bumping of the wagon, but she enjoyed learning a new skill.

An hour later, they stopped to give Amber a break and let the horse rest. Josh reached for the basket and handed it to her. "You've done so well for your first lesson, I'm going to reward you with a snack," he teased.

Amber laughed. "How thoughtful!" She ripped two chunks off the bread and handed him one, and then grabbed a piece of chicken. "I think we're making better time on this trip."

"We're covering the same terrain. It should take us the same amount of time unless we stop more often."

"I guess I'm just eager to get back...and see Emma when she returns to Whisper Creek, whenever that'll be."

He touched her hand. "I know you miss her and you're worried, but you'll see her soon."

Amber turned to Josh. For the short time that she had known him, he seemed unflappable. She wished she could be more like that at times.

"I'm really glad you're here," he told her, and his face reddened. "I mean, that you came back for Emma. You're a true friend. I admire that. She's lucky to have you."

And just like that her heart skipped a beat...or two. "I'm the lucky one."

Chapter Eight

The mid-afternoon sun cast hints of shadows over Whisper Creek's bustling Main Street. Like Deer Lodge, the town boasted boarded sidewalks and a variety of similar establishments from saloons and inns to a blacksmith and doctor's office. The bank and livery sat toward the far end of town, along with a water tower, tall windmill, and other buildings. Whisper Creek was cleaner than the prison town they just came from. It reminded Amber of one of those Old West living history museums she had visited in her own time, complete with false-fronted stores, hitching posts, and horse troughs.

Only this wasn't a museum. This was real life. *Her* life.

The Whisper Creek of 1883 looked nothing like it had when she was there a week ago in her own time. There were no parking meters, street signs, or LED streetlights. Gone were the souvenir shops, noisy bars, and cafés. Nothing familiar remained.

Josh slapped the reins, and they continued into town. A small cloud of dust swirled as the wagon bounced along the dirt road. The smell of horse dung pervaded the air, the same exact stench as back in Deer Lodge.

"Do all towns smell like horse crap?" she asked.

Josh laughed. "Pretty much, considering horses are the main mode of transportation."

"Super."

"It's better than sniffing exhaust fumes in a big city."

She made a face at that. "If you say so."

"After I drop you off, I'm going to meet with the marshal."

"Whoa, you're leaving me with a stranger?"

He grinned. "Just for a little bit. You'll be fine. Anne is great. She'll make you feel at home, especially if she serves you her *special* tea."

"Emma told me all about that."

"At least you're forewarned. Once I'm done with my rounds, I'll come back for you."

"Okay," she said, studying each building as they rode down the street. "So tell me about your boss. What's he like?"

"Marshal Charlie Reed is a good man. He's both town marshal and US Marshal."

"How does that work exactly?"

"He's a federal marshal," Josh began, "and the town marshal, appointed by Whisper Creek's Sheriff Calder, mainly to keep the peace. This town is a small dot on the map in a vast territory, so both positions are needed. And not everyone wants to fight danger. When necessary, Reed deputizes others to either help hold down the fort or ride out in a posse. Our nearest towns, which truthfully aren't all that near, are Helena and Montana City. That's why we need both."

"Makes sense," she agreed. "What about Wyatt? Isn't he a deputy, too?"

"He was. Wyatt resigned a while back."

"I'm glad. Knowing Emma, she was probably beside herself with worry when he wasn't home."

"Aside from the pursuit with Grey and his minions, Wyatt didn't get involved in much. Our line of work can be dangerous, especially out here."

"They don't call it the Wild West for nothin'," she remarked.

The wagon pulled up in front of a quaint two-story building. The large, wide window featured gold lettering, *Designs by A, Dressmaker*. She studied the wood structure from top to bottom. No such buildings existed in her own time, except on a movie set or a living history museum. This entire journey was way too bizarro for her to wrap her mind around. One minute she was in her own time, and the next, she walked through a time portal and ended up in 1883.

Josh set the brake lever and got out. He rounded the wagon to help her. Amber put her hands on his shoulders, like she'd done many times before, while he took hold of her waist. Her body slid down against his until her feet touched the ground. She didn't pull away.

His gaze rested on her mouth before he met her eyes. "You're going to love Anne," he said, then offered his arm.

"Oh, right. Emma's new best friend," she smirked, linking her arm with his. Amber couldn't wait to meet the woman who had become so important to Emma.

Josh opened the door, and the bell above it rang. Inside they were greeted by a demure petite woman dressed in cream muslin with a long matching skirt. She appeared to be in her early twenties. Amber's clothes looked nothing like hers. In fact, the younger woman's dress looked much finer in quality and style.

"Hello, Mattie," Josh said, bestowing a wide smile. "Is Mrs. Wilson here? I have someone I'd like for her to meet."

"Deputy." Mattie smiled, and a tinge of red touched her cheeks. "I'll let her know you're here." With a quick glance at Amber, she left.

Amber wiped her sweaty palms on the sides of her skirt. She shouldn't be so nervous to meet Anne. Last year, Emma had told her all about her new friend, and Amber was genuinely happy she had found friendship in another century. After all, she and Emma had a long history of sisterhood, going all the way back to birth. It was important she made a good impression.

While they waited, she forced herself to think about something else, so she focused on the interior of the shop. It was charming. Beautiful gold sconces and wide gold-framed mirrors adorned the rich, wood walls. Flowy drapes billowed from a gentle breeze blowing in through the windows. Neatly arranged bolts of fabric ranging from linens and ginghams to silks and taffetas covered the wide counters. A glass case displayed a collection of stunning jewelry, featuring gems, silvers, and golds that Amber would know anywhere—they were Emma's designs. She sighed. Her friend was so close, yet so far.

Through the portiere, stepped a beautiful woman in her late thirties, with rich dark hair and a curvy silhouette any woman would envy. Her burgundy dress fit her to perfection, accentuating her hourglass figure. *Shit, she's gorgeous*. And, based on Emma's description, Amber knew this would be Anne.

The woman smiled at Josh. "Delighted to see you, Josh." Her gaze shifted back and forth questioningly between Amber and Josh.

Josh removed his hat and put a hand on Amber's

back, nudging her forward. "Anne, there's someone I'd like you to meet—"

He didn't get to finish the introduction because in the next instant, Anne had her arms around Amber, pulling her into a warm embrace.

"Amber!" Anne cried, rocking her like old friends who hadn't seen each other in years. She set Amber away, clasping her by the arms. Anne's gaze swept over her from head to toe, and tears glistened in her eyes. *Tears.* "We meet at last! Emma always speaks so fondly of you. I feel like I've known you for a thousand years."

Amber smiled in return and found herself liking Anne immediately. "How'd you know that I'm Amber?"

The woman released her arms and grasped her hands instead. "Emma keeps a tintype of you in her reticule. It's astonishing how much color it shows—and how much you look like the image, smiling, perfect, and beautiful with your mane of auburn tresses."

Emma kept a photo of her—and showed it to Anne? *Aww.*

"Besides, you have that same look in your eyes as Emma did when she first arrived here last year," Anne went on. "Lost, uncertain, and well—" She indicated her attire. "—garbed in, how shall I say this, outdated fashion."

Amber glanced down at her travel-rumpled blouse and skirt. Apparently, Millie's clothes weren't in style either. "These are borrowed. I hope you won't hold it against me. I had to come here in a hurry."

Anne frowned. "Why the rush, dear?"

"Oh, well, I, um—" *Josh, help me!* She pleaded with her eyes.

"Amber was detained due to family matters," Josh

chimed in. "Unfortunately, her bag fell off the stage from Helena, which they didn't discover until it was too late. You can imagine the rest."

"Oh, dear." Anne clasped her hands in front of her chest. "It's a shame you came all this way, and Emma isn't even here. On the bright side, it gives the two of us time to get to know each other."

"I've got to run, ladies," Josh said, tugging on his hat. "I need to speak with the marshal. In the meantime, Anne, please measure Amber for some clothes, and, of course, some shoes. I'll be back in a few hours."

"A few hours?" Amber cried.

He cuffed Amber on the sleeve. "You're in excellent hands. See you later, sweets." He gave her a wink and headed out the door.

Amber was at a momentary loss for words. Rare, but it happens. Thankfully, Anne spoke first.

"Let's have some of my tea, shall we?" Anne suggested.

Emma had told Amber all about Anne's *special tea*. She could certainly use a cup after this week.

****

Josh ambled down the dusty boarded sidewalk toward the marshal's office. He removed his hat to wipe the sweat off his forehead. The air was dry, and the sun was hot. Typical for this time of year, but it got him thinking again. Until Amber showed up on his doorstep, he had no idea what the future would hold for him or his family. Now that she arrived with evidence that his brother and Emma would be six feet under sometime this year, he had to act. He was tired of waiting for something bad to happen. The notion that harm could befall the people he loved most weighed on him heavily. While

Wyatt took his family away for a little respite, Josh thought maybe it had more to do with the hunch it could be Grey and his men making attempts on their lives.

Griffin Grey. Josh hated him. The man was a fucking psycho, to say the least. After meeting with him in the prison, there was no doubt in his mind that he was seeking his revenge from the confines of his cell. There was no one else apart from that lunatic who hated Wyatt enough to want to hurt him—or his family. He just needed proof.

Donning his hat, he walked up the steps and into the office. "Hey, Marshal."

Charlie Reed looked up from the mess of papers spread across the large, wooden desk. His blue eyes weren't as vibrant as when Josh first met him, and his face had a few more lines. "Deputy," he said with a nod, clearly distracted.

Josh eyed the scattered papers. "Lose something important?"

Reed mumbled, then ran his hand over his careworn face. "Nothing I won't find sooner or later. How did it go with Grey?"

Josh crossed the stuffy room to the coffee pot on the stove. The marshal never used it in warmer months. The daily coffee was compliments of Davis Cooney, the owner of the Coppered Pan Saloon down the street. The man was grateful to have a new business after Grey burned his former one down last year, and he'd do anything for Marshal Reed.

He poured himself a mug of the lukewarm liquid and turned back to Reed. "I don't have solid proof yet, but my gut says it's Grey making the threats against my family. Anyway, you may want to ask the warden about a guard named Carson. I can't put my finger on it, but there was something off about the guy."

"I'll do just that. Anything else?"

Josh hesitated. "That prison is tighter than a drum. The warden has it under control, but…I worry about Grey. I can't explain it."

"You're too close to this," Reed told him. "Maybe we should get Cadmus or—"

"No way," he said, cutting him off.

"All right." Reed sat back in the chair, his gaze lingering on Josh for a moment. "When did you get back?"

"About fifteen minutes ago."

"Usually, you're there and back in two days. Why so long?"

"I had company." He couldn't help but smile. "Emma's best friend from the—from back home came to pay her and Wyatt a visit. Amber didn't know they would be away, and I didn't know she would be coming, so I wasn't about to leave her at the house unprotected. Now that we're back, I want to get her settled in."

Reed stood up and smiled. "At least, you'll have company now. I know you miss having your brother and his family around. Bring her by to say hello."

"I will do that," he said, touching his hat. "Later, Marshal."

He frowned. "Later for what?"

Josh chuckled. "I'll see you later."

He left the office and walked down the center of Main Street, kicking stones and rocks in his path, avoiding piles of horse dung. It was too soon to collect Amber from the dress shop. Fittings took a while, and he was sure she and Anne were chatting up a storm which would delay the process. It's what women usually did. He just hoped Anne wouldn't serve Amber more than a cup of her special tea.

****

Amber stumbled out of Anne's shop onto the boarded sidewalk, grabbing the post to keep from tumbling down the steps. Falling would've been a major embarrassment. She burst out laughing at herself. Anne's *special tea*—a combination of a teeny-tiny hint of black tea, lots of sugar, and a hefty dose of whiskey—was great and just what she needed after a crazy week of traveling through time, riding by horse and wagon for four days, sleeping outdoors, and fighting her attraction to a hotter than hot cowboy-slash-deputy who happened to be related to her bestie. Amber always loved a good cocktail, but modern-day booze had nothing on nineteenth-century whiskey. She was a bit tipsy after all that "tea" and needed to get her footing.

Once she was comfortable enough that she wouldn't stagger, she gathered her skirt and took slow, tentative steps along the boarded sidewalk. The afternoon sun gradually made its way toward a beautiful colored sunset of orange and purple. There was no direct sunlight baking her skin, but the air was still warm and dry. Her clothes already stuck to her from the heat and sitting in Anne's office for hours. She licked her lips with her dry tongue. Ugh, cotton mouth. Her head throbbed, too. Josh had mentioned there was no aspirin in this damn century, but maybe she could find some kind of anti-inflammatory meds. Water would help, too.

Across Main Street, a stand-alone building with a large shingle across the front caught her attention. *Doctor*, it read simply. Maybe she could get something for her headache there. She crossed the street and was just about to knock on the door when it swung open.

"Oh. Hello." The woman inside the doorway was taken by surprise. She had beautiful green eyes, and her ink-black hair was pulled into a neat, loose bun. "Pardon me. I hope you weren't waiting long. Do you need medical assistance?"

"Hi." Amber glanced at the small shingle nailed to the wall next to the door that read, *Dr. Jonas Wilson.* Maybe she was the nurse? "Um, yeah. I guess so. I have a…headache."

The woman, who was about her age, smiled. "Come in. I can help you."

Amber walked into the office and stopped inside the doorway. The waiting room looked like something out of an old Western movie. Wood was everywhere—the floor, the walls, the ceiling. There were two upholstered wing chairs flanking a small round table. Three tall windows lined the walls, and they were all open, letting in the fresh air. But the smell of antiseptic and medicine filled the room.

"This way." The nurse led her through an open doorway on the other side of the room. Once inside the examination room, she closed the door and patted the table. "Please, sit."

Amber glanced around at the shelves of countless glass jars filled with liquids, tablets, and specimens she couldn't decipher. Some looked like body parts, like tiny fingers, others appeared to be plants or roots of some kind. Roots? Hard to tell. Sharp and scary looking instruments were laid neatly across a leather mat on top of a wood counter, and the exam table had a long, white blanket over it. *Maybe this wasn't such a good idea after all.*

The smell of something medicinal filled her nose. If it kept up, she might vomit. Her head spun, and she rubbed her temples.

"I'm Dr. MacKenzie," the woman announced, slipping a starchy white medical apron over her head, and tying it behind her back.

"You're the doctor? I thought you were the nurse. I mean, it's great that you're a doctor."

The doctor gave her a quizzical glance. "I think so, thank you."

"Who's Dr. Wilson?"

Dr. MacKenzie smiled. "Dr. Wilson has been the town doctor for the last ten years. He's the reason I came all the way from Boston. Whisper Creek is a growing town, and as such, he needs more help. Now, tell me, about this headache."

Amber rubbed her forehead. *Hello, splitting headache.* "I'll take whatever you've got. It's getting worse. Plus, I think I might be dehydrated, too. It's been a rough few days."

"A headache can stem from multiple causes—"

She held up a hand. "I drank too much alcohol."

"Ah, I see."

"Yeah, I didn't think Anne's special tea was so…special. Just way too sweet and much too strong."

The doctor watched her with a scrutinizing squint. "There's only one Anne in town I know who makes special tea. She serves it exclusively to her friends, and she also happens to be Dr. Wilson's wife."

"That's her, and I've had too much of it," Amber admitted.

"How do you know Anne, if you don't mind me

asking?"

"She's friends with my best friend, Emma."

"Emma…Kincaid?" Dr. MacKenzie's sculpted features softened. "Is your name Amber?"

Amber nodded. "Yeah, Amber Harrison. How did you know?"

"You're Emma's Amber!"

"That's me."

The doctor reached for Amber's sweaty hands and gently squeezed them. "It's wonderful to meet you at last. Anne and I have been hearing about you since we each first met Emma."

Amber smiled, warmed to hear that her bestie hadn't forgotten about her, despite the centuries separating them. "I miss her," she admitted, blinking away the sudden burning in her eyes. "I wish she was here. This so sucks without her."

The doctor put her arm around Amber's shoulders. "Emma will be back soon. She and Wyatt were in need of a belated honeymoon. I'm sure she will be thrilled to find you waiting for her."

Belated honeymoon, my ass. "Thank you, Doctor. She will certainly be surprised."

Dr. MacKenzie poured a glass of water from an earthenware pitcher and handed it to Amber. "Please, call me Caroline."

"It's great to meet you, Caroline," Amber said, raising her glass in a salute. "I, um, haven't heard from Emma in a while, so you'll have to forgive me. I don't know who her friends are here, only Anne." She gulped down the water.

"I've only been here about six months." Caroline refilled the glass, which Amber downed in seconds.

"You may want to drink a little slower, so you don't get too nauseous."

She nodded, and then took a few small sips. The cool water was refreshing, especially after being on the road for days. "So tell me, what's it like here?"

"How do you mean?"

"This town is out in the middle of nowhere. It's not a city like New York or Boston. What's it like living here?"

Caroline thought for a moment. "Whisper Creek is a bit...slow. I'm used to the world moving at a faster pace back in Boston. The town is very different from a big city. However, I do enjoy meeting all the townsfolk and making new friends, like Emma and Anne and now you."

Amber liked Caroline and Anne. Emma certainly did all right making new friends in a different century. "That's nice."

There was a knock at the outside door. Caroline left the exam room, her thick heels clunking across the wood floor. While she couldn't see her any longer, Amber could hear her.

"Deputy," Caroline said. "How can I help you?"

"By any chance is there an Amber Harrison in there?" Josh's voice carried into the exam room, and Amber's pulse quickened. "I just went to Anne's shop, and she said Amber left a while ago. Your office is nearest, so I thought she'd come here first."

"Yes, she's here," Caroline replied. "Please, come in."

Amber's gaze shot to the doorway. Josh stood there with a parcel under his arm. He looked upset. "I've been looking all over for you," he told her.

"Sorry," she said. "I just needed a walk after all that *tea*." She rubbed her temples again. "That woman kept the cups coming, that's for sure."

"You left this at Anne's shop," he said, gesturing to the parcel.

"My clothes. Thanks. I was going to go back for it before coming to you at the marshal's office. I just needed some air."

"It's been a long week," Josh explained, turning to Caroline. "I took Amber with me to Deer Lodge for a few days, and now I think it's time I get her back to the house."

"It was lovely getting to know each other," Caroline said. "You should've told me Emma's dearest friend from back east was visiting. Anne and I would've brought around the welcome wagon."

"There's a wagon for that?" Amber asked, licking her lips. "I need more water." Caroline poured her another glass.

"What…did I miss?" Josh asked, his gaze volleying between her and Caroline. He put the parcel on the counter.

"Too much tea," Amber explained.

"I'm not surprised." Josh plucked the glass from Amber's fingers. "I think you need to get some rest."

"That I do, cowboy," she said, yawning. *Time travel certainly does make one tired.* Then again, it could've been all the wagon riding or the nineteenth-century alcohol. Maybe it was both. She followed Josh to the door.

Caroline squeezed her arm. "Amber, if it's all right with you, I'd like to pay you a visit."

"I'd love that," she replied. "Any friend of Emma's

is a friend of mine."

Caroline pulled her into a hug before saying goodbye. Josh adjusted the parcel under his arm, and he walked Amber outside.

She blinked a few times at the fading afternoon sun. The headache was catching up to her, and she turned to Josh. He had an unreadable look on his face. "What?" she demanded.

A grin tugged the corners of his mouth but then quickly vanished. "Nothing."

She stepped closer, and lifted her gaze, her insides hummed with warmth. "You know, you have the most amazing green eyes I've ever seen. They're really emeraldy." She scrunched up her face. "Is that even a word, emeraldy?"

"Did you, by any chance, eat at all or have anything other than tea to drink?"

"Um, no," she said. "Well, I had the few biscuits Anne served me and the water Caroline gave me. Other than that, nope."

"No wonder you have a headache. We best get you home." Josh ushered her to the wagon. He tossed the parcel in the back, hoisted her onto the bench, and then climbed in on the opposite side. Before she could settle herself, he slapped the reins. She fell backward, and they headed out of town.

After riding for four days back and forth on that sorry excuse for a bench, it was next to impossible to get comfortable. Her butt hurt. She probably had a dozen bruises by now.

An eternity later, Josh steered the wagon onto the property. Her head pounded, and all that water and whiskey-tea in her stomach swirled, making her more nauseous than she'd been at Caroline's office.

Josh pulled the wagon to a halt and came around to help her out. Her feet touched the ground, and she swayed. She clenched her eyes and willed the nausea to go away.

"Considering you traveled back in time last week," Josh began, "rode by wagon to a prison town, and chased all that down with Whisper Creek's finest whiskey today, I'd say you did pretty well for your first week in 1883."

She met his gaze. "Gee, thanks."

"Why don't you take a nap? I'll let you know when it's time for dinner."

"You're the bestest." She swatted him on the arm and stifled a yawn. "And then you can draw that bath you promised me." Backing away toward the door, she said, "I just need an hour or two…or ten."

"Sweet dreams," he called out.

Amber stumbled into her room and collapsed on the bed without stripping out of her travel clothes. Her head was a muddled mess of time travel flashbacks…and the handsome deputy with the emeraldy eyes.

Chapter Nine

Today marked three weeks since Amber arrived in the nineteenth century, and that was three weeks too long. All this waiting around for Emma and Wyatt to return did nothing to allay her fears. Amber wanted answers, and more importantly, to protect her best friend from the danger of dying an untimely death. The image of Emma and Wyatt's names on those tombstones clouded her mind. She needed to know how and why they were engraved. If there was no word from either of them soon, she would have to take matters into her own hands. Then again, with no personal means of transportation or money, that might not be so easy.

The smell of coffee drew her into the kitchen where Josh just poured a steaming, hot mug. He handed it to her.

"Thanks," she said. Since they returned from Deer Lodge two weeks ago, drinking coffee together first thing in the morning had become their ritual. And by now, Josh knew how she took it, light and sweet. She sipped it and smiled. "Maybe it's my imagination, but every day your coffee tastes a little bit better."

"Of course, it could just be that you're getting used to the taste."

"I hope not. It's godawful." She stuck out her tongue playfully. "Please no more coffee talk. It's making me crave a latte. What's on the docket for today? Are you off to town, leaving me to sit here all by my lonesome and read through Emma's collection of old books?"

He grinned. "Nope. Today, I'm taking you with me."

"How will I ever contain my excitement?" she joked. "Any word from Wyatt?"

After a sip of coffee, he said, "You've been asking me that every day, and every day I tell you the same thing."

She huffed. "One of these days, give me a different answer, will you? This is so frustrating. All I'm doing is sitting here, reading books, and sipping shitty coffee. Sorry. I don't mean to be bitchy." She scowled in frustration. "I've got to find Emma. She and Wyatt could be in major danger."

"It's okay, and you're not bitchy. I get it. You came a long way, and you want to see your best friend." He placed his mug on the counter. "Let's take your mind off things for a while. Meet me outside in fifteen minutes so we can get going. I've got a busy day, starting with Reed. You'll like him."

Amber stopped in mid-sip. "You don't think he can tell I'm from another time just by looking at me, do you? These lawmen have a sixth sense and pick up on clues like that," she said, snapping her fingers.

He smiled. "If he didn't pick up on me and Wyatt coming from the twenty-first century already, I'm quite sure he won't figure it out with you. Unless, of course, you say something stupid to give us away."

"I get it. What about other people?"

"Not likely. Anyway, after you meet Reed, you can pay Anne a visit and check on your new wardrobe, then maybe see the town sights."

"All while traipsing about in my stunning nineteenth-century attire," she mumbled.

He gently stroked her arm. "I'm sure you'd look beautiful in anything."

"Aww," she said, touching her face, burning at the sweet compliment. "Thanks."

Amber freshened up while Josh hitched up the wagon. When she was done, she went outside to meet him. At the bottom of the steps, a long, black snake with light yellow coloring slithered right in front of her. She let out a blood-curdling scream.

"It's just a snake," Josh announced, rushing over to her. He grabbed a nearby stick, lifted the disgusting creature, and tossed it out of her sight. "Don't worry, it's nonvenomous."

"It doesn't matter if they're venomous or not," she managed. The snake slithered into the bushes, vanishing in record time. She shuddered. "I-I hate s-snakes."

"That was a garter snake. It doesn't bite. I'll let you know which ones do."

"But what if you're not around next time?"

"I'll give you a lesson in Montana snakes on the ride, okay?" He helped her into the wagon before he came around the other side and got in.

For the rest of the ride, Josh explained the differences between venomous versus nonvenomous snakes, certain colors to be aware of, and what signs to look for.

The wagon jostled over the road until they reached their destination. Everything about Main Street was unique. There were false-fronted frame buildings, sounds of horses and wagons bouncing over the road, the godawful smell of horse dung and smoke, and the gritty taste of the air.

Josh extended his hand to help her out of the wagon, but her damn skirt got caught. She tripped and fell hard against him. When her feet touched the ground, she gazed up into green eyes, beaming with amusement.

"I knew you cared, but I didn't think you'd fall for me," he teased.

Heat burned her cheeks. "Yeah, well…these freakin' skirts are a pain in the ass."

He leaned over to whisper against her ear. "But you look great."

A sweet shiver skipped down her spine. Before she could form a verbal response, he reached for her arm and led her up the wooden steps.

Inside, the one-room office smelled like coffee and old, damp wood. Even though the windows were open, the air was stuffy. On the back wall was another door with bars on the top half. That must be where the prisoners were kept. A gentleman with silvery hair behind the desk was deep in thought and clearly didn't hear them enter. He rubbed his face with one hand as he got up to pace.

Josh coughed, and the marshal looked in their direction. A smile spread across his features, and the truth in his expression softened the years of careworn lines on his face. "Josh! Why, this must be the lovely Miss Amber you've been telling me about." The marshal crossed the room to take her hand.

"Yes, sir." Josh beamed. "Marshal Charlie Reed, I present Miss Amber Harrison."

"I've been hearing so much about you, both from Miss Emma and Josh here," the marshal said, his light blue eyes sparkling with kindness. "It's a pleasure to make your acquaintance at last. I can see why Josh has been keeping you away from town."

Amber smiled. "It's lovely to meet you, Marshal. Josh speaks highly of you."

"He's the best thing to happen to Whisper Creek law enforcement since I deputized him. Can't explain how he knows things that no one else does. Makes me wonder, sometimes, though he says it's his gut." He waved them over to the counter. "Coffee?"

She held up a hand. "No, thanks. I already had some."

"Mine's not as good as Josh's," the marshal admitted.

"His isn't all that good," she whispered.

"Hey, I heard that," Josh said.

"Lordy, mine must be terrible then." The marshal laughed. "It's a pity you came a long way to see Emma, and she's not here. They'll return soon enough."

"I've been here for three weeks already, and we haven't had any communication with them."

Reed waved a hand. "They're safe. If anything transpired to say otherwise, Kane would let Josh and me know immediately."

Amber's gaze shifted to Josh. "Who's Kane?"

"Remember I told you about our friend there, Marshal Kane?" Josh explained. "He's trustworthy and reliable. Marshal Reed, Wyatt, and I would stake our lives on that."

"Indeed," Reed agreed.

"I still don't get why you haven't had another wire in weeks," she argued. "Why wouldn't Wyatt send something further?"

"There's no reason to," Josh said. "Wyatt will wire

me when they're ready to return."

"Maybe if you told him that I'm here…"

Josh raised an eyebrow and tilted his head, giving her that we'll-talk-about-this-later look, so she bit her tongue. After that, neither of the men spoke again, and she took that as a hint that it was time for her to make an exit. They probably wanted to discuss whatever it is lawmen discuss in the nineteenth century, most likely outlaws and horse thefts.

"And on that note," Amber said, "Mama's gonna get goin'."

Reed frowned. "Pardon?"

"I'm sure you two gentlemen have business to discuss, so I'll be on my way. Marshal Reed, it was wonderful to meet you."

"You as well, ma'am," Reed replied, and then sat behind his desk.

Josh led her to the door. "In case you see something you want to buy." He handed her a few coins. "Meet me here when you're done."

"Thanks," she said, dropping the coins into her skirt pocket. "See you kids later."

Before she closed the door behind her, she heard the marshal say, "Did she just call us kids?"

****

Time to check out the town. After all, once Anne started pouring her special tea, there would be no escaping. Amber liked Anne, but her sweetened whiskey was a little much. Instead, she would begin with one of her favorite pastimes, window shopping. The shops of 1883 were quite different than those in her own time. They were much smaller, to say the least. Most of the window dressings featured thick, plain curtains and simple displays. Nevertheless, she enjoyed taking a walk through the bygone era. A confectioner's shop beckoned her, and she couldn't resist purchasing a few sweets with the coins Josh gave her.

By the time Amber reached the end of the street, she was parched. The sweets she ate in record time were delicious but left her craving something to wash down the sugary aftertaste. The dry mountain air and hot summer sun added to her discomfort. She tugged at the bra stuck to her dewy skin, and her icky boob sweat made it even more unpleasant. If only this century had a chain drugstore where she could pop in and grab a bottle of water and deodorant, she'd be all set.

Piano music came from somewhere down the street. It sounded lively and fun, so she walked in the direction from which it came. The sign Coppered Pan Saloon hung across the front of a large, tall, wooden frame building. From what Emma had told her, the original Copper Pan burned in a fire and the townsfolk got together to rebuild it. The entire structure was brand new with shiny, clean windows and the customary boarded sidewalk. Now, she listened from the street as the piano played a different catchy tune.

Two filthy cowboys burst through the set of swinging doors and, drunk, stumbled down the steps. They landed in the dirt right in front of her before struggling to their feet. Upon seeing her, both men tipped their hats and staggered to their horses tethered to a nearby post. One man attempted to hop into the saddle three times before finally getting it right. He couldn't stop laughing at himself. *Small things amuse small minds*. The other man managed to get into the saddle but hugged the horse's neck to keep from falling. They waved at her and rode off, cackling all the way.

"I hope they have RWI laws here—riding while intoxicated," she mumbled under her breath.

She climbed the steps and peered over the double swinging doors. Saloon. Bar. All the same. Maybe she could sit for five minutes and have a drink and even chat with some of the locals just for laughs. That is, if there were no other inebriated men stumbling around the place.

Amber pushed open the doors. The music stopped, and the doors swung closed behind her, bumping her on the butt. Most of the tables were taken up with customers drinking and playing cards. Big brass spittoons sat on the floor by each of the tables with small mushy puddles next to them from those who had missed. *Eew*. To top it off, the place smelled like sweat, tobacco, and stale booze, even with the windows open.

"Hey, guys!" she said with a friendly wave. "I heard the music and wanted to see what all the fun was about."

A voluptuous, overly endowed woman sat behind the upright piano, her long fingers resting on the keys. If she wasn't wearing so much makeup, she would look a lot prettier. Her shiny, dark hair was arranged into a half-updo with the rest draped like a curtain around her shoulders. Too bad she was a saloon girl, but she wasn't half bad at playing the piano.

"Oh, hi," Amber said. "I hope I didn't interrupt anything."

The woman at the piano responded with a catlike smile as she ran her fingers expertly over the keys. She played an old love song from the nineteenth century, one Amber recognized. Lorelei, or something like that. It had been turned into a hit in the 1950s with different lyrics.

It was one of her mom's favorite songs.

"Howdy, ma'am." A shabby looking cowboy doffed his hat, revealing a sweat-stained forehead and stringy greasy hair.

Judging by the stench, he hadn't showered in a year. His gaze raked over her, and she wanted to run to the nearest bathroom to give her skin a thorough scrubbing.

"Mightn't I buy you a drink, missy?" he asked with a toothless smile.

Amber backed up a bit, covering her nose. "Oh, no thanks. I'm just going to have a quick soda and be on my way. Appreciate it, though."

She walked over to the long wooden bar. Tugging up her skirt a notch so her shoes wouldn't get tangled in the hem again, she perched a foot on the rail. Bottles of booze lined the counter below the wide mirror spanning the length of the wall behind the bar. Most of them were orangey brown in color. It didn't seem there was much of a selection. They were probably different types of whiskey.

The bartender leaned over the counter and whispered, "You lost, missy?"

She leaned forward, too. "Um, no. Why?"

He glanced around the room. "I don't think you should be in here, ma'am."

She peered over her shoulder and turned back to him. "This is a bar. I'm thirsty, so I'd like a drink, please. Whatever soda or cola you've got will be fine."

"Sorry, ma'am. Your choices are whiskey or beer."

Amber didn't like beer, but it was better than whiskey, especially if it was anything like Anne's special tea. "I'll take the beer, please."

"Comin' right up." He poured Amber's drink then

slid it in front of her. "On the house, ma'am."

"Really? Thanks." She took a sniff and scrunched up her face at the bitter smell of grass and herbs wafting up from the glass. Something about the aroma reminded her of urine. But, hey, it wasn't whiskey, she reminded herself. "Cheers!" The first sip was stronger than she expected, but it was sweet and smooth…and warm. "Not bad," she added, pleasantly surprised at the taste. "But it could be colder."

Nineteenth-century bars were quite interesting, from the scruffy men in their wrinkled and stained attire to the women with their lowcut bodices, hanging seductively over the men. The atmosphere certainly wasn't dull. The piano player started singing about the Red River Valley, and she hummed along. She closed her eyes and lost herself in the melody.

When the song was over, she opened her eyes. Three men stood before her. Clearly this town had a dirty cowboy problem. "May I help you?" she asked.

The man with the black bandana around his neck stepped forward, crowding her personal space. "Just makin' sure you're all right, ma'am."

Amber backed up and turned her head aside. The stink emanating from him was vomit worthy, and the worst she'd smelled thus far. *I'll be better once you leave.* "I'm peachy," she said instead.

All three men exchanged a glance. The middle of the three men asked, "Where're you from, Peachy?"

"Leave her alone," the bartender barked. "She's too good for the likes of you three."

The trio glared at the bartender, mumbling incoherently. Reluctantly, they returned to their seats at one of the poker tables, but they kept casting glares in her direction.

She turned to the bartender. "What's with them?"

Concern crossed his features. "Ma'am, you shouldn't be in here by yourself. Where's your husband?"

She rolled her eyes. "Does every woman in the world need to be married? Geez. I don't have a husband."

The piano player's next tune had a foot-tapping rhythm, and one of the women grabbed Amber's hand and pulled her up to dance. Three more women clapped along from the sidelines before joining in on the fun. Amber got into the dance and showed the ladies some modern moves, shimmying, and shaking her butt, which the women tried to emulate, laughing as they did so. Before she knew it, a crowd gathered around them, clapping, stomping, and whistling, trying to get closer.

The woman banging out the tunes on the piano finally ended the song. Cheers went up. She took a bow, and then came over to Amber to give her a quick hug. To the crowd she said, "That's enough, gentlemen. Our new lady friend here needs a drink. Excuse us."

She led Amber to the bar where two glasses of whiskey awaited them. The woman pushed one in front of Amber, and they toasted. "You are quite a delight," the woman said, tossing back the drink in one quick tilt.

Amber shrugged, followed suit, and chugged down the strong, dark liquid before slamming the glass on the bar. She pounded on her chest. Her throat burned with the trail of fire the liquid left as it settled to scorch her stomach. "Whoa, that's strong stuff."

"I'm Veronique," the woman said, tilting her head to study Amber. She smelled like a bouquet of roses, the kind that people with allergies didn't like. A sneeze attack was imminent. "And you are…?"

Amber rubbed her itchy nose then licked her lips. Cotton mouth. "Amber," she replied at last.

"Did you recently arrive in town?" Veronique asked, a dark eyebrow arching in question. "I haven't seen you before."

"Yes," Amber said, pushing the glass away. "I, uh, got here a few weeks ago to visit friends, but they're not here right now."

"Miss Veronique," the bartender said, "you'd best let me handle this one."

"Nonsense." The woman waved her hand in a dismissive fashion that implied she was used to getting her way. "She's perfect and will do quite nicely. As you can see, the men here already have their eyes on her. And she's…friendly."

"Not in the way you think," he snapped.

"Whoa, hang on," Amber said, holding up a hand. "What are you two talking about? I'll do nicely for what?"

Veronique's lips slowly curled into a smile. "Do you see those rooms upstairs? I think you'd make us both some good money. You're the prettiest one here."

Amber glanced at the second-floor landing with all the rooms. How did she not see what type of place this was? She turned to the bartender. "I thought this was a dive bar in a hotel, not a whorehouse!"

Veronique stiffened. "Please refrain from using that word. My ladies are not whores. They are companions, and this is a respectable saloon." She shoved her chin into the air, and then sashayed her way back to the piano to pound angrily on the keys.

The bartender scrambled around to Amber's side of

the bar. He put a hand on her arm. "I'm sorry about that, ma'am," he shouted over the loud music. "I don't think you belong in here. I'm Davis Cooney. This is my saloon, but Madame Veronique is temporarily occupying the upstairs with her girls. If you need anything, you holler for me or Marshal Reed. Deputy Kincaid can be of assistance, too."

"Deputy Josh Kincaid?" Amber nodded. "Yeah, I already know him. His brother's married to my best friend."

"Miss Emma is your best friend?" The old man broke out in a wide grin. "Well, why didn't you say so? Don't you worry about Madame Veronique. I'll put her straight. What's your name, miss?"

"Amber Harr—" The music came to a halt once again. She followed everyone's gaze and turned in the direction of the swinging doors. "Josh!" she cried, waving at him. "Over here!"

Josh marched over to her. His face was tight, and his jaw, clenched. *Uh-oh*, he did not look happy. "What are you doing?" he demanded.

"Just having a little fun."

"You're in a saloon," he hissed.

"Yep. I figured that one out all by myself."

"It's also a brothel."

Amber snapped her fingers. "Brothel. That's the word. Yep, figured that out, too." She leaned close to whisper, "This place is filthy and stinky, and the guys all reek."

Josh glanced around the room. His gaze stopped on a pretty, young woman sitting alone, in the corner, fanning herself. "We best get going," he told her, hauling her to her feet.

"Ouch!" Amber cried when his fingers wrapped around her arms a little too tight. "All right, all right." She shouted over her shoulder, "Buh-bye, ladies. It's been a slice. Thanks for the drink, Davis."

"Bye, Peachy!" someone called out.

Josh shoved her outside and down the sidewalk until they reached the side street. "Dammit, woman, you cannot go back in there," he ground out.

She rubbed her arm where his fingers had gripped her. "Why are you so angry? I was just dancing."

"Yes…in a *brothel*."

She made a face. "So what?"

He took a step closer, and their noses almost touched. "So what? You were with *Madame* Veronique." He flung a hand in the air. "One look at you and that woman would want you to be one of her girls. Don't you get it? The men who were in there have now branded you a whore. What the hell made you go in there, anyway?"

"This outfit is so freakin' uncomfortable. I needed something to drink. I asked for soda, but Davis didn't have that. And I hate beer." She looked down at the ground and sighed. Her shoulders slumped a little. The last thing she wanted to do was make him mad. "Josh—"

"I didn't mean to be rough on you," he said, his voice softened. "I apologize, but things are different here. We've already been over nineteenth-century propriety. As innocent as you think your actions may be, they aren't so innocent to the men in that saloon. Since you're going to be staying here for a while, I think we should have a refresher course."

Josh was right. Until she was reunited with Emma—and they got the portal up and running—there was no telling how long she'd be in 1883.

"I think we best get you home," he announced, and his voice was velvety and quiet.

"Please don't be mad at me. I just had a little fun in there."

He put his hand under chin and tipped her face toward his. "I'm not mad, Amber. I'm just…I don't want other men ogling you."

Why did he always have to look so irresistibly handsome? His eyes reminded her of endless Irish meadows. And his lips, those lips, full and kissable…*Kissable*? That one tall shot of whiskey was getting to her. Her pulse quickened. She clenched her eyes for a hot second, and then opened them. He was mere inches away.

"I'm going to kiss you, Amber," Josh told her, and his breath fanned her face.

Could he read her mind? She licked her lips and sighed. "You are?"

"Yes, but it won't be out here on the street. No, when we do kiss—" He lowered his head even closer. "—you will forever crave the taste of my lips when I'm not with you."

"Ohhhh." She sagged against him.

Josh held her against him and gazed into her eyes. "I mean what I say, sweets. I do want to kiss you…but not here." He traced an invisible line from her cheek to her neckline. A slow smile touched his lips. His voice was low and smooth. "And I always keep my promises."

Chapter Ten

Amber grabbed the basket from the picnic table and walked toward the chicken coop. Josh waved at her as he closed the gate to the paddock. She sighed. Oh, how she wanted him to make good on his promise. *When we do kiss, you will forever crave the taste of my lips when I'm not with you.*

A blue-white light lured her gaze to the barn. The building didn't have any electricity, nor did the house, so she was quite curious how the light got there. However, the portal was inside, and she hesitated.

The light intensified. Her curiosity got the best of her, and she headed for the barn.

Once inside, she tossed the basket aside and looked around. A cold, gentle breeze whirled into a gust of wind. The hair at the back of her neck stood up, and she shivered. Suddenly, a shimmering blue-white light appeared on the far end of the barn wall. Her fingers tingled, and a whirl of anxiety shot through her. What if she got too close and sucked through the time portal? No, she couldn't allow that to happen.

Spinning on her heel to flee, she plowed right into Josh. She hadn't heard him come into the barn. He gripped her upper arms to keep her from tripping. "Whoa, what's the hurry?" he asked. "Are you all right?"

"Yeah, fine. I saw a strange light."

"I saw it, too."

An odd noise, like a heavy, steel door sliding open, gained their attention. The back wall vanished, replaced by a tall, wide doorway filled with that same bright blueish light.

Amber took a step back, clutching Josh's arm. "W-what's happening? I-I have to save Emma. I don't want to go back, not without her."

He took her hand and wrapped one arm around her waist, giving her a gentle squeeze. "It'll be all right."

"Hello." A tall, slender man in a dark charcoal metallic jumpsuit appeared. The light behind him vanished, though a wavy flickering outline of the doorway remained. His white hair was short and thick, a stark contrast to his young, wrinkle-free face.

Amber leaned into Josh and whispered, "Am I totally losing it or what?"

"No, you're not," the man replied first. "My name is Malachi, and I'm here to help you, all of you, return home." He glanced over his shoulder like he was half expecting someone to be there, then ran his fingers over the colorful techy band with the tiny buttons and prisms sewn into his sleeve. It beeped and flashed.

"So you're for real," Amber mumbled, clutching Josh's arm tighter. She met his gaze. "For a hot second, I thought you were losing it. Sorry."

"I know," he said, squeezing her arm. "It's okay."

"Yes, I'm for real," Malachi said, checking his armband again. "And I think you should know that I'm the one responsible for you being here this long."

A ripple of apprehension danced along Amber's spine. "You?"

Malachi nodded. "Yes, and I apologize for that; but I'm going to rectify the situation. I should've come sooner; however, it was difficult for me. And now, we only have a short amount of time to correct this…without repercussions."

"What sort of repercussions?" Josh asked.

He hesitated. "The kind that would be the end of the world you left, the world as you knew it." His armband flashed. "I don't have the time to explain right now."

"Whoa," Josh said. "You can't just drop that bomb on us and expect to vanish into thin air again. That's not fair to us."

His armband beeped, and he spared it an impatient glance. "The time portal is scheduled to shut down on New Year's Eve. I've been running the Project for a few years now. As you can imagine, the government doesn't like private endeavors and has threatened to take over if we—me and my team—don't cooperate and hand over operations. We can't allow them to gain control. The result would be catastrophic. The only way to prevent that is if we discontinue funding the Project. Before they can act, we must shut it down."

"You said the government knows about the portal?" Amber asked, her fingers as cold as icicles.

"Yes, in my year, they do."

"And what year would that be?" Josh asked.

"I'm from the year 2234. I will tell you more when I return," Malachi promised. "I came now because I wanted you to know help is on the way." He glanced over his shoulder, walking backward and into the open shimmering doorway bright with the blueish-white light once again. "Everyone—you two along with Emma, Wyatt, and their baby—needs to be *here* at the same time in order for this to work. That is, unless something else goes wrong."

"Hang on a second," Amber said. "How come we can't just use our tokens to go through the portal? Why are we stuck?"

Malachi explained in a rush, "I'm afraid the tokens don't work. They never did. Farewell for now, friends." He took one more step backward and disappeared into the light.

Instantly, everything grew dim and returned to normal. The once-shimmering doorway disappeared like it had never been there, and the barn wall looked as it had before Malachi's arrival.

Amber moved on wobbly legs and collapsed on a bale of hay. Her hands trembled. "What...the...hell...was that?"

Josh rubbed his temples and sat down next to her. "No clue."

Amber looked at him. "Do you believe him?"

Josh thought for a moment. "Clearly, he knows about the portal, and he came through it. It's logical that he's telling the truth."

"So what if he came through it?" she scoffed, rising to her feet. "You and I did, too, along with Emma and Wyatt. We have no idea who this guy Malachi even is. For all we know, he'll kill us when we go back through the portal. He's given us a deadline. When Wyatt and Emma return, I say all of us should try going through the portal *together* with or without him."

Josh stood up and stared up at the ceiling. It was a long moment before he spoke. "All right," he agreed. "First, we have to make sure everything is secure with Grey and whoever he's got working for him. I won't risk Wyatt and his family's lives for anything." He walked over to her and put both hands on her shoulders. His voice softened. "We can't take any chances or unnecessary risks. This all has to be planned strategically. Okay?"

She sagged against him and inhaled the soapy scent emanating from his skin. Sandalwood. He smelled so good. "Okay," she said, slipping her arms around his waist.

Josh reached under her chin and tilted her face up to his. His gaze dropped from her eyes to her lips and remained there. "Timing has to be perfect...for everything."

"Everything...?" she asked, breathlessly.

Josh lowered his head and pressed his mouth against hers. His tongue traced the outline of her lips before slipping into her mouth. Amber leaned into him, sliding her hands around his neck, tugging him closer. He drew her against his rock-solid body while his searing tongue continued its exploration, colliding with hers in a perfect, eager rhythm. And, oh, did she drink in the delicious taste of him. His lips were warm and sweet. Jolts of fire spread through her body in all directions, heat surging to her core.

For days, weeks, she wondered what it would be like to kiss him, to feel his lips on hers, to be in his arms. He did not disappoint.

Her heart pounded, and her senses short-circuited. She reveled in the delicious taste of his kiss, until he pulled away but continued to shower her with more kisses around her lips and along her jaw. Heat sizzled in her veins. Her mind tuned out everything wrong in their world...except this moment. This moment was perfect. She savored every kiss, every heartbeat, every breath.

Josh's lips returned to hers. Her knees weakened,

and she tightened her grip so she wouldn't fall. He groaned and slowly pulled away, leaving her body on fire and barely able to stand.

His eyes were heavily lidded, and his breath came in short bursts. "I've been wanting to do that for a while now, sweets."

She licked her lips, trying to get her breathing under control. "Oh?"

"Don't give me, oh. If your response to my kiss now is any indication, I'd say you wanted me to kiss you for a while, as well."

She gazed up into his mesmerizing eyes and smiled. "You bet I did."

He smiled smugly. "Good."

She couldn't recall the last time she felt like this, where butterflies erupted in her belly and her insides were all a hot mess. And if she gazed into his eyes much longer, she would totally lose herself forever. "Josh…"

"Hello…?" A strong female voice shouted outside the barn. "Josh…? Amber…? Is anyone home?"

Amber groaned and sagged against Josh. "Who's that?"

He raked a hand through his hair and headed for the door. "It sounds like Caroline."

Amber exhaled a deep breath, hoping her heartbeat would return to a normal rhythm. After wiping her lips, she patted her chest, and then followed Josh out of the barn to greet their visitor.

Caroline climbed down from the wagon and reached for a small basket on the bench. "Hello to you both," she called out.

"Caroline," Josh said, approaching the wagon. "What brings you out all this way?"

"I came to have a visit with Amber," she replied. Her gaze shot from Josh to Amber. "I hope this is a convenient time?"

Amber self-consciously folded her arms across her chest. Could the doctor tell she'd just been thoroughly kissed? Oh, hell. She was acting like a teenager now.

"Yes, of course," Josh replied. "We were just…"

"All good, sista," Amber told her, linking her arm with Caroline's. "What do you say we have our visit outside? It's too hot in the house. There's a nice little shaded area with table and chairs just over there."

"Sounds wonderful," Caroline replied. "I brought some savories. Matilda at the general store makes these delicious little mini pies. I thought you might like them."

Amber stole a peek into the basket. "Mmm, looks delish. Thank you."

"Ladies," Josh began, "this is where I shall bid you both farewell. I've got to head back into town to meet with the marshal." He touched Amber's arm. "Sam is a gunshot away if you need urgent help. See you later."

"Later, gator," Amber said, watching him amble away. Josh had the hottest swagger and the nicest ass. The idea of grabbing those naked cheeks while he was on top of her—*Stop it*! She turned back to Caroline. Her new friend was smiling and had a glint in her eye. "What's the matter?"

"I think you and Josh are well suited," Caroline stated with a nod.

"Well suited for what?"

"Don't be obtuse. It's clear Josh is sweet on you. And it doesn't take a medical degree to see that."

Amber's stomach fluttered. She sank her upper teeth into her bottom lip, glancing at Josh. He was riding off the property in a full gallop. Tugging on a lock of hair, she coiled it around her finger.

Caroline squeezed her free hand. "I'm always right about these things. Now, tell me. What kind of expression is 'later, gator'?" she asked. "I've never heard that before."

****

Josh tethered his horse to the post and then went inside the marshal's office. He waited a solid fifteen minutes for Reed. No sign of him. His boss was probably out making his rounds—that or dealing with some drunken idiot stirring up shit. Just like the marshal, Josh liked to check in with the locals at different establishments, especially the saloons. There, he would usually discover some interesting tidbit of information, whether it was about the drifters coming and going, who won a gunfight in a neighboring town, or any other gossip. People liked to talk, particularly when drunk.

He ambled down Main Street, observing the townsfolk, along with a few seedy-looking drifters here and there. More than one young lady batted pretty eyelashes in his direction, giggling behind cupped hands when he tipped his hat in greeting.

Since he'd come to Whisper Creek, a few fathers begged him to marry their daughters. While he appreciated their high regard for him, and as lovely as the women were, Josh had no intention of marrying any of them. He was as fine flying solo in the nineteenth century as he was in the twenty-first. Not that he never wanted to marry; he just hadn't found the right woman. Over the years, he had a few girlfriends and was even serious about Ashley, almost married her, too, but it wasn't meant to be. He held all relationships up to the one his parents shared, and he knew that if he continued with her, he would be settling. And he was not one for settling.

Moments later, he stepped inside the Coppered Pan, and the doors swung closed behind him. With his experienced eye, he surveyed the room for trouble. Finding none, he headed for the bar where Cooney already had a beer waiting for him.

He held up a hand. "I'm on duty, but thanks."

Cooney gave a curt nod and then moved down the bar to serve his other customers. It was a quiet day, just before noon. There wasn't much happening yet, no music, no dancing, but at least business was good overall. Josh was glad the townsfolk pitched in to rebuild the saloon after the fire that took Deputy Allen's life last year. If it hadn't been for that greedy bastard, Griffin Grey, Deputy Bobby Allen would still be alive.

He spotted Daisy, the woman he'd occasionally spent time with, at the back of the room, waving a colorful fan. She had a sweet face but was much prettier without all that makeup. He had told her so, too. Over the past couple of years, he'd visited her from time to time. Daisy was fun, lively, and adventurous, but she was paid for her services and not the type of girl to ever settle down with.

Daisy saw him, and her face lit up. Zigzagging her way around the tables, she finally reached him. "You haven't been around lately, Deputy." She tilted her head to study him. Her smile faded, and she pouted. "I bet I know why, and it has nothin' to do with work."

"Then what does it have to do with?"

She moved closer and slid her hands up the front of his chest. "The pretty lady you escorted out of here a few days ago."

Amber. He let out a long, slow breath. While he had lost track of the days and weeks since Amber's arrival, Daisy was right. Amber had come to mean so much to him. Suddenly, merely talking to this woman felt all wrong.

"You don't have to say anything. I know I'm right." Daisy sighed, pressing a finger over his lips. "I knew it the moment you whisked her out of here. She's one lucky lady—a real lady, at that." She kissed his cheek, and then sashayed through the saloon to perch herself on the lap of an eager customer a few tables away.

He signaled farewell to Cooney and then left. With the arrival of the railroad in Helena a few months ago, more and more people were moving in; some staying for good, others just visiting. He'd been in nineteenth-century Whisper Creek for over two years now, and already, he could see a difference in the population. The community itself had grown with dozens more establishments, spreading the town limits even wider. He knew what this place would look like a hundred and forty years from now, and he could already see how that would come to be.

He continued his rounds on Main Street before crossing over to First Street. Most of the newer establishments—smaller restaurants, inns, shoemaker, and hatmaker—were located there. Not much going on, so he cut back to Main Street.

"Deputy." It was Cadmus, one of the town's firemen and telegraph operator, walking across the street to meet Josh. "I've got something for you." He handed him two small envelopes. "One of them's from Deer Lodge."

Josh thanked him, and then walked away to open the

messages. The first one was from the warden at Deer Lodge. *Carson harmless but strict*. Strict isn't the word he'd use to describe that idiot. Clearly, the warden at the prison where Grey was incarcerated didn't think he had an issue with the guard. He'd give that to the marshal to deal with.

The second one, though, was from Marshal Kane in Montana City. *Settled in. Secured*. And Josh knew his message meant that Wyatt and his family were safe in their little cabin on the outskirts of town.

Now, all he had to do was tell Amber about his brother's wire and hope she wouldn't want to rush over there in a New York minute.

Chapter Eleven

Amber hadn't laughed so much in ages. The last time she had one of those belly-buster-giggle-fits was with Emma before she moved to the nineteenth century. As it turns out, Caroline was funny, too. Who knew? When she first met Caroline a few weeks ago, Amber thought she was a brilliant and sophisticated woman ahead of her time but a little too cerebral. She was glad they were getting to know each other.

"Oh, my gawd, *stoppppp*," Amber howled, unable to quit laughing. She grabbed her sides.

"You have me in stitches," Caroline admitted, giggling, and wiping the corners of her eyes with a monogrammed handkerchief. "Ah, the phrases you say! Really, Amber. 'Later, gator.' And what was the other? Oh, yes, 'grab a straw because you suck'." She shook her head with amusement. "Why, I haven't had such a laugh in—I can't remember when. Now, what were we discussing?"

Amber's laughter finally subsided. "Birthing and babies. Personally, I don't get it, and maybe that's because I don't have kids, but why is it when a baby is born women always say, boil water? Are you making soup for the newborn? Kind of like, 'hey, the baby's here. Let's eat'!"

Caroline appeared to hide a smile. "Of course not. The water is to clean the baby when it comes."

"But if he or she doesn't show up for hours or even a day, you've got to keep boiling the water over and over and over."

"It was like that with Emma and Wesley," Caroline said softly. "She had a long labor."

"I didn't know you were there when she gave birth."

Caroline nodded. "I had just arrived in Whisper Creek. As I settled in, Doc Wilson told me about his wife's dear friend who was expecting her first child. A few days later, he was away on an urgent house call at a ranch treating what turned out to be a fatal injury. Anne came running into the office with the news that Emma was in labor, and I had to hurry. We rushed out to the Kincaid place. It was the first time I'd met Emma. She looked lovely and beautiful, but she was nervous about giving birth. Her labor was a bit longer and more painful than anticipated, but thankfully, little Wesley arrived the next day."

Amber's stomach clenched. When she had first learned through Josh that Emma was a mom with a healthy baby boy, she was relieved that Emma had survived childbirth. She had heard nightmare stories over the years and watched nail-biting documentaries on what women endured in the nineteenth centuries and earlier. Thankfully, Emma didn't fit into that category. "Josh never told me about her delivery."

"He was away with Marshal Reed at the time. And you know men. It's not something they discuss."

Amber wrapped her arms around herself. "Emma must've been beside herself with worry."

"If she was, she didn't tell me or let it show." Caroline looked off in the distance, a small smile tilted her mouth. "What surprised me most was that Wyatt stayed by her side the entire time, holding her hand, wiping her brow, giving her sips of water. When the contractions came, he told her to push and breathe. Emma did some kind of breathing practice that she said was used back where she came from. Considering I'm from Boston, and she is from a city only a few hundred miles away, I'm not quite sure what this method was. In any case, it worked. Twenty hours later, little Wesley was born, and he was healthy and perfect."

The fact that Wyatt was at Emma's side the entire time warmed Amber's heart to the man she had yet to meet. Knowing this, she was even happier for Emma now. "I'm so glad you were there for her, Caroline. Thank you."

"No need to thank me. This is part of my job." She paused. "Since you haven't met Wyatt yet, I think you will be pleasantly surprised. He is one of the kindest husbands I've ever met in my life. He puts Emma and Wesley first. Most men don't do that."

Amber was already burdened with guilt for how she left things with Emma last year. Even though they had a bittersweet and tearful goodbye, Amber remained angry with Emma for leaving, for choosing Wyatt and the nineteenth century. After hearing Caroline say all these wonderful things about the man Emma chose to go back in time for, Amber was genuinely happy for her friend and family.

"And speaking of husbands," Amber said. "What about you, do you have a husband or boyfriend, uh, suitor, back in Boston?"

Caroline shook her head. "Medicine is very important to me. I didn't spend all those years in medical school to give up my work just so I could dedicate myself to maintaining a household for a husband and children."

"You can always have both."

"Yes, that's a possibility. I just choose not to." She took a sip of tea. "I adore Emma. In the months I've known her, she has become dear to me. Did you know she made me a cameo choker as a thank you for delivering Wesley? Unfortunately, I haven't had a chance to wear it yet. It's too precious to put on when I'm working."

"Aww, that's so sweet and so Emma. If she made it, I'm sure it's gorgeous. How about wearing it at a special occasion? Are there dances or community gatherings here?"

"Yes, there are," she replied, and her eyes sparkled. "And there's one in next month to celebrate autumn. From what I hear, the fall is harvest time and very busy here. Once winter arrives, people don't go out much, except to town if they can make it. When it snows, no one travels anywhere. It's impossible to get through."

Amber shuddered inwardly. She hated to think of Emma and Wyatt getting stuck in Montana City and not returning by the deadline that Malachi gave them, which was two and a half months away.

"It's been a lovely visit," Caroline said, standing up. "I wish I could stay longer, but I should be getting back."

"I'm so glad you came," Amber told her, walking Caroline to her wagon. "Next time I'm in town, I'll pop in to see you. Josh wants me to ride more often. It'll be a good excuse to practice and not take the wagon."

"Wonderful." Caroline gave Amber's arms a squeeze. "I've enjoyed spending time with you and getting to know you." She climbed into the wagon, slapped the reins, and rode toward town.

Now that she was alone, Amber headed back to the chicken coop to complete her chore. Only she didn't make it there. She went to the barn instead, though this time, there was no blue-white light. The damn portal took up a lot of her thoughts, and she had a bazillion questions about it, the mysterious Malachi, and all the inner workings that no one knew. If only the damn thing came with a user manual.

She walked inside where it was cooler. Damp hay and the musky odor of horses filled the air. Quite a contrast from its twenty-first century counterpart with the smells of paint, motor oil, and rubber tires. For a moment, she closed her eyes, picturing the garage in her real time, silently wishing that when she opened them, everything would be normal again.

If—when—they all made it through the portal together, she wondered what life would be like for them in the future. Emma and Wyatt would most likely stay in Montana. Wyatt's construction company was in Whisper Creek, but Emma's business was in New York City. Emma could run her company remotely from anywhere; Wyatt couldn't. Josh would return to practicing law at the family firm. And Amber...? She bit her bottom lip. If Emma ended up moving her business to Whisper Creek, would Amber give up the city life to move there, too? Everyone would be there. Everyone...as in Josh.

She opened her eyes and sighed. It was getting more difficult to push Josh from her thoughts these days. He had become someone important to her.

"Hey," came Josh's sultry voice from behind.

Amber turned around. Josh removed his hat, and his windblown hair hung messily over his forehead. Damn him for being so handsome. "Hay is for horses," she teased.

He walked over to her, glanced at the barn wall where Malachi had last appeared. "I know you hate being inside the barn. Did you see Malachi or the light again?"

"No, I was just…thinking about the portal and…things."

"I've been doing a lot of that, too." His eyes searched her face before meeting her gaze. "Marshal Kane wired me. Wyatt and family are all settled in and doing fine."

"That's great, but when are you going to send them a wire about me being here?"

"I should've done so today. I'm sorry. I was more focused on the second wire I received. Work related. I promise I'll get a wire off."

"I get it. So are Wyatt and Emma coming back soon?"

"His wire didn't say."

She glanced up at the beamed roof and sighed. "Great. Well, what about Grey? Any news on that front?"

"Not yet, I'm afraid." He walked toward the door. "How about we go for a ride?"

"You're good at the changing the subject." She thrust her hands on her hips. "I think you're afraid my riding skills aren't up to your standards."

He chuckled. "Something like that. C'mon."

****

Amber considered herself an okay though rusty rider, considering she hadn't been on a horse in quite some time. Galloping was something she had yet to fully master, and after an hour into their ride, she learned— and quick. The ominous clouds that had teased the sky in the distance moments before suddenly shifted in their direction and grew darker, swallowing up the sun behind them. Distant thunder grew louder, closing in on them. A loud boom hit the air, shaking the ground. Winnie threw back her head and took off toward the property like hell was chasing her. Within seconds, the rain came down in torrents, soaking everything. By the time they reined in the horses under the barn eave fifteen minutes later, they were both utterly drenched.

"Oh my God, that was crazy!" Amber cried, sliding out of the saddle. Pools of water collected on the ground beneath her skirt. She grabbed the hem, wrung out the material, shook her arms, and then wiped wet hair off her face. "Well, that was a first, getting stuck on a horse in the torrential rain."

"For you, maybe. Me, not so much."

"It's a good thing the horse knew where to go. I couldn't see anything!"

Josh chuckled, removing his sodden hat, letting the water run off the sides. He stomped his feet, and water splashed everywhere. His white shirt was glued to his tanned skin. "You better get out of those wet clothes. I'll take care of the horses."

"I'm not going into the house like this. My clothes are beyond soaked. Plus, it's still raining. I'd be mopping for days."

He grinned and took the reins. "I've got another idea. Follow me." When they got inside the barn, he canted his head toward the end of the aisle. "Wyatt keeps extra clothes in the last stall. He sometimes does his woodworking in the barn and needs an extra shirt. Help yourself."

Amber wasn't about to argue. She hated being wet

and was already extremely uncomfortable. The skirt material was much heavier and thicker than anything she wore back home, especially in summer. It would've been nice to be wearing a waterproof jacket instead.

The last stall looked more like a combination of an old-fashioned office and closet with a bale of hay thrown in to give it some character. A wood desk with two drawers sat in the corner. Three shirts hung from pegs on the wall, along with two sets of leather chaps, and riding breaches. She grabbed one of the shirts, tossed it on the desk, then peeled away her wet clothes.

The skirt was easy to remove, but the blouse was another story since the buttons were on the back. *Thanks, Anne.* This morning, she was able to button the bottom few but needed Josh to finish the top four.

"Need some help?" Josh asked from the doorway.

"Just in time," she said, turning her back to him. "I was about to rip off this damn blouse." She lifted her hair, giving him access to the buttons.

He walked up behind her, and her stomach swirled with his nearness. Slowly, he popped the buttons, opening them one at a time. Strong fingers brushed against her skin in a featherlight touch. Her body tingled from the contact.

When he was done, she craned her neck to look over her shoulder. "Josh…" she whispered.

He wrapped an arm around her waist, pulling her back against his hard chest. His whiskers teased her, rubbing against her shoulder. He nuzzled her neck, and goosebumps spread up her arms. This time, she didn't rub them away.

"Amber," he groaned. His breathing was ragged, and his face, pressed against her skin, was warm and damp from the rain.

Slowly, he tugged her sodden sleeves down her arms. He tossed her blouse aside, leaving her with just the chemise covering her 1883-style bra that Anne had custom made and her modern panties.

Josh swung her around in his arms, and she met his gaze. The smoldering fire in his eyes didn't startle her; it thrilled her. Her hands slid up his chest, and she clasped them around his neck, entwining her fingers. Oh, how she wanted more than just another lip-burning kiss. Josh's grasp tightened around her waist, and his lips crashed down against her mouth. Her body molded to the contours of his wet, lean form. He showered kisses around her mouth and along her jaw, all the while, drawing her farther into the stall.

"I want to tell you something," he whispered against her lips. "God knows I probably shouldn't but...I think I'm falling for you."

Her breath caught, and she tilted her head back to gaze into his eyes. She swallowed. "Really?"

He nodded. "Big time."

"Good, but let's not talk about it right now," she said. "I'd like you to kiss me again."

"My pleasure, sweets."

He gathered her in his arms and held her against his wet frame while his lips claimed hers in a slow, thoughtful kiss that sent tremors of reckless desire through her. The caress of his mouth set her body aflame, first nibbling on her earlobe before kissing his way down her neck, her shoulders. She clutched his hair in her fingers, holding him closer, but suddenly, he pulled his lips away, leaving her burning with fire.

"Amber," his hot breath whispered against her

heated flesh. "I need to get out of these wet clothes."

His words finally registered. "Oh, right. Let me help."

He grabbed her hands that were well on their way to unbuttoning his shirt. "I've got this," he said, yanking the shirt over his head. Tossing it aside, he pulled off his boots and stripped out of his pants until he stood completely naked.

Amber took a long, slow drink of Josh's deliciously hard body, especially his six-pack abs, corded muscles on every limb, and his throbbing desire. Heat flooded her, burning all the way to her core. "Hell-o, gorgeous."

He chuckled. "You're next."

She was quick to strip out of her chemise, bra, and panties, giving him a full view of her entire body. His eyes shimmered with desire, and his little groan of satisfaction set her body off in a blaze.

"God, I want you so much," he told her.

He pulled her to him, and they fell against something crunchy and pokey. Hay. Before she could protest the jabs of dried grass, he reached for her skirt and spread it out beneath them.

Josh's hand slid down her stomach to the swell of her hips. Excitement tingled along her skin when his lips followed the same trail, stopping at her breasts to taste and tease her already puckered nipples. His hands moved magically over her, sending currents of desire racing through every inch of her body.

Amber curled into the curve of his body while his hands continued to search for pleasure points and found them. Each one ignited into an inferno, sending fire pulsating within, bringing her to the brink of ecstasy.

"Josh," she begged, digging her fingers into his

shoulders. Her body squirmed beneath him, responding to his expert touch. His tormented groan was a heady invitation. Within seconds, she lay panting, her chest heaving.

He continued his sweet torture, kissing one breast and then the other before slowly making his way down to the hottest part of her. His finger slipped inside her, and she bucked beneath him.

"You are so beautiful," he whispered. "I could feast on you all night." Josh kissed her hungrily.

He eased himself between her thighs before thrusting himself deep inside her, taking her to another height of bliss. Their bodies rocked together in a sensual rhythm, and moans of pleasure escaped her lips.

The feeling was more than sexual desire, his touch was divine ecstasy. A wave of pulsating warmth enveloped her, and she clung to him, begging for release as she met his every thrust. A surge of heat coursed through her, and she squeezed Josh tighter. Passion pounded the blood through her heart, chest, and head, until her body shattered.

Josh called out her name, shuddering his release and burying his head next to hers. After a moment, he rolled onto his side and gathered her against him. She rested her hand on his heaving chest, snuggling closer. He tucked the scratchy blanket around them and said, "I think we should do that all night, sweets."

She leaned up on her elbow and traced his lips with her finger. "I think so, too," she agreed.

He grinned and squeezed her against him.

She didn't tell him, but she had fallen for him, too.

Chapter Twelve

Josh tipped his hat and whistled a peppy tune while making his morning rounds. Damn, he felt good. Alive. It was amazing the difference one night could make—or more specifically what one particular woman could make. There was no denying now how hard he had fallen for the blue-eyed beauty. He had dated many women, but never anyone with the spirit, sense of humor, and determination of Amber. Sure, he'd loved a few women, but it never felt like this—like he couldn't breathe when she was around. Being away from her, even for a few hours, ate him up on the inside. He wanted to see her, be with her, talk with her every minute of the day. She filled his thoughts. His body rattled with excitement. The lavender smell of her hair teased his senses. And the taste of her sugary kiss tempted him even now. Everything about her and his reaction to her made him feel like he was a kid in junior high.

In a way, he felt like he had already known Amber from the countless stories Emma had told him and Wyatt. Amber's loyalty to Emma brought her through the time portal and into his life. And he would always be grateful to his sister-in-law for being the reason Amber traveled through time and into his arms.

His heart tugged in a new direction it hadn't gone before. Not only was he falling for Amber, but he needed to protect her, guard her. Not because he had to, because he wanted to. There wasn't anything he wouldn't do for her. She had a shitty childhood, losing most of her family at an early age. And he wanted her to feel special, secure, and wanted, because Christ, did he want her.

"Good morning, Deputy."

Josh turned toward the direction of the feminine voice. Caroline stood outside Doc Wilson's office, leaning against the post, garbed in her doctor attire of white apron with an old-fashioned stethoscope in hand. Whenever he was on duty, she called him deputy.

She gave him a wave, and he walked over to her. "Mornin', Dr. MacKenzie," he said with a tip of his hat. "Beautiful day out."

"It is." She spared the sky a quick glance and rubbed her arms. "But it's going to be an early winter."

He followed her gaze then looked back at her questioningly. "How can you be so sure?"

A smile spread across her lips. "Call it intuition."

He chuckled. "You women have that nailed, that's for sure. I'll take your word for it." He cocked his chin toward the office. "Are you working alone today?"

She descended the steps and stood next to him on the street. "Just until Doc Wilson returns. I'm not all that busy. Unfortunately, the locals still think of me as the nurse and don't consider me a real doctor."

"Nonsense, you're one of the best doctors Whisper Creek is lucky enough to have," he told her. "Not all towns in the territory can boast they have two outstanding medical professionals at their fingertips. Don't let the ignorance of some of the old timers get you down. They'll come around."

"I do hope so."

"I've got to get back to my rounds." He touched two

fingers to his hat. "See you later."

Josh continued along Main Street, checking in at a few more establishments before making a U-turn and heading back to the office. When he stepped inside, a bitter chill hit him like winter arrived without warning. It wasn't the temperature; it was the vibe. Marshal Reed had a look on his face Josh knew too well. *Bad news.*

"Hey," Josh said, walking over to his boss's desk. "What's going on?"

Reed rubbed a hand over his weary features, then snatched a paper off his desk. He pushed out a breath as he handed it to Josh. "This just arrived."

Josh spared the marshal a glance and quickly read it. The wire came from the warden at Deer Lodge. A lead fireball shot into his stomach, burning a hole. Disbelief collided with anger. The wire contained four simple words: *Grey escaped. Whereabouts unknown.*

Marshal Reed stroked his forehead. "I'm planning to ride over to Deer Lodge to find out what in tarnation happened. I want to see the warden's eyes so I can read the truth in them. If he or one of his bastard guards knew anything about this before it happened or is responsible—"

"I'll go with you," Josh cut in.

Reed shook his head. "No, you need to stay low and get word to Wyatt. Until we have proof that it was Grey threatening your brother and his wife, I want everyone to be extra careful now that this bastard is on the loose."

"Fine." Josh's insides turned cold. His fingers clattered like the icicles hanging from his father's old barn in winter. "I'm on it," he said.

Reed scratched his head. "You're on what?"

Josh waved a hand. "I'm going to see my brother

and let him know about Grey."

"*See* him? I don't advise that. It's best you stay in one place. Because if it does turn out to be Grey that's been threatening your brother, there's no telling what he could do—to either of you."

"Marshal, Wyatt's my brother. I'd give my life for him."

"Let's just hope it doesn't come to that."

"It won't," he swore, but even Josh couldn't know that. "I'll leave for Montana City in the morning—"

"Josh, that's not a good idea."

"I know what I'm doing." He headed for the door. "Let me know what you find out. You can send word to me through Kane. I'll be back in a few days."

Reed nodded. "Be careful."

With a tip of his hat, he walked out and headed for home, racing as fast as his trusted horse would take him. When he got back to the property, he stopped and surveyed his surroundings before approaching the house. His gut clenched. The hair on his arm prickled. Winnie grazed in the paddock, soaking up the sun as she did every day, but he couldn't shake the feeling something was…off.

He led his horse into the paddock, and then first checked the house. "Amber!" he shouted.

There was no response.

Searching one room at a time, he came up empty. When he got to his room, everything was perfectly in place. The bed was made, erasing all signs of his and Amber's incredible night of passion after they made their way in from the barn. The windows were open, letting in the soft breeze. Amber's robe lay at the foot of the bed. Where was she?

He turned to go, but something made him give the room another survey. There was a piece of paper tucked halfway under her pillow. He snatched it up and read it—twice.

Don't be mad. I have to do this for my own sanity. I'm tired of waiting.

XO

Amber

A heaviness tightened in his chest so much that he could hardly breathe. The only place he could think of that she headed to was Montana City. *Shit*.

****

Amber couldn't sit idle anymore. It was imperative she get to Emma. Josh was going to kill her, but she didn't care. That wasn't one hundred percent true. She did care what he thought, and she would explain everything when she returned. Hopefully, he would understand and forgive her.

There was no train travel yet between Whisper Creek and Montana City or even Helena, as she'd learned, so she would have to take two stagecoaches: the first to Helena and the other from Helena to Montana City. It would be an overnight trip, but that didn't matter.

At the depot in town, the stagecoach driver grabbed her carpetbag and tossed it on top of the conveyance, securing it with other passengers' belongings. She nodded her thanks, and then climbed into the old-fashioned stagecoach complete with dirt-stained burgundy curtains, two narrow benches, and dust-covered floor.

Settling on the empty bench, she smiled at the couple across from her. Judging by the amount of googly eyes they were making at each other, they were newlyweds. "Hi there," she said, arranging her skirts. Even though the carriage had some fancy bench padding, she had a feeling it was going to be a rough ride since her knees almost touched them.

"Ma'am," the young man said, doffing his hat. "I'm Elmer Gregory, and this is my wife."

"Pleased to meet you both. Amber Harrison."

"We're on our way to Helena to ride the railroad," Mrs. Gregory squealed, clutching her husband's arm. She looked like she was barely eighteen. "It's my first time on a train! I wonder what it'll be like."

Amber smiled at the young woman's excitement over something so simple as a train ride. In her own time, she rode trains and subways nearly every day. Not once did she give a second thought as to how the railroad came into existence or what a novel opportunity it was for the people in its early days.

A figure filled the doorway, blocking out the midday sun. A man climbed inside and settled into the only available seat next to Amber. *So much for comfort.* She scooted toward the wall of the coach and grunted. It was definitely going to be a tight ride. The man doffed his hat, revealing thick grey hair. His skin was pale, and his suit appeared a size too large. He might have been handsome once, but he looked like he had seen a few rough years.

"Good day, everyone. Marcus Whitcomb." When the man's gaze turned to Amber, he smiled. "And you are…?"

He had an accent of sorts, not from the West or Midwest. She couldn't quite put her finger on it. "Amber Harrison."

"Charmed," he said, taking her hand. "And would

there be a Mr. Harrison?"

In the nineteenth century, it was best to make mention of a husband, whether there was one or not. That is, according to Anne. "Yes, there is," she said at last.

"Pity," Whitcomb remarked, and his gaze remained on her.

He seemed pleasant enough, but Amber gave him a fake smile. There was something intense about the way he was looking at her, almost like he knew something. Then again, it could be her New York paranoia setting in.

The coach lurched into motion, and she second-guessed herself for her hasty decision. Knowing that Emma and Wyatt were safe and settled in Montana City wasn't good enough for Amber. No, she had to see Emma in person.

Throughout the ride, conversation ebbed and flowed with her seatmates. The young Mrs. Gregory drifted off for a nap, and Amber couldn't understand how the woman was able to sleep throughout all the bumping and jostling.

"Mrs. Harrison," Whitcomb whispered. "What takes you to Helena without your husband?"

Dust blew in from the open window, and Amber waved a hand in front of her face. She coughed, then cleared her throat before responding. "I'm, um, meeting him there. He had some business to conduct."

"Are you both from Whisper Creek?"

"Um, yeah. I mean, yes. And you?"

"I lived there for a spell," he said, playing with the rim of the hat on his lap. "What sort of business is your husband in if you don't mind me asking? I may know of him."

That caught her off guard. She didn't know what sort of occupations were abundant in the Old West, other than lawman, blacksmith, or saloonkeeper. While not her husband, she decided to refer to Josh when speaking of a pretend spouse like she had done back in Deer Lodge. "Law," she said simply.

Whitcomb shifted in the seat, tapping his foot. "I don't recall a marshal or deputy or even a sheriff by the name of Harrison. I'm sure you're happy to be reuniting with him."

"Of course."

He nodded; his gaze returned to hers. "Is Helena your final destination?"

Amber hated lies, but this guy was getting a little too nosy for her liking. Instead, she turned the tables and said as pleasantly as possible, "You've been asking all about me, Mr. Whitcomb, and yet I feel I haven't asked you anything. How rude of me, so let me reciprocate. Is there a Mrs. Whitcomb waiting for you?"

He stared down at the hat in his lap. "I had hoped there would be, but she…" He cleared his throat and turned his gaze out the window.

"Sorry, I didn't mean to pry. I was just trying to make conversation."

"It's quite all right." He paused and looked at her. "I was engaged a long time ago. She perished in a fire. And most recently, the woman I had hoped to marry chose another man."

"I'm so sorry."

"I am too. It would've been an advantageous marriage, for certain."

Hearing that, Amber was relieved that whomever this woman was escaped a lifetime of misery. What a creep. Then again, men in this century married mainly for wealth, she reminded herself, not love.

After that, Amber watched the passing scenery of hills, mountains, trees, and a few wild animals here and there, until the stage slowed. She was seated backward, and as Helena came into view, she craned her neck to see the sights. It was a miracle she didn't get motion sickness or vomit on her seatmates. The clippety-clopping of horses and bouncing of wagon wheels turning up dirt in their wake filled her senses. Countless cement buildings stood three to four stories high. A handful of smaller buildings, like the ones in Whisper Creek, had false-fronts and boarded sidewalks.

The town bustled with two-horse wagons, riders on horseback, and city goers strolling along Main Street. The more fashionable men wore three-piece tailored suits, while the drifters or local cowboys wore casual shirts, vests, and pants with high leather boots. Women looked stunning in tight bodices and overskirts that accentuated their hourglass figures. She stuck her head out the window and inhaled the smells of dirt, horses, and smoke.

"Be careful you don't fall, Mrs. Harrison," Whitcomb said, tugging her arm.

She laughed, plopping back against the bench. "Knowing me, that's quite possible. Thanks, though."

They arrived at the stage depot. Whitcomb emerged first and offered his hand to Amber. She accepted, stepped down, and then stretched her aching limbs. The driver tossed their bags down one at a time. Whitcomb caught each one and placed them neatly on the boardwalk, leaving them for their respective owners.

"It was a pleasure to meet you, Mrs. Harrison."

Whitcomb took her hand and kissed it. "Until we meet again." He turned and walked away.

"Later, dude," she mumbled, and turned in the opposite direction. "Much later."

****

The coach to Montana City didn't leave Helena until the next morning, so Amber took a stroll around the city before checking into the nearest hotel for the night. It was a good thing she had borrowed a few coins from Emma's jewelry box stash. Back in their own time, that's where her friend hid small bills. Thankfully, some things never changed.

The clerk gave her a room on the third floor. She paid extra for hot water so she could take a long, hot bath. The hotel reserved a small room on its own for female guests to bathe and refresh themselves since the rooms were too small to fit individual tubs. She waited several hours for her turn, then waited even longer because she insisted the tub be cleaned before she used it. The clerk gave her an odd look but kept his comments to himself.

After enjoying her first bath in an Old West hotel, she returned to her room and settled in for the night. It was time to go over the crazy plan in her head.

She had obtained a map from the stage depot and studied it by lamplight. According to Josh, Wyatt and Emma were staying outside Montana City limits in a secluded cabin. While the map gave an indication of how the town was laid out, there were no markings or symbols denoting properties on the outskirts of town. Dammit. She would have to find Marshal Kane and start name dropping, beginning with Josh and Marshal Reed. Of course, she would explain that she traveled all the way from New York to begin with. If that didn't work and he refused to divulge any details, she would use all her womanly wiles to persuade him. It wasn't a great plan, she knew that, but it was the only one she had. And, boy, did that sound better in her head before she took off. What was she thinking? Clearly, she wasn't. Her impatience was getting the best of her.

A persistent knocking on the door startled her, and she dropped the map. There was no time to scramble and replace her thin robe with something more conservative to wear. Without warning, the door burst open. Sheer fright sent an explosive banging in her chest until her gaze focused on the intruder.

"Josh!" She clutched her chest, her breath heaving in a panicked rhythm. "You scared the crap out of me. What are you doing here?"

"You left." Josh closed the door and turned the key, locking them inside. He didn't look happy. His jaw was clenched, and he was breathing hard. He leaned back against the door, holding her gaze. The lamp cast a warm glow on his face.

"Mrs. Harrison?" a man called from the other side of the door. "Are you all right in there? It's Mr. and Mrs. Gerald from down the hall."

Amber cleared her throat. "Yes, Mr. Gerald," she replied loud enough for him to hear her. "All is well. Thank you. I appreciate you checking on me. My, uh, husband forgot his key."

"Good night, then," he called back.

It was a moment before the sound of their footsteps faded away down the hall.

Josh still hadn't answered her yet. When he didn't say anything, she feared the worst.

"Well?" she demanded. "What are you doing here?

Say something!"

"I thought everything was fine between us," he began, his voice a tight tone. "We had an amazing night last night—the first of many, I'm hoping. Early this morning, I kissed you while you slept, and off to work, I went."

"Josh—"

"I get there, and my boss proceeds to tell me…Grey escaped prison."

She gasped. "What?"

"Thinking it can't get any worse, I come home to tell you the news and make sure you're all right. Instead, I find a note, saying you left."

"Yeah, about that…"

He pushed away from the door and paced. "I knew you would go to Montana City to find Emma. That's where you're going, right?" He stopped in front of her, waiting for her response.

She nodded. "Yes."

"You're lucky Fergus, Sam's stableman, saw you getting into the stagecoach, otherwise I never would've found you in time to catch up with you. I busted my ass to get here as fast as I could to make sure you're safe."

She bit her bottom lip and looked away. "I am safe."

"That's what you think. Grey is on the loose now. It's why I came for you. I'm worried that he might start inquiring about about Emma and Wyatt. If he does, there's a chance he could find out you, Emma's best friend, is in town. And then that would put you in danger."

She flopped down on the bed. "How would he find out? He doesn't even know I exist."

"Grey is cagey and calculating. He has a knack for

digging up information. And now that he's out of prison, his main goal will be to exact revenge before going back through the portal—or at least, attempting to." Josh paused. "Marshal Reed went to Deer Lodge to find out what happened. I'll wire him when we get to Montana City."

She quirked a brow. "We?"

He sat down next to her and reached for her hand. "I was planning to take you with me there at some point. That's why I wanted to make sure you could ride without falling off the horse in case we were forced to…flee quickly."

"I'm sorry," she admitted. "I was going to tell you about my plan and leave you a long letter or something, but I'm not good with details. I was even going to write something sweet and mushy to you but, well, that's more Emma's thing than mine."

His voice dropped in volume. "Define sweet and mushy."

She gazed into those emerald orbs that had the magical power of tripping her heart. "Damn it, Josh. I'm crazy about you, and I don't want to be. I mean, I do, but it complicates things. My main goal here is to prevent Emma's name from appearing on that damn tombstone. But, shit, you're making it difficult with all sorts of yummy distractions and your kindness and deputy-protection-mode and all that. You're wearing me down."

He kissed her hand and let out a slow, deep breath. "When I first discovered you were gone…my heart shattered until I realized what you were up to. I had to come for you."

"I'm glad you did."

Amber's simplest plan to warn her best friend about

the tombstones, and then head right back with her through the portal had more than one wrench thrown into it. Emma and Wyatt were out of town, the damn portal didn't work, and now Grey escaped prison. The anxiety and worry eating at her regarding Emma's safety was rivaled by the burgeoning feelings she had for Josh. They took her by surprise, especially that the walls she had built around her heart and her sanity for so long were slowly being chipped away. Could her feelings for Josh and the anxiety over Emma's safety coincide without driving her crazy?

"Let me hold you tonight," he told her.

She flopped back onto the bed and within seconds, he was at her side, pulling her up against the hardness of his body where she would be safe and secure.

He leaned back to caress her cheek and gaze into her eyes. "I'm not letting you out of my sight again, sweets." He pressed a kiss to the side of her head and held her tight. "I'll work out a plan by morning. Close your eyes and get some rest."

She closed her eyes and fell asleep to the comforting sound of his breathing.

Chapter Thirteen

Josh rented a horse for Amber from the local livery so she could keep up with him and Delorean, allowing them to reach Montana City sooner. While he had no idea if Grey had anyone on his tail, he wasn't going to take any chances. Unfortunately, with Grey on the loose and Malachi giving them a deadline, Josh wouldn't feel completely safe until they were back in their own time. If Malachi truly was the answer to returning to their own century, why hadn't the man shown up sooner? Still, the deadline rankled him. There had to be something special about that date…but what?

"You and Emma are my heroes," Amber commented, wiping her neck and face with a handkerchief.

He smiled. "Why is that?"

"Emma makes everything seem so effortless, like you do. It's like you both were born in this century. Me? Not so much. Don't get me wrong. It's been a unique opportunity to travel through time and witness Old West history in the making; but I'd never choose to live here, not in a bazillion years."

"It's a rough life, I'll admit. Sometimes, survival mode is all that's on your mind."

"Do you ever wonder what brought you here to this place in time? It's not like we had to program a time machine to bring us here."

"It's funny you should ask that. When we were kids, Wyatt and I used to pretend we were cowboys, and James was the mean old marshal out to get us." He chuckled. "Since I've been here, I've wondered if the portal somehow connected into our subconscious or memories. I'm reaching here. I really have no clue why this place was chosen for us. Maybe we accidentally got sucked in. Who knows? I'm hoping Malachi will have an explanation."

"If he shows up again," Amber mumbled.

"You don't think he will?"

She shrugged. "Let's just say I'm not banking on him. All I want is for us to go home. Plus, the more I think about Malachi, the more I think he's not telling us the entire story. I don't know why, but I think he's withholding pertinent details that we need to know in order to access the portal."

He turned to her. "Such as?"

"If I knew, I'd tell you. It's just a hunch." Facing forward again, she asked, "Are we there yet?"

He knew when a woman was done with a conversation, and Amber certainly was. Relenting, he cocked his head toward the town. "Just about."

They rode down Main Street until they reached the livery where he paid for their horses to be fed and watered. That done, he offered his arm to Amber and escorted her to the marshal's office. They strolled down the dusty boarded sidewalks, arm in arm.

"This town is different," Amber announced after the third block. "It's not like Whisper Creek, that's for sure. For one, it smells even worse." She crinkled her nose. "I didn't think that could be possible; and two, it's grimier. I feel like we're in a developing country here."

"The Old West was, I mean is, anything but clean. There are no street sweeping machines or rubbish removal services. There's horse shit everywhere. And don't forget," he said, leaning close to whisper, "people sometimes don't bathe for weeks. If they do, the water in the public bathhouses is usually reused unless you pay extra."

"I just threw up a little in my mouth."

He squeezed her hand. "Toughen up, sweets. You're from the Big Apple, or did you forget the awful stench of the New York City subway system in summer? Nothing should faze you."

She swatted his arm with her free hand. "Listen, cowboy. You might be used to living in the Old West with all its interesting odors and whatnot, but I've only been here for five or so weeks. Cut me some slack."

"If it makes you feel any better, we won't be in Montana City long." They reached the office, and Josh opened the door. "C'mon, I'll introduce you to Marshal Kane. You'll like him."

The office set-up was pretty much the same as Reed's office in Whisper Creek with bare wood floors, a large wood desk, stiff chairs, and a sideboard. The box stove had been put to good use in colder months. The room, though, was quite stuffy, despite the open windows. Even he had to admit, air conditioning would feel good right about now.

The man behind the desk looked up from his newspaper and grinned. "Well, if it ain't Deputy Kincaid." Emmett Kane rounded the desk to shake Josh's hand. "How are you, my friend?"

"I've been better," Josh replied. He and Wyatt had become friends with Kane in the short time they'd been involved with Reed and the law, though they didn't see much of Kane unless it involved outlaws and shootouts. The three of them were cut from the same cloth, all loyal to the oath they took to protect and serve. And they were always honest with each other. "It's good to see you."

"You, too." Kane's gaze traveled from Josh to Amber. "And who do we have here?"

"Ah, I'd like to introduce you to someone special," Josh began. Were his cheeks on fire? It sure felt like it. "Marshal Emmet Kane, this is Miss Amber Harrison; Emma Kincaid's dearest friend."

"Pleasure to meet you, ma'am," Kane said, taking her hand. "That you're a friend of Emma's means you're a friend of mine."

Kane was in his early forties, but the man's eyes held two lifetimes of sadness. Josh never understood why.

"Thank you." Amber smiled. "I've heard good things about you from Josh."

"That's very kind of you to say, ma'am."

"I guess you know why we're here," Josh announced.

"Your brother," Kane stated with a nod.

"That," Josh said, "and Grey."

"I ain't got much to report on him, considering he's still rotting over at Deer Lodge."

Josh frowned. "I take it you didn't you get my wire?"

Kane scratched the back of his neck. "Nope, no wire. We've been having some trouble with telegraph wires lately—or maybe it's the delivery boy."

He pushed out a long breath, then turned to Amber. "Why don't you sit down? This could take a while."

Amber fanned herself. "If it's all right with you, I'd rather go for a walk. I'm sweating to death in these clothes."

"I don't think that's such a good idea."

"Please, I'm so sticky, I can't take it."

"All right." Josh sighed and walked her toward the door. "Just stay close. Don't go any farther than the next corner. I'll be watching you from this window. And come back as soon as you've had enough air."

"You got it," she said and left.

Josh watched her from the window for a moment. He removed his hat and shoved a hand through his hair. "I'm surprised you didn't hear. Grey escaped."

"Shit," Kane swore. "What happened?"

"I was convinced Grey had someone on the outside working for him." Josh paced but kept returning to the window to check on Amber. "There were accidents, threats on Wyatt's and Emma's lives. I'm sure Wyatt must've filled you in."

His friend nodded. "Wyatt told me he had his suspicions. Don't worry. No one will ever find them at my cabin. They're safe."

"We can't thank you enough."

Kane shrugged a shoulder. "I merely gave them a roof over their heads. And when you and Miss Amber are ready, you can ride over. I'm sure they'd pleased as punch to see you both. I'd suggest you not linger in town. I'll have my deputy make some inquiries about Grey, discreetly, of course."

"I'd appreciate that."

"I'll wire whatever information I can rustle up over to you and Reed in Whisper Creek. With any luck, we'll apprehend Grey and get him back in prison in no time."

****

Amber's stomach grumbled. While she and Josh had a quick breakfast of biscuits and cheese before they departed for Montana City, it was well past lunchtime. Between the layers of clothes, the heat, and her hunger, she was hangry. A nutty chocolate bar would be ideal right about now.

Strolling down the dust-covered sidewalk to the next corner, she admired the false-fronted buildings on both sides of the street. While Montana City was similar in layout to Whisper Creek, it lacked the vibe of its somewhat metropolitan counterpart. Not only that, but Montana City was about half the size of Whisper Creek, and it was far from being clean and tidy. She only hoped she could find a decent place to grab a bite—one with a clean kitchen. Somehow, she doubted that was a real thing here.

After her initial escapade into the Coppered Pan, Amber knew better than to seek sustenance at a saloon, but she spotted a café half-way down the next block. Josh would be mad if she ventured too far, but her hunger was getting the best of her.

Someone called her name, and she turned around. *Whitcomb.* "Mr. Whitcomb, what are you doing here?" she asked, surprise evident in her voice. "I thought you were staying in Helena."

Marcus Whitcomb doffed his hat and smiled. His silver hair was neatly combed. Out in the bright of day, the pallor of his skin and the dark circles under his eyes were more prominent than she had noticed in the shadows of the coach they had shared the day before.

"Lovely to see you again, Mrs. Harrison," he said. "Helena was not my final destination. Alas, neither is

Montana City. And you?"

"Oh. Um, I'm visiting…friends."

Whitcomb got distracted by something across the street. Amber followed his gaze. A tall, skinny cowboy with dusty boots, stained vest, and dirty chaps leaned against a post. The man tipped his hat slightly back, revealing straight greasy hair. His eyes were scary, like he wouldn't mind shooting off a few bullets into any nearby object just for the fun of it. His steely gaze remained on Whitcomb as he spit out a wad of tobacco. It splattered across the front of the man's shoes.

"Yes, that, er, sounds nice." Whitcomb was clearly distracted. "Perhaps, our paths will cross again. Good day, Mrs. Harrison." He bowed his head in farewell before hurrying across the street. Joining up with the cowboy, the two men engaged in conversation before disappearing down a nearby alley.

"What a weirdo," she mumbled.

"*Psssst…*"

Amber turned toward the sound.

A tall cowboy stood by the alley with his hat tugged low over his eyes. A black bandana tied around his neck was pulled up to his nose, covering the lower part of his face. He pulled it down and waved her over.

"Dude, are you nuts?" Amber lifted her hem, about to make a mad dash.

"Wait! Are you Amber?"

The man knew her name, but how? She backed up a few steps. Shards of panic sliced her. What if this man turned out to be that psycho, Grey? "Who…who are you?"

"I'm a friend of Emma's, okay?" His voice was calm, but his hand clamped around her arm in a vicelike grip. "Come with me, *please*. I'll explain who I am and how I know you."

Amber's instinct was to bite the man's hand, grind her heel into his foot, then knee him in the balls, as she had learned a million times over in self-defense classes through the years, but she thought better about it. This was the Old West, so it was more than likely this brute would be carrying a gun, like all the other men she'd seen around town. And this man knew her name—and Emma—and she needed to know why.

"It's me," the man told her at last. His grip on her loosened as he led her into a narrow passageway. "Wyatt. Emma's husband. Wyatt Kincaid."

His words sank into her brain. She blinked. *Wyatt*?

He pushed his hat back, letting it dangle on the string around his neck. Blue eyes pierced her. Thick blond hair fell over his forehead. He could do without the scruffy beard, though. But holy shit, he, James, and Josh looked so much alike—except for the color of his eyes. There was no denying they were brothers. Hot gene pool, indeed.

"Shit, Amber, I can't believe you're in the nineteenth century. What are you doing here?"

"Me?" Her initial shock wore off, and there was no doubt she would have an ulcer at the end of this trip. "You scared the hell out of me! What's the matter with you? What are *you* doing here? Where's Emma? What happened? Is she okay?"

"Take a breath. It's all right. Come here." Wyatt grabbed her hands and pulled her into a brotherly hug. Some of her anger dissipated. Hugging him wasn't as good as Emma, but close enough…for the moment. "I'm sorry if I frightened you. I'm just shocked you're here."

"How do you think I feel?" she countered, pushing away to study his face. "I don't get it. How'd you recognize me?"

"Emma has a photo of the two of you she brought back from the future."

"Oh, right," she replied.

"When I saw you on the street, I thought my mind was playing tricks on me. I watched you for a bit, hoping you wouldn't notice." He paused. "Why are you here…in Montana City…and more specifically, in this *century*? And where the hell is Josh?"

"Why am *I* here?" she scoffed, having zero patience to hold it all back now. "I'll tell you why—you're in danger. You and Emma. *That's* why I'm here—to warn you both."

His blue eyes narrowed. "Warn me about what? I don't understand."

She drew in a deep breath, and then let it out slowly before replying. "Back in our time, I found two tombstones at the old Whisper Creek cemetery. They had your names on them…yours and Emma's."

Wyatt scratched the back of his neck, slightly amused. "I know I'm not the first to tell you this, Amber, but we all die at some point. Maybe—"

"The year on them was *1883*," she cut in. At this point, she'd had it being patient. "I know it's not a lot to go on, but with all the threats against you and Emma, Josh thinks this dude Grey has something to do with that. Whether he does or doesn't have anything to do with the tombstones, you two cannot die *this* year!"

"Well, I have no intention of letting that happen, but, shit, this changes everything." Wyatt's jaw tightened. "I've got to get back to Emma, and then move her and

Wesley somewhere else, somewhere safe. I can't take the chance of Grey finding my family. If Josh is here with you, the two of you should return to Whisper Creek. Now."

"And just where are you going? Where are you taking Emma and Wesley?"

He raked a hand through his hair. "I don't know yet, but I'll figure it out."

"Figure it out *after* you see your brother, because I'm not going anywhere until I see Emma first."

"Amber, I know how far you traveled to get here," Wyatt said, gently holding her arms. "No one knows that better than me, Emma, and Josh. I can't thank you enough for bringing this information, but I will not risk my family's welfare. When the time is right, we'll all be together. I promise you."

"No," she said and grabbed his hand. "You're not leaving here without talking to your brother first. He's over at the marshal's office. Let's go."

"I can't go in there," he protested, pulling away. "I'm in hiding. I just came into town to pick up supplies."

She glowered at him. "I thought you took Emma on a getaway…not to run off into hiding?"

He hesitated. "True, I did take her and Wesley away. Emma was anxious with all the incidents happening, so it was best we leave town for a while. It's been great spending time at the cabin. It's super cozy and…anyway, knowing Grey may have hired a man or two to do his dirty work, I'd still like to keep a low profile."

"Then use your bandana and your hat to hide your face like you did before," she suggested. "Do whatever you have to, but you're not going to walk away without seeing Josh. Besides, there's a lot going on that we have to tell you about." She clamped her hand around his wrist and marched off in the direction of the marshal's office.

"Woman, you're as stubborn as Emma," he remarked with a chuckle. "All right, I'm coming."

Chapter Fourteen

On the brief jaunt to the marshal's office, Amber updated Wyatt on everything that had transpired, starting with her trip through the portal, Malachi's appearance, and what she knew about Grey's recent prison break. During their conversation, she found it difficult to take her eyes off him. He had such a strong resemblance to Josh and James that they could almost pass for triplets.

"Aside from the tombstones and Grey's escape," Wyatt said lightly. "What else you got?"

"I'll let Josh fill you in on everything else," she replied. "It's been an interesting month, to say the least."

His eyebrows shot up. "You've been here that long?"

"Technically, sixish weeks. I'm starting to lose track."

He smiled. "So what do you think of the Old West?"

"Let's just say, if I had found Emma the minute I got here, I'd have left minute number two."

"Oh, come now. It's not that bad."

"You, Emma, and Josh seem to have adapted quite well," she said. "Me? I like the comforts of home, my home, in the twenty-first century."

"Considering this may be a once in a lifetime occurrence, maybe you should try to enjoy it more."

She cuffed him on the arm. "Oh, sure. I'll just sit back and relax while we wait for the locals to round up the prison escapee and toss him back in the hoosegow," she said, with a twang.

Wyatt chuckled. "All right. Have it your way, but once you go home, you may dream of returning to 1883, Whisper Creek."

"When pigs fly, pal," she said with a laugh.

They arrived at Kane's office, and Wyatt opened the door. Amber walked in first and immediately wanted to remove every ounce of clothing. It was hot inside, nearing sauna-like temps. She had worked up a sweat on the way over, and already her clothes were sticking to her.

"Hey, kids," Amber announced waving both hands, and then pointed in dramatic fashion. "Look who I found."

Josh and Kane were in deep conversation. Josh turned and crossed the room. "Wyatt! How the hell—?"

"Good to see you, big brother." Wyatt pulled him into a hug.

Josh tugged Wyatt's scruffy beard. "The beard isn't a good look for you, sorry to say," he teased. "You look like Dad after a week of camping."

Wyatt scratched his jaw and shrugged. "Had to do something a little different to disguise myself."

Josh glanced at Amber and smiled. "I guess it's safe to assume that you've met Amber."

"Yeah, at last. She filled me in on everything."

He quirked a brow. "Everything?"

"He means Malachi," Amber added.

Wyatt crossed the room and shook hands with Kane. "Emmett, thanks again for your hospitality."

"No need to thank me," Kane said. "It's what friends do. And now that we're all here, why don't we discuss

185

what we're going to do about Grey."

"When we get back to the barn," she whispered to Josh, "I'm sure all this will just work itself out."

"What does a barn have to do with anything?" Kane asked, folding his arms. Clearly, there was nothing wrong with his hearing.

Josh cast Amber that squinty-eyed we'll-discuss-this-later warning look and shook his head. "I know you're eager to return, Amber, but first we need a plan in case Grey's men are out there looking for us."

"Well, your genius brother here thinks you and I should head back to Whisper Creek while he takes Emma and Wesley elsewhere," Amber said.

"That's not a bad idea," Kane remarked. "If Grey's men are looking for Wyatt and find Josh instead, that could buy some time. We could use Josh for leverage."

"Are you nuts?" she scoffed. "Sorry. What part of that sounds like a good idea? Swap one brother for the other and sacrifice Josh's and my safety. Grey doesn't care if it's Josh or Wyatt. He's an equal opportunity villain. I mean, he's got it in for both of them."

"I agree with Amber," Josh announced. "We all stay together. Safety in numbers."

Wyatt sighed then nodded. "You're probably right."

All Amber wanted was to get her friends back to the barn as fast as humanly possible for this century. That way, they could go all go home through the portal together. There was no reason to wait any longer. However, with Grey out of prison and his whereabouts currently unknown, they had to take extra precautions. It was time to get the hell out of Dodge, so to speak. They'd been there long enough, according to her, anyway.

The men droned on with different scenarios on how

to capture Grey, but all Amber could think about was Emma. There was no way of knowing if Grey was the one responsible for Emma and Wyatt's names appearing on the tombstones. And now that he was out of prison, things just might be even more dangerous than she had imagined.

Josh held out his hand to her. "Ready?"

"What did I miss?" Amber took his hand and stood up, glancing at all three men. "Where are we going?"

Wyatt donned his hat. "To get Emma and Wesley."

"Finally!" she cried, running toward the door.

"Wait!" Josh tugged her hand and pulled her to him. "You can't leave my side or my sight, not even for a second, and not until we get back to Whisper Creek. Understood?"

"Stick to you like glue," she agreed, tipping her head back. Damn those emerald eyes. They burned right through her. "Got it, cowboy. Now, can we please go? I haven't seen my best friend in a year, and my patience is about zero."

"You've certainly got your hands full," Kane said with a chuckle.

Josh grinned and cast a wink at Amber. "Indeed, I do."

Wyatt's gaze volleyed between Josh and Amber. "What did I miss?"

****

"Are we there yet?" Amber shifted in the saddle. The trip to Wyatt and Emma's secret hideout was farther from town than she expected. She, Josh, and Wyatt had been riding for a solid hour, and still no sign of a house or cabin. No wonder there was no indication of the structure on her little town map.

Wyatt chuckled. "You sound like Josh when he was a kid, always so impatient."

"Me, impatient?" Josh scoffed. "Never."

"Always," Amber added with a laugh. "I can't wait to see Emma. She's going to flip when I tell her about the tombstones."

"That's not going to happen," Wyatt warned.

"Of course, I'm going to tell her. That's the main reason I came here—to warn her and you. You know her. She'd get it out of me anyway. Emma and I don't keep secrets. Plus, it's not like she's going to think I'm in town just visiting. There's a reason for me being here."

Wyatt pulled up next to Amber and tugged her reins. The horse came to a stop. "All I meant is we will tell her *together*," he said.

"Oh."

"Emma's strong but she keeps everything on the inside, as you well know. She worries too much about me when we're separated, especially now. We've got to do this strategically. All right?"

"Got it," she agreed, albeit reluctantly.

"He's right, sweets," Josh added.

"Sweets?" Wyatt's head swiveled to Josh. "Hell, I definitely missed a lot."

Josh chuckled. "More than a lot."

Amber's patience was wearing thin. Emma needed to know everything, especially about the tombstones. If it were up to her, she would grab Emma and Wesley and head right through the portal, leaving the men trailing in the proverbial dust to follow. Now, the stupid thing was broken, and they all had to wait and travel together. This trip back in time was nothing but a long series of rotten luck.

She snapped the reins, jerking the horse into a trot. "You're lucky Emma loves you as much as she does," she grumbled.

"Yes, I am lucky, and I don't take one second for granted. You can be sure she and Wesley are my whole world." Wyatt pointed. "We're here."

At the bottom of the hill was a circular line of trees surrounding a small log cabin with a stone chimney and a sorry excuse for a barn with a wagon at its side. From their viewpoint, it was barely visible. If it wasn't for the white paint on the porch, she would've missed it.

"Let's go!" she cried, nudging her horse.

Josh reached across and yanked her reins. "Not so fast."

"What are you doing?" Amber demanded.

"Emma doesn't know you're here," Wyatt said. "Let me go in first."

"Why? Emma's not some fragile little flower. This is Emma we're talking about. She gave up her life in the future to live here with you in a backward century. You think she's suddenly going to faint because of my presence?" Amber rolled her eyes. *Men.* "Puh-leeze."

Wyatt smiled. "I'd like to say hello to my wife and son with a kiss first. Is that all right with you?"

"Geez, why didn't you just say so?"

Wyatt stole a glance at Josh, shook his head, and then rode ahead of them. When they all reached the dilapidated barn, they dismounted and tethered the horses.

Wyatt came up to her and squeezed her arm. "Give me a few minutes, then come in. Despite what you think, I can't wait for Emma to see you. She's going to be thrilled, and seeing her happy makes me doubly happy."

He walked around to the front of the cabin, opened the front door, and called out, "Honey, I'm home."

Amber paced, coiling her hair around her index finger. Her stomach was all aflutter. It had been a year since she'd seen Emma, and since they'd spoken. While she had wished her friend the best of luck on her journey back through time, Amber hadn't been sincere. She wanted Emma to remain in the twenty-first century with her, not gallivanting across time for some hot guy. Now that Amber had met Wyatt and based on what Caroline had told her about him, she understood why. They were suited for each other. She was truly happy for her friend.

"You're pacing," Josh said.

"I know. It helps me to calm the anxiety." Sparing him a quick glance, she grabbed another tendril with her other hand and started twirling. "Sixty seconds ought to be enough time for them to greet each other, smooch, and for Wyatt to give her a heads up. Right?"

"I'd give them another minute." Josh reached for her hands, pulling them free of her hair, and she stopped to face him. "I'm really glad you came for Emma. Don't get me wrong. I miss James, but…I'm happy you were the one who traveled through time for her."

"I am, too." She touched his cheek, and he bent to press a kiss to her lips. Pulling away, she said, "Okay, that's about sixty seconds, right?"

He laughed and swatted her butt. "Go on. I'll follow."

Amber walked up the front steps, but her feet were heavy, like they were made of lead. Her stomach swirled with excitement. Inside, Wyatt and Emma were talking, but she couldn't hear what they were saying. She sucked in a breath and swung open the front door. "Honey, I'm home, too!"

The tiny one-room cabin had minimal furnishings: a small wood table with two chairs, pot-bellied stove, wood counter, and a bed as small as the one she and Josh shared at Mrs. Roth's boarding house. But that's all she saw since her gaze was fixated on Emma. Wyatt snatched Wesley from Emma's arms in record time. The glass bottle filled with milk that Emma was holding in her other hand slipped out of her grasp and crashed onto the floor.

"It's me," Amber announced, swallowing back the tears. "In the flesh…in the nineteenth century."

"I can't believe this!" Emma flew into Amber's arms.

They hugged each other like drowning swimmers clinging to life preservers thrown into a storm-tossed sea. Amber squeezed Emma tight. Her knees wobbled; relief washed over her. She had waited a year to see her best friend—the woman who was her sister, her confidant, her everything, the yin to her yang, the chocolate to her chip…her person—the one she loved above all else.

The ugly cry began, and tears streamed down her face. Amber rambled, "I'm so glad you're safe…I've missed you…I'm sorry…"

They held tight to each other for endless moments. Emma was the first to pull away. She wiped her eyes with a small handkerchief she kept up her sleeve, like her mom used to do when they were little, and then touched Amber's face.

"You have no idea how happy I am to see you," Emma admitted, her voice trembling. "I have missed you beyond words…but for you to be here, something must be terribly wrong. You can't tell me you're dropping by because you're in the neighborhood."

"Darlin', why don't you sit down?" Wyatt pulled out a nearby chair while bouncing Wesley in his arms. The baby played with the bandana around his neck, babbling away.

Emma shot a look at her husband. "You leave me for the day to get supplies in town an hour away and come back with my best friend who's supposed to be in the twenty-first century. How the hell did you two meet up, anyway?"

"It's a long story." Wyatt pressed a kiss to her head. "And we will tell you everything."

"Wait, first, I want to meet Wesley!" Amber said, making a fuss over the baby in his daddy's arms. He was absolutely gorgeous, as she knew Emma's baby would be. He had the sweetest smile and wettest chin dripping with that adorable baby drool. He was all Emma, except for his eyes. Those were like his dad's. "Aww, Wesley, it's me, your Auntie Amber." The baby smiled and reached out to touch her face with his wet fingers. She kissed his forehead over and over.

Emma tugged Amber's sleeve. "Okay, spill it. Why are you here?"

Amber spared both brothers a quick glance, then took a deep breath. "Back in our time, I came across two tombstones in the small cemetery in town that had…your name and Wyatt's name on them."

"Holy crap!" Emma cried. "That's more than a little creepy."

"You're telling me," Amber agreed.

"I can imagine how you must've felt when you saw them. If I were you, I probably would've freaked." She rubbed her arms. "Did they say the year? No, wait. I don't think I want to know when we die."

"Knowing that you went back to 1882 last year, and based on you two living a long, happy, and healthy life," Amber said, "I might agree with you, but…"

"But…?"

"The year engraved on them is…*this* year, 1883."

Emma's hand flew to her mouth. "That…can't…be!"

Josh nodded. "I'm afraid it's true."

Amber sat down in the chair next to Emma and reached for her hand. "It's why I convinced James to help me come here. I had to warn you and Wyatt. James and I wanted to make sure you were both safe. I couldn't live with myself if…if anything happened to you. I can't—I couldn't…I love you—"

"I know," Emma said, squeezing her hands. "I love you, too, and I'm so grateful you came for me, but right now it's not safe for you to be here."

"I know all about Grey," she said.

"We've got a plan, honey," Wyatt added. "We spoke with Kane before coming here."

"One thing is for certain," Josh chimed in. "With Grey out of prison—"

Emma gasped. "How the hell did he escape?"

"We're still trying to uncover all the details," Josh explained. "Reed went to Deer Lodge. Anyway, with Grey out of prison, we do know he'll eventually head to Whisper Creek if he hasn't already. All he wants to do is go back to his own time. That means he'll make an appearance sooner or later when he tries to use the portal."

"And with him heading to Whisper Creek," Wyatt supplied, "that means we are, too. We've got to stop him." He plopped Wesley into Amber's lap. "Here, get to know your godson."

Wesley immediately ran his wet fingers over Amber's face, and then giggled. Her heart melted. "My sweet godson," she whispered, fighting back more happy tears. "You look just like your mommy." She kissed his forehead, inhaling his addictive baby scent.

Wyatt grunted, then placed a kiss on Emma's cheek. "I'll go hitch up the wagon," he said. "You ladies have five minutes to get ready, and then we're off. Josh?"

"Coming," Josh said, following Wyatt.

"I don't know, Wyatt," Emma began before he could exit. "With Grey heading to Whisper Creek, don't you think all of us would be safer here?"

"In a perfect world, yes." Wyatt paused at the door. "But we have to protect the portal, and I can't be in two places at once. If you're with me, my eyes and attention are on you. Josh and I are going to nail that bastard, once and for all." The brothers walked out.

"Stubborn husband," Emma muttered, rubbing her eyes. She turned back to Amber. "Knowing all this insanity, aren't you afraid?"

Amber shook her head. "Me? Nah."

"Well, I am. Ever since the wheel went flying off my wagon and Wyatt was shot at, I've been living in a constant state of worry. I try not to let Wyatt see that, but sometimes, I can't help it. I'm only human."

"A brave human," Amber added. "You've managed to live in this backward century for a year and a half. I don't think I could do it for that long. It's been less than two months for me, and I was ready to split on day two."

"I'm surprised you've been here so long," Emma admitted. "But right now, I don't want to talk about all that." She got up to collect their belongings and pack a small basket with food. "Tell me *everything* that's been going on at home. How's James? How are you? And how's my business?"

Amber bounced the baby up and down in her lap, lifting him high above her head. He responded by bestowing baby drool on her, dripping onto her blouse. She just met the little tyke and already she was in love with him.

"Business is great. I hired a new veep about six months ago, and she's done wonders for our sales. You're rolling in the dough, girl." She hugged Wesley close. "James is the same. Lonely. He misses his brothers."

"He's an amazing guy," Emma said, beaming. "I know both Wyatt and Josh will be thrilled to see him again. Oh, did you get a chance to meet Anne yet?"

"Yep, I met her and Caroline. Love them both, by the way."

"You met Caroline, too? Oh, I'm so glad. She's a brilliant woman. All the women in town adore her. And she's all about the suffrage movement and equal rights."

"I'm really happy you made a life for yourself here," Amber began, "and have all these wonderful new friends. You can thrive anywhere and adapt to any situation in a New York minute. I wish I could." She paused. "Now, it's time to go home. You've been here too long. Hell, I've been here too long."

Emma stopped packing and sat down at the table. "I don't know if Josh told you this, but the portal…it's not working."

"I know," Amber said, and made funny faces at Wesley, who replied with that adorable baby giggle. "We might have a solution."

Emma sat up straight. "What sort of solution?"

"Oh, it's a good one. Wesley, how about we tell your mommy a story?" Amber kissed Wesley's cheek and turned him to face his mom. "Once upon a time, in a century far, far away, there was a man from the future," she said in a storyteller's voice fit for babies. "And his name was Malachi."

Chapter Fifteen

Amber and Emma shared the front bench in the wagon while the brothers rode alongside them on horseback. Despite all the bumping, little Wesley was nestled comfortably in his mom's arms. From time to time, Josh or Wyatt would disappear ahead to scout the area before returning. They didn't want to take the chance of being ambushed by Grey or any of his men. Amber felt she was living out her life like one of the characters in a favorite western romance novel. When she first arrived, she couldn't wrap her head around the experience; but now, it was time to forget all this Old West nonsense and get back home to where they all belonged. Nineteenth-century living was interesting for a short time, but it was quickly getting old.

"Penny for your thoughts," Emma chimed in.

"You sound just like your mom. She'd always say that."

"She did." Emma smiled. "Well, care to share?"

"I'm thinking about everything that's happened since I arrived here," Amber admitted. "It's so weird, Em. I don't get how you and I and Wyatt and Josh could all be here...in 1883." She shook her head. "It's so surreal."

"You're not kidding," Emma agreed, glancing at her husband riding ahead of them. "At first, I thought it was so romantic. I loved everything about Old West Whisper

Creek. I met the man I wanted to spend the rest of my life with. We had a baby on the way. Unfortunately, living in a past century got old quick. I'm homesick." She turned to Amber. "Back at the cabin, you started telling me about someone named Malachi, but the guys interrupted us. Who is he?"

"Malachi came through the portal…from the year 2234."

"That's amazing!" Emma's face lit up. "Imagine all the changes in the world that he's seen and witnessed, events that we'll never get to see. And all the technological developments, maybe even the cure for cancer. What did he say? What did he want? Is he a good guy or bad guy? What's the deal?"

"He didn't have time to say much, but he did admit to being the one responsible for us getting stuck here."

"How could that be possible? I thought the portal was something that was just there, and we discovered it."

"Good question, but I don't know. Malachi was very cryptic when we met and kept looking over his shoulder like someone was watching him. He said something about the portal no longer being *funded*," she said, using air quotes. "They have to shut it down before the government takes over. Whatever that means." She filled Emma in on the rest of the details, including their approaching deadline.

Emma frowned. "I don't get it. What's so special about New Year's Eve?"

"No clue. All I know is, if the guy returns, he better cough up more details. Otherwise, we're storming the portal. We have to try to get back home, no matter what."

"And if that doesn't work?"

"Then we're stuck until New Year's Eve, I guess."

Up ahead, Josh turned his horse, circling back to wink at her and blow her a kiss. Amber smiled back, and her heart did a little dance. She caught Emma staring at her, eyebrows almost up to her hairline. "What?" she demanded.

"Lucy, you have some 'splaining to do," Emma said, smiling. "I want to know what's going on with you and Josh! Tell me *everything*."

Amber couldn't hide her smile. She relayed all the details of the first terrifying moments she had met Josh at gunpoint, then their trip to Deer Lodge, their growing attraction, and of course, a few juicy details of how close they've become. Emma was the only one she would ever spill her heart out to. It felt good to talk to her again in person, instead of just out loud, pretending Emma was still there.

"Wyatt and I are gone for a couple of months, and here you and Josh are hooking up." Emma watched Amber intently. "Judging by that lovestruck look on your face I can tell this isn't anything casual. You really care for him."

She let out an unsteady breath. "More than you know."

"Josh is a great guy. I've gotten to know him really well this past year. I think you two are good for each other."

Amber's gaze pivoted to her. "I hear a but coming."

"No but. I love you more than anything, Amber, and I also love my brother-in-law." She paused. "If Josh's heart is in this, he's yours forever. He's not the type of guy to settle. And I know you won't settle either, which is why you've never said I do yet."

"You've known Josh longer than I have, and you've

met my previous boyfriends, even though they were few and far between. He's not like them," she went on. "I never felt this way before, Em. It's freaking me the hell out. I never wanted to fall this much for a guy. I mean, I did, but…you get it."

"I do get it." Even though Emma spoke softly, her voice carried over the rickety sounds of the wagon. They sat in companionable silence for a while before Emma spoke again. "I've got to be honest; something's been bugging me."

"What's that?"

"The tombstones," Emma said. "You said they have this year engraved on them, yet Wyatt and I are still very much alive."

"Yeah, but it's only September. We have a few months until the end of the year."

Emma clamped a hand on her arm. "Did you have to say that?"

"I'm sorry. I don't mean to scare you, but it's the facts. This whole thing is a conundrum. I'm hoping once we get back to the property, we won't have to worry about it. With any luck, we can try the portal, and it'll work this time."

"From your lips to the Time God's ears."

Amber bit the inside of her cheek. "I know we talked about this briefly when you came back home last year, but do you ever wonder how traveling back here would affect you, us, in the future? You know, like the grandfather paradox—you go back in time and do something to kill off your grandparents or parents before they're even born, so you're not born? That kind of quantum physics science mumbo jumbo that I'll never understand. I'm asking because Malachi gave us the impression that we did something wrong in either this time or our real time, and he was trying to fix it."

"Like what?"

She shrugged. "He said he had a short amount of time to correct the situation…without repercussions. I have no idea what situation he was talking about. That was unclear. Maybe when he shows his face again, he'll tell us."

"You mean *if* he shows his face again. What if he doesn't come back?"

Amber swallowed the sudden lump in her throat. "If he doesn't, then we'll have to figure out the damn portal ourselves. I refuse to be stuck here for the rest of my life." She touched her friend's arm. "I'm sorry. I ramble on too much."

Emma looked like she was about to say something, but her gaze shifted. Josh rode back toward them. He circled the wagon, and then pulled up on Amber's side.

"All clear," he announced. "If we keep this pace, we should make Whisper Creek after nightfall."

****

The wagon bounced onto the Kincaid property around midnight. Wyatt rode ahead to make sure there would be no surprises waiting for them inside the house, while Josh stayed with the wagon. After several minutes, Wyatt waved, indicating it was safe. Amber steered the wagon toward the barn, pulling the brake lever after it stopped. Wesley was sound asleep in his mother's embrace. He traveled like a champ, only waking once for Emma to nurse him. With her little bundle secure in her arms, Emma managed to get down with Josh's help.

Amber jumped off the bench, forgetting she had removed her new hideous shoes hours ago, and landed on some pebbles. "Ouch!"

"You wait here, and I'll check the barn," Josh announced.

Amber stretched her arms and rolled her hips to release some of the achiness. "Do you really think Grey waited to sneak into the barn after Wyatt made a sweep of the house ten seconds ago? Why are you being so paranoid?"

"The bastard told me he wanted to use the portal," Josh bit out. "Now that he's escaped prison, that's his goal. So yes, I do think it's possible he could be waiting somewhere on the property to surprise us."

"Wonderful," she said.

"Sit tight." Josh kissed her cheek. Gun in hand, he walked into the barn.

"I can't get used to seeing guns on the men here," Amber remarked. Even though she hated guns, Josh somehow made it look sexy.

"It's not just the men," Wyatt said, joining them. He tapped Emma's hip. "Show her."

Emma rolled her eyes, then hiked up her skirt with her free hand, revealing a holster strapped to her right thigh. In it was a smaller version of Wyatt's revolver. "My over-protective husband insists I carry this."

Amber's eyebrows shot up. "Do you even know how to use that thing?"

Emma smiled. "Of course."

"Josh and I taught her," Wyatt explained. "We wanted to make sure she could protect herself and Wesley if ever we weren't around."

"It's even weirder seeing *you* with a gun," Amber told her best friend.

Josh returned to the group. "All clear."

"Good," Wyatt said. "Let's get inside now."

They went into the house. Before Amber had left there the other day, she wasn't worried about her surroundings. She'd be lying if she said she wasn't worried now. Grey's escape changed her outlook on what safety meant. Even though the kitchen lamps Wyatt had lit gave off a cozy, warm glow, a chill wrapped around her. She shook it off.

"Wyatt and I will take care of the horses," Josh announced. "Why don't you ladies rustle up some food?" He kissed Amber on the cheek, and then walked out.

"I'm going to put Wesley to sleep," Emma said with a yawn. "Would you mind fixing something to eat?"

"You got it." Amber reached for the baby, cuddling him close. "But first, I'll go put my beautiful godson to bed while you have a bath. You need your rest, especially for Wesley. Besides, you know better than to argue with me, particularly when I'm hangry and tired."

Emma smiled. "Love you."

"Love you more." She blew her friend a kiss and then took Wesley into Emma's room. She changed his little cloth diaper before putting a clean onesie on him. Emma had sewn a twenty-first century style assortment of them. A small hand-carved wood cradle sat next to their bed, and she put the baby in it, tucking the little blanket around him securely.

How long did she stand there, watching him breathe? She dreamed of someday having her own babies. Leaning over the cradle, she inhaled his delicious baby scent and sighed. In just one day, Wesley managed to steal her heart.

"You don't belong in this backward century," she whispered. "None of us do. When we get home, I'm going to spoil you rotten. Your mommy and daddy won't be able to stop Auntie Amber." After pressing a kiss to his smooth little forehead, she padded down the hall, wincing from the blisters. Emma's melodic voice came from inside the bathroom, along with the sound of water splashing.

Returning to the kitchen, she rummaged for food. She was hungry but even more exhausted. Inside the basket they brought back with them were a loaf of bread and a small parcel of fried chicken. It was more than enough. She set four places, equally distributing the food onto the plates. By the time Emma joined her, she'd managed to polish off her portion.

Emma sat down in the chair next to her. "I'm too tired to eat."

"I thought I was, too, but one bite and it was all over. I inhaled mine." She wiped her mouth with a napkin. "Eat up and then hit the sack. You need to rest."

"Thanks, I will, and the tub is all yours. I cleaned it out and let some fresh water run. It's not warm, but it'll do."

Amber squeezed her hand, then pressed a kiss to her head. "Love you, girlfriend."

Emma squeezed her hand in return. "Love you, too."

Blinking back happy tears, Amber walked down the hall, and into the bathroom. After their long, bumpy ride, she was eager for a bath and didn't have the patience to wait for boiling extra hot water. She scrubbed her body from head to toe, and her thoughts went directly to Josh. Her body ached for him, his touch, the safety that embraced her when she was with him.

When she had decided to come back in time, never in a bazillion years did she expect to fall for someone from such a backward century. Technically, Josh wasn't from the nineteenth century, but he was the first man she had a connection with. He was a genuinely great guy, and he made her feel important, special, and…desired.

"Hello, sweets." Josh's sultry voice broke through her thoughts.

Startled, Amber gasped. "Josh!"

He walked over to the tub. His gaze traveled over her body submerged in the water, lingering on her breasts, and then moving lower. "You are beautiful."

Her nipples hardened under his scrutinizing gaze, and the rest of her caught fire. Slowly, she stood up and got out of the tub. Water sloshed over the edge and sluiced down her body, creating a puddle at her feet. "I'm glad you think so."

Josh pulled her into his arms, holding her tight. He lowered his head, resting his forehead on hers. "I know we haven't known each other very long, and I'm not expecting for you to say anything back so soon, but…I need you to know."

"Know what?"

"I love you, Amber."

Her heart bounced in her chest, and she could barely catch her breath. Aside from Emma, she had never said those three little words to anyone. This was different, of course. Sure, she had been in lust before, but never truly in love…until now. She couldn't get enough and always wanted more from Josh.

"I-I…" she stammered. "I've never…felt this way before. Ever. But…I'm not ready to label my feelings. I know that sounds like a copout, but I hope you know—"

"Shh." He pressed a finger to her lips. "It's all right, sweets. I can wait to hear you tell me. There's no rush.

I'm not going anywhere. Now," he said, planting a kiss on her lips. "I need a bath, and I need you."

Amber appreciated that he wasn't expecting to hear the same words echoed back. She would tell him, in her own time, when she was ready. There was no rush, like he'd said.

Quickly, she dried herself off and slipped into her robe. Josh peeled out of his clothes and stood before her in all his naked glory. God, he was delicious in all the right places. She wanted to admire him, but he gave her a quick kiss and climbed into the tub.

"Join me," he said.

Amber laughed. "Are you kidding? The two of us in *that*? We'd never fit."

"There's plenty of room. C'mon. We can certainly give it a try," he offered, and then splashed her when she didn't hop in. "Wait until we get back home to our time. I've got a tub big enough to party in. We'll have to christen it together."

"Sounds like fun," Amber said. She kneeled beside the tub and lathered a small cloth using Emma's homemade soap. The one with a woodsy scent. Josh leaned forward, giving her ample access to scrub his back. Using circular motions, she gently made a trail from his broad shoulders down to his tapered hips. There wasn't an ounce of fat on him. How was that possible?

He leaned back against the rim of the tub, closed his eyes, and sighed. She washed his long, strong neck. He tilted his head even further back, giving her fuller access. The broad expanse of his smooth bronzed chest was next. She tenderly scrubbed him, admiring his firm pecs. Her hands traveled downward to his perfect six-pack stomach. The room wasn't hot by any means, but she was melting. She closed her eyes, pushing the cloth farther down his body until she touched the hardest part of him.

Josh grabbed her hand. "If you do that now, touch me there, I won't be held responsible for what happens next."

A smile curled her lips. "Good." She dropped the cloth into the water then took him in her hand, gently caressing his swollen flesh. His eyes grew heavy lidded, and he moaned. "Is there a problem?" she queried with mocked innocence.

"Yes, I'm still in the tub and you're not." He stood up and the water streamed down his perfectly sculpted body. He reached for her and pulled her against him. "I can't wait anymore. I need you."

She laced her fingers around his neck, and he swooped her up and into his arms. "Wait! You need a towel. You can't just traipse down the hallway all naked and wet."

"Watch me," he told her.

"But Wyatt and Emma—"

"Wyatt is outside taking the first watch in case Grey or his men show up," he said, cutting her off. "And Emma is most likely asleep by now."

He stopped long enough for her to grab the towel she had laid out on the counter. When they got inside his bedroom, Josh kicked the door closed and put her down. He quickly dried himself off, tossed the towel aside, and closed the distance between them. God, he was incredibly sexy. If Amber lived a hundred years, it would never be enough to get her fill of him.

His lips came crashing down on hers in a heated frenzy. He tasted like the sweetest honey and fresh mint. The deep scent of sandalwood soap emanating from his smooth body was a heady sensation. Her hands slid up his chiseled chest to clasp around his neck. She tore her lips from his to gaze up into his eyes, gleaming with desire.

He reached for the sash around her waist and slowly untied it. Her robe opened, and he pushed it off her shoulders. The soft fabric slid down her arms until it pooled at her feet.

"I could feast on you all night," he whispered against her ear.

Josh took her by the hand and gently laid her on the bed. He lowered himself, covering her with his body. His skin felt so good against her, like hot steel molding perfectly to her every curve. The sweet torture began at her mouth. He nipped and teased, nudging her lips open until their tongues collided. She pulled him tighter and hooked a leg around him, urging him closer.

He stroked one of her breasts, tenderly kneading and molding, before giving attention to her other. His mouth and tongue soon followed. He sucked on her nipple, biting and tasting, until she gripped his hair, tugging him against her. Moaning at her response, he trailed kisses slowly down to the hottest part of her. Surging blazes built up within, and it was more than she could bear.

"Josh," she cried, tugging at his hair. "I want you."

"Good, because I can't wait anymore." He tore his mouth away from her and settled himself between her legs. He slid into her warmth and grabbed her thigh to give himself fuller access.

Their bodies moved together in harmony, climbing higher and higher. Heat flowed through her like lava until she found her release. Josh called her name, shuddering. He lay on top of her for a few moments, and then leaned back to gaze into her eyes.

"That was super yummy," she said breathlessly.

"Indeed, sweets. And this was much more comfortable than a bed of hay, wouldn't you agree?"

She smiled. "Yes, but I wouldn't mind a romp in the hay from time to time."

"Your wish is my command." He chuckled, rolled onto his back, and gathered her in his arms. "In the meantime, I think we should do this all night."

"I think you're right," she agreed, then covered his body as she straddled his hips.

Chapter Sixteen

Josh followed the aroma of coffee until he walked into the kitchen. Hell, he could use more than his usual dose of caffeine this morning. He barely got any sleep. The minute he carried Amber into the bedroom, he knew he wouldn't be able to get enough of her. The effect she had on him was overwhelming. He had spent most of the night showing her how much he adored her, worshipping her delectable body. This was the first time in his life that everything felt right.

He went directly to the coffee pot, poured himself a hefty serving, and then sat down across from Wyatt, who had Wesley on his lap. Four muffins on a plate made his mouth water, and he swiped one up. "Morning," he said, tearing off a bite.

"It's weird hearing you and Amber going at it," Wyatt scoffed.

"Unfortunately, you and I never considered sound-proofing the house when we first began renovations, so there's that."

"Who knew we'd need to?" Wyatt joked. He yawned, stretching his neck left to right. "You owe me a few hours of shuteye, big brother."

"Would someone please tell me why we're up at this *ungodly* hour?" Amber mumbled, padding barefoot into the kitchen. Her hair was a sexy mess of auburn, and she had that just-loved look on her face. She clasped her robe tighter and smiled at Josh in a way that got his blood heated and his heart bouncing in his chest. What had she done to him?

"It's nearly seven," Wyatt replied. "This is late for us nineteenth-century folk."

Josh got up, poured Amber a cup of coffee, and gestured to the table.

She took a sip and made a face. "Ugh, who made this? It's terrible."

"You're welcome," Wyatt said, raising his mug.

"Sorry." She put the mug down and devoured half a muffin in a single bite. "We need more than muffins to eat. I'm starving. You boys want something else? Eggs, maybe? I think the hen laid enough for a month."

Both Josh and Wyatt raised their hands. Amber finished the muffin and grabbed a bowl from the cupboard. She cracked a dozen eggs and reached for a pan.

"You can use the outdoor grill," Wyatt told her. "The fire's already burning."

"Mmm, I smell coffee," Emma said, gliding into the room, already dressed. She went straight to Wesley who was enjoying being in his daddy's arms and gave him a kiss.

"I'm making a real breakfast," Amber announced, gesturing to the pot and bowl of eggs. "Interested?"

"Not if you're cooking." Emma gave her an I'm-joking-look, poured herself some coffee, and sat down. "I'm not in the mood for breakfast now. I've been up all night, thinking about the portal…and Grey. What are we going to do?"

"Forget Grey," Amber announced, putting the breakfast accessories down on the counter. "Let's try the portal first. Malachi told us we must be here *together*. Well, we're together now, so there's no reason why it can't work. I say we just go!"

Wyatt held up a hand. "Not so fast. Don't get me wrong. I'm just as eager to return home as you are, but how do you know that we can trust this Malachi?"

"For one, he came through the portal," Josh explained.

"So what?" Wyatt scoffed. "All four of us—and Grey—came through the portal, too. Don't tell me that just because Malachi waltzed on through unexpectedly in a blaze of light that makes him legit on sending us back to our own time."

"He's also from the future," Amber added. "The future from our future, like the twenty-third century."

"Again, how do we know he's being truthful? And if he is, so what?" Wyatt repeated. "What if all of us go through together and something wonky happens because he didn't warn us?"

"Wonky, like what?" Josh asked.

"I don't know," Wyatt replied. "What if the portal suddenly shuts down while we're traveling, and we get trapped in time...or we get stuck between two times? Or what if we get separated and sent back to the dinosaurs or someplace crazier than here?"

"All I can say is," Amber began, "he appeared to be authentic. Hear me out. Aside from his weird futuristic-styled outfit and the electronic armband with colors that I can't even describe, there was the sound of the portal when it opened. Creepy. If you had been there, you'd think probably think he was the real deal, too." She huffed. "I had doubts at first, but at this point, what choice do we have?"

"I agree with Amber." Josh exchanged a glance with his brother. "Maybe the worst that could happen is…nothing. We're either going to get home safely or be stuck here. I think we should give it a go."

Wyatt's gazed touched on Emma before turning to Josh. He nodded. "Okay."

Emma took Wesley from Wyatt and bounced him up and down on her lap. "Yay, we're going home, Wesley. We're going home."

Once they were all back in their own time, Josh would never see this house as it is now or the nineteenth century again. And once he returned home, he wouldn't be looking back. While he was here, though, he still had responsibilities. He was a man of the law, after all, and a man of his word. "Before we do anything hasty," he began, "I want to talk to Reed and tell him…something."

"Why?" Emma asked. "The less he knows the better."

"If we just disappear, he might think it had something to do with Grey," Josh explained. "And I don't want to leave him hanging. Reed's a good man, and I have the utmost respect for him. I can't just vanish on him."

Amber touched his arm. "You're going to miss him, aren't you?"

Josh nodded. "Yeah, and Sam. They've both become good friends."

"I'd like to see Anne and Caroline before we leave, too," Emma added. "Anne has been so good to me since we first met, and I adore Caroline. I would feel awful if I didn't say goodbye to them either and we just vanished without a trace."

"All right." Wyatt got up and shoveled both hands

through his hair. "Then we better come up with the same story to tell everyone. That way, there are no mistakes."

"Let's keep it simple, and say we've decided to return to New York," Emma offered.

"Wouldn't they be curious to know why everyone is suddenly taking off?" Amber asked.

"Aside from running away from Grey, we could say that James needs Josh to return to work in the family firm," Emma went on. "That wouldn't be too far from the truth. It would only be natural for Wyatt and me to go along. And since Amber, my best friend, came here from New York with the plea from James to return, they wouldn't question her leaving."

"Shouldn't we consult with stagecoach and train schedules so you can tell them which ones we'll be fake leaving on?" Amber probed. "And don't you have to sell the house or board it up to make it more believable?"

Josh nodded. "You're right. We need a few days to make it all seem plausible. Wyatt, what do you think?"

Wyatt rubbed his chin thoughtfully. "Okay. Let's all stick to that story. In the meantime, you two ladies will need to be armed at all times. And you will not be allowed to go off alone."

"Excuse me," Amber said, waving a wooden spoon. "*Allowed*?"

Josh stood next to her. "Wyatt means, if you venture outside the house, you'll need an escort."

"Let me be clear as to what I mean," Wyatt stated. "No riding into town alone. No hanging laundry outside alone. No playing with Wesley in the garden alone. No going to the lake alone. No walking or riding alone. You two are not to do anything alone. One of us needs to be with you. Got it?"

"We're keeping you safe, sweets," Josh told her, laying a hand on the small of her back. "All three of you."

Amber pushed out a breath. "I know, but you're making it sound like we're in prison."

Josh grinned. "If you like, I could lock us both in the bedroom and tie you up—"

"Josh!" Her face flamed.

God, he loved making her blush. He pulled her to him and kissed her soundly on the lips. "Okay, so once we're done with breakfast, I'll head into town and speak with the marshal. Over the next couple days, we can make our rounds and say goodbye to our friends."

Everyone raised their mugs in a silent toast. Josh hoped that they could go through without Malachi's help, but most importantly, that there would be no repercussions from their time spent in another century.

****

After breakfast, Amber slipped into one of the lighter dresses Anne had made for her and returned to the kitchen. Wesley was giggling and drooling while his mom tossed him in the air. His laughter melted her heart.

"How's my favorite and only godson?" Amber swooped him out of Emma's arms. The baby giggled and waved his hands. Clearly, she had a fan. "You are just the best, my sweet boy." She kissed his forehead and placed him into the wooden playpen. "Where's your shadow?"

"Wyatt went to take care of the horses," Emma replied, pouring each of them a cup of tea.

"Thanks," Amber said, taking a sip. It was a bazillion times better than the coffee. "I have a feeling the next few days are going to suck while we're under house arrest. We can't go anywhere or do anything without the guys."

Emma smiled. "It won't be for much longer. Before you know it, we'll all be back home." She closed her eyes and sighed. "God, I can't wait."

"When we get back, what's the first thing you're going to do?"

Emma's face lit up. "Are you kidding? I'm going to book a spa day, order a pizza with everything I love on it, and enjoy some of my favorite ice creams by the gallon." She laughed. "Then I'll go buy Wesley a bunch of toys and clothes and sightsee in the Montana of my own time. Of course, I'll have to return to New York to pack everything up and even do some sightseeing there, too. Never in a million years did I think I would ever miss home as much as I do."

"You seem to have adapted well to country living in this century," Amber told her. "If I had just met you, I'd think you were born and raised here."

"I wanted to fit in and not look or sound like an outsider."

"You've mastered that."

"Survival," she said simply. "I'm so glad you came back for me. I've missed you. There's only so much I can talk to Anne and Caroline about. They don't know the real me."

"How could they? You're keeping the biggest secret of your life from them." She paused. "What do you think they would do if you told them where you're really from?"

Emma's eyes widened. "They would probably want to take me to the nearest insane asylum and have me committed. People wouldn't know what to make of our story. They would think we're insane."

Amber thought about that for a moment. "I always wondered what it would be like to travel ahead in time. If I had my choice, I would've gone a few hundred years into the future not back."

"Explore the unknown. I like it."

Horses neighed in the distance. Emma went to the window and giggled. Amber joined her. Wyatt was trying to teach Winnie how to bow, and the mare was not following commands. Instead, she was butting him on the shoulder.

"He loves those horses." The tenderness in Emma's eyes for her husband was palpable. Amber wondered if she, herself, gazed at Josh like that.

"You can always get a horse or two when you go home," Amber suggested. "You'll be moving to Montana permanently when we get back, right? After you stuff your face with New York's best pizza, that is."

Emma turned to her. "Before coming here and meeting Wyatt, I wanted to return to the city and run my business there, but now everything is different."

"Of course, it is." Amber squeezed her hand. "You belong with Wyatt in Montana. We can move your business out here. It makes sense."

Emma's eyebrow arched. "We?"

"Do you honestly think I'm going to let you leave me for a second time? I may not be the biggest fan of nineteenth century Montana, but the Montana of our own time is pretty nice. Besides, I have a godson to spoil now. I have my responsibilities as the coolest auntie on the planet. I can't go back to New York City without you. That would just suck big time."

"Are you sure?"

While she had been mulling over this idea in her head, she never really committed to it until the words were out of her mouth. "Absolutely."

Emma threw her arms around Amber; they hugged and cried. "I'm so glad. And I'm happy for you and Josh."

Amber pulled away. "Me too. He's amazing."

Emma's eyes narrowed. "But...?"

She twirled her hair. "He told me he loves me."

"That's wonderful!"

"I know. It is wonderful, but...I didn't say it back. Is there something wrong with me?"

"Nothing is wrong with you, except a little fear of commitment." Emma squeezed her hand. "And it's all right. You'll tell him when you're ready. He loves you; he'll be patient. Does he know about...your family?"

She nodded. "I told him about Mom and Grandpa, yeah, but not Caitlin."

"Everything in its time," Emma assured her. "But it's important you tell him. It might make him understand a little more about why you're a little gun-shy."

"I know," she agreed. "It's just not something I like to talk about."

"Loss and grief are never easy. Josh is crazy about you. I can see how he looks at you. He is one of the very few good ones left. He'll want to know and help you remember the good times."

"Why are you always right?"

Emma laughed. "Now you're mocking me, sister. Come on, let me teach you how to handle a gun. I think it's wise to be prepared...for anything."

Amber bit on her lip. "Do you think Grey will show up before we're out of here?"

"It's possible. Think about it. If he's on the run now, where's the first place he'll want to go? The man wants to return to his own time, and he can only do that from our property."

Emma was right. No matter what, they had to be prepared for Grey and what he could potentially do to them. It was difficult to shake the icy shivers of fear and anxiety flowing through her veins.

For the next hour, Emma taught her the different parts of a revolver, how to load the bullets, the easiest way to cock the gun without snapping her finger off in the process and aiming with precision.

When Wesley fell asleep, they went outside for target practice with Wyatt's approval and oversight. He scouted the perimeter constantly, always keeping them in sight.

An hour later, after hitting bottles, cans, and whatever else Wyatt lined up on the fence, Josh rode up in time to witness her shooting three bottles into oblivion.

"I can hit the target!" she cried.

Emma retrieved her gun from Amber and said, "Yay, you. It's not as bad as you thought, right?"

"It's still daunting, but while Grey may be lurking in the shadows, I feel better about knowing I can actually shoot a target without killing myself in the process."

Josh dismounted and walked over. "Not bad for a beginner." He drew her into his arms and kissed her soundly on the lips. "You're a fast learner."

"Thanks to my wonderful instructor," she said, nodding to Emma.

"It was all you," Emma told her.

Wyatt joined them and asked Josh, "How did it go

with Reed?"

"Not good, I'm afraid." Josh's smile turned into a frown. "We've got a problem. Reed just received a wire. Grey was spotted in Helena the other day."

"What's he doing there?" Amber asked.

"Who knows? But considering the marshal in Helena didn't discover that until after the fact, Grey might be in disguise and making his way to us."

"Hang on," Emma said. "Deer Lodge, where he escaped from, is west of Helena. Why would he bypass Whisper Creek to go directly there? It doesn't make sense that he's going out of his way to get here."

"That's why we've got to be prepared," Josh said. "It's only a matter of time before he shows up on the property."

"The portal can't be left unprotected," Wyatt announced. "We can't take the chance of him getting through." He glanced at Josh. "And we can't leave you ladies and Wesley unprotected either."

"Agreed." Josh turned to Amber and Emma. "Wyatt and I will take turns keeping guard. Later, Wyatt can go and bring Sam over to say farewell. Tomorrow, one of us will take you both into town to visit with Anne and Caroline. After that, we head for the twenty-first century."

Chapter Seventeen

The next morning, Amber, Emma, and Wesley rode to town in the wagon, with Josh up ahead leading the way on horseback. Wyatt remained behind in case Grey showed up at the property and attempted to go through the portal. One of them had to be there to guard it and prevent him from succeeding. There was no telling what could happen to them, or their futures, if Grey somehow managed to get through ahead of them. While anything was possible, she didn't want to admit that maybe Grey and Malachi knew each other and were in cahoots.

Amber pulled the wagon to a stop outside Anne's dress shop. The threat of a thunderstorm hung in the air and ominous clouds hovered overhead. The weather certainly didn't match their moods. Today should've been bright and sunny. After all, this was the last day they would all be in the nineteenth century and heading home. That meant happiness for Amber, but for her friends, it would be a sad day, saying goodbye to those they came to care for.

"I'll be back in a couple hours to meet you. Until then, stay at Anne's," Josh warned. "Before I take care of business, I'll be sure to tell Caroline to swing by because you two have news." He kissed her cheek. "Later, sweets."

Amber enjoyed watching him walk away, letting her mind drift to the moments when those hips were settled between her thighs. She sighed. He turned around once to wave, and then kept walking.

"I so love how he adores you," Emma whispered.

"And I adore him," she admitted. Her insides were all aflutter. She felt like a lovesick fool. This is probably how Emma felt about Wyatt when they first met.

When she and Emma entered the dress shop, Anne was busy with a new customer. Mattie led them to the back room where they settled on the sofa. "Anne will be with you shortly," she told them, and then disappeared.

Emma gazed around the room, bouncing Wesley on her hip. He was busy sucking on his fist. There was a wistful gleam in her eyes. "I have so many fond memories here. I'm going to miss Anne and this place."

Amber squeezed her hand. "I know."

Mattie returned with a tray of tea and biscuits. "Anne will join you momentarily. In the meantime, why don't you ladies start with some tea?" She poured them each a cup and then left.

Amber arched a brow. "Is this…?"

Emma smiled. "But of course."

She poured the sweet whiskey back into the tea pot. "What?" she said, when Emma gave her a questioning look. "I'll tell Anne I already drank a cup while we were waiting. That way, she won't keep on pouring."

Emma giggled. "Oh, yes, she will."

The lush velvet portiere parted, and Anne breezed into the room. Amber had almost forgotten how stunning she was. Her rich dark hair was swept up and impeccably coiffed. Her dark green dress fit perfectly, and the skirts rustled as she walked. Regardless of the century, she was a woman who could definitely turn heads.

"You've been gone way too long, dear," Anne told

Emma and pulled her into a hug. "I've missed you terribly."

"I've missed you, too," Emma said, shifting Wesley on her hip. Amber picked up on the catch in Emma's voice.

Anne turned to Amber and gave her a hug. "And my dear Amber. Lovely to see you again."

"You too," Amber replied. "I wanted to thank you again for making the clothes for me. They're all beautiful. I really appreciate it." With all the work that went into fitting her for a small wardrobe, it was a shame that she would have to leave it all behind in this century.

Anne waved a hand. "Think nothing of it. You wear it well, my dear. Now, let's sit and have tea," she said, shooing them toward the sofa. She leaned over to kiss Wesley's head. "How is little Wesley?"

The baby gurgled and tugged on his bib. "He missed you," Emma replied, snuggling him close.

"And I missed him and his sweet mama." Anne inspected Amber's teacup and refilled it. "No need for you to have an empty cup, dear."

Amber cast a quick glance at Emma. "Thanks," she said.

Anne sat on the sofa, filled a cup for herself, and then raised it in salute. "To dear friends."

Amber and Emma clinked cups with each other, and then Anne. Emma wouldn't meet Anne's gaze. Amber knew why. She, herself, was swallowing back the sadness at saying farewell to new friends.

Mattie stuck her head through the portiere and announced. "Dr. MacKenzie is here."

Anne got up to greet Caroline. The doctor was a striking woman. Her silky ink-black hair was pulled in a tight bun, and her flawless complexion would make any woman jealous. Perfectly sculpted brows shadowed green eyes fringed with the blackest lashes that put the best mascara to shame.

"Hello, my dear doctor," Anne said.

Caroline smiled. "I hope I'm not interrupting your visit, but Josh came into the office and said Emma and Amber were here with urgent news for us both."

Anne turned back. "News?" She led Caroline over to the sofa. "Please, sit. Tea?"

Caroline raised a hand. "I'm fine, thank you."

Anne arched a brow, eyeing Emma and then Amber. "Ladies, what news do you have for us?"

Amber glanced at Emma. There were tears in her friend's eyes. She didn't think Emma would be this broken up about saying goodbye. Instead of leaving it to her friend to make the announcement, Amber took in a deep breath before blurting out, "We're going home…to New York. All of us."

Anne's hand flew to her chest, and instantly, her eyes watered. Caroline's shoulders slumped. Amber felt a pang of sorrow for Emma who had grown to care for these two women. It would be a difficult goodbye all around.

"When?" Caroline rasped out.

"This week," Amber replied, giving Emma a minute to collect herself. "Josh and Wyatt's older brother James has been running the family law firm on his own for a while now. But, uh, there are a few big cases that have come up, and he needs Josh to come back sooner than later."

"Naturally, Wyatt and I want to be with our family now that we have Wesley," Emma added, keeping her eyes downcast. "He has yet to meet his Uncle James. And since Amber traveled all this way to deliver the news, we plan to take the train back together."

"I see," Anne said, wiping at her eyes with her handkerchief. "I'll admit, this comes as a surprise, though I did harbor the sad thought you might return home someday. I only hoped someday wouldn't be this soon. I'll miss you, both of you." She reached for Caroline's hand. "Thankfully, Caroline and I will still have each other."

"I'm going to miss you both, too," Emma said, blinking her tear-filled eyes.

"I wish I had known you longer," Amber admitted. She, too, felt the pang of sadness at their upcoming departure. "Emma speaks so fondly of you both. I'm sorry we won't have a chance to get to know each other better."

"Well, I, for one, will not accept this as goodbye," Anne announced. "Jonas and I have been wanting to travel since we wed. And I see a trip to New York City in our future."

"Oh—" Emma began.

Amber patted Emma's hand before she could say another word. "Well, once we get home and settled, we'll send you all the details and our addresses and all that good stuff."

"Wonderful. This news calls for a toast." Anne poured a cup for Caroline and handed it to her. "To eternal friendship."

They clinked cups. And it was Amber's turn to wipe away the tears.

****

Josh stepped out of the marshal's office. Today

would be the last time he'd walk these dirt-lined streets, the last time he would witness history in the making. It was bittersweet. Maybe that's why his stomach was knotted up. While his time in the nineteenth century was filled with countless adventures and constant manual labor that he'd never experienced before, he enjoyed every drop of sweat. He would miss hopping in the saddle every day, helping the marshal bring outlaws to justice, and witnessing life firsthand in a long-ago century. This was a place he had dreamed about since he was a kid. And living here had really blown his mind. Who else could say they traveled back in time to live out their childhood fantasies?

He pondered what his friends and colleagues would say once he and Wyatt returned. They'd been gone for a few years. While they hated to lie to everyone, it needed to be done to protect them and James, who remained behind. They didn't want anyone thinking their brother was crazy. Hopefully, their friends would accept their story about an extended survivor-man type trip across Africa. He and Wyatt would find out when they got back. If they told their friends about their time travel journey, they would probably laugh him and his brother right into two straight jackets and padded cells. Perhaps Amber could assist them in doctoring up some photos of them in the African jungles.

Josh ambled down Main Street, taking his sweet time, treasuring his final stroll. He decided to have one last drink at the Coppered Pan Saloon and share a goodbye toast with the owner. There were certain people he'd miss; and Davis Cooney was one of them.

A commotion across the street grabbed his attention. He tipped his hat back to get a better look at a grimy-looking cowboy pawing at one of Madame Veronique's women. She was garbed in a simple burgundy dress with a super lowcut bodice. He couldn't recall her name, but he'd seen her at the saloon plenty of times. The cowboy managed to trap the young woman's hands behind her back. She squirmed, trying to escape, but the man leaned his filthy face over hers, slobbering his tongue across her cheek. Josh's blood boiled. It didn't matter what the woman did for a living, she didn't deserve to be treated in such a way—not by anyone.

She struggled to free herself. "Let me go, you vile—"

"Hush up, woman. You ain't nothin' but a filthy whore."

Josh palmed his gun and marched over to the offender. He pressed the weapon to the side of the man's head. "The lady said to let her go."

The cowboy released her with a shove, and then slowly turned to face Josh. His eyes focused on the tin star on Josh's vest. Slowly, his hands went up. The putrid odor emanating from him was a clue had hadn't had a bath in months. "Oh. Deputy. Apologies. I was just gettin' acquainted with, er, the lady here."

"Go on, miss," Josh told the young woman, his eyes never wavering from the cowboy.

"Thank you, deputy." She picked up her skirts and ran off.

"We don't like anyone harassing our women." Josh deftly removed the cowboy's revolver from his belt and stepped back, but he kept his gun trained on the man. "State your business."

The cowboy's eyes flared. "I was just having some fun, is all. No need to get all riled up."

"I'll get riled up when filth like you take advantage of Whisper Creek's women." He paused. "What are you in town for?"

"I's just passing through," he replied with a shrug. "Meetin' a friend first. Can I lower my hands now, deputy?"

"I don't know, *can* you?"

The cowboy frowned. "Huh?"

"Lower them at your own risk, but if you flinch, I'm going to shoot you. What's your name?"

"Earl...Lester." Slowly, Earl lowered his hands. Sweat beaded down his face, dripping onto the dirty bandana tied around his neck. Ripped and dusty chaps, stained shirt, and mud-caked boots were a giveaway that Earl was bad news. Keeping up appearances wasn't something men like him were known for.

Josh didn't remember seeing Earl's name on the wanted posters, but there was something familiar about the stranger. "Where'd you ride in from?"

Earl glanced behind him nervously, like he was expecting to see someone over his shoulder. His Adam's apple bobbed up and down. "Came in from...Helena."

"Who's the friend you're meeting with?"

"What's it to you? I don't need to answer no questions. I ain't under arrest...am I?"

"Not yet, but that could change, depending on your answer."

He cursed, and then uttered, "Name's Whitcomb. Marcus Whitcomb. Once I see him, I'm leaving. I swear."

"Whitcomb?" Josh ran the name over in his head. He didn't recall anyone in town by that name. "What do you need to see him about?"

"Ain't none of your business," Earl spat, lifting his hat to stroke back his greasy hair. The hat had left an imprint in his forehead. Josh advanced on him, and Earl backed up, throwing his hands into the air, flinching. "All right. All right. He owes me money. Once I collect, I'm leavin' town. I swear."

Josh met the man's gaze. His dark eyes held a glint of fear, but he seemed to be telling the truth. "Go about your business, then. You can pick up your gun at the marshal's office on your way out of town."

The man stomped his foot. "That ain't fair, Deputy."

"It is if you prefer to stay out of jail for the night."

His jaw clenched. "Yes, sir."

"When you leave this town, Earl Lester, never come back. Got that?"

The filthy cowboy nodded and walked backward a few steps before running away down a nearby alley. Josh didn't like the man, and his gut told him he had seen him before. He just couldn't recall where.

Josh followed him and came out the other end of the alley. Earl was a few streets ahead of him, and there, he stopped to speak to with another man. Unlike Earl, the other man was sharply dressed in a fine suit, shiny shoes, and a hat. He wondered if this man was Whitcomb. The two men spoke for a moment, and then walked hurriedly toward the far end of town. The cowboy had a hard time keeping up the pace.

If Earl planned on leaving town anytime soon, he would have to double back to the marshal's office first to reclaim his gun. In these parts, a man couldn't defend himself without one.

Chapter Eighteen

In the two months that Amber had been in the nineteenth century, she had grown fond of Anne and Caroline and considered them friends. However, Emma had a longer bond with each of them and would miss them even more.

"Are you all right?" she asked, walking arm in arm with Emma, while Emma's other arm clutched Wesley to her hip. They were walking the few blocks to the marshal's office. Josh moseyed a few steps ahead, giving them a moment, but kept glancing back at them and their surroundings.

"No," Emma replied, blinking away tears. "This is harder than I thought. I've been here nearly a year and a half, and I've come to care so much for Anne. And most recently, Caroline, too. They're both wonderful women."

"I know." She squeezed Emma's arm. "It sucks we'll never see them again."

"Wouldn't it be great if the two of them could travel forward in time to see us someday?" Emma mused. "Could you imagine Anne and Caroline traveling over one hundred and forty years into the future? They would probably die of the fright. It's hard enough going back in time, but…maybe traveling forward wouldn't be too bad."

"At least, they'd have running water, hair dryers,

and great coffee," Amber joked.

Emma laughed. "Yes, there's definitely that."

"Now, you've got me thinking. What if *we* went ahead in time by that amount? How different would it be for us? Would there be flying cars or instantaneous travel? Maybe, even, a cure for terminal diseases?"

"Who knows? Maybe it would be post-Apocalyptic or something insane like that."

"Hell, I hope not!"

They reached the marshal's office. Josh stopped at the open door, peeked inside, and turned back to her and Emma. "Why don't you ladies wait out here for a moment? The marshal's got someone in with him." He gave Amber's hand a squeeze and walked inside.

She and Emma waited on the bench just outside the office. It was sturdy enough but looked like it had taken a weather beating. After a few minutes when Josh didn't return, Amber peered through the doorway. "Hey, I know that guy," she said.

Emma got up and craned her neck to see who she was talking about. She swung Wesley to her other hip, rocking to keep him quiet. "How would you know him? He looks like trouble."

"Don't most of the men in this town?" she quipped.

The cowboy was hard to forget. With his dirty clothes, slimy hair, and the way he spit out that wad of tobacco, he had totally grossed out Amber. He was just as filthy now as he'd been on that Montana City street. What she'd never forget was the look in his eyes, like he wouldn't mind killing just for sport.

"I don't *know* him, per se, but I've definitely seen him before."

The cowboy holstered his revolver, muttered

something, and then marched outside. He saw Amber and stopped in front of her. His grin widened, and his eyes were hollow with sparks of evil. "Afternoon, ma'am." He lifted his hat, and then walked away without looking back, his foul odor gagging her.

"Yuck, he stinks," Emma said, wrinkling her nose. "I sure wouldn't like to meet him in a dark alley."

"An alley is exactly where I saw him," Amber told her.

Josh waved at them from the doorway. "Ladies, come on in."

Amber and Emma walked into the office. The smell of the cowboy lingered. Emma made a face at Amber, pinching her nose, and stayed close to the door, gulping down fresh air.

Amber hitched a thumb. "Who was that guy?"

"No one you need to concern yourself with," Reed said dismissively.

"No, really. Who was he?"

Josh's brows furrowed. "Why are you asking?"

"I saw him when we were in Montana City. He gave me the creeps then just as he did now."

Reed glanced at Amber, and then Josh. "It could be a coincidence. We all know thieves move about quite a bit."

"I don't go for coincidences," Josh said, shaking his head. "I trust my gut, and my gut says this guy is hiding something."

"He said he has some business with a man named Whitcomb," Reed told Amber.

"Marcus Whitcomb?" Amber asked.

The only one who didn't look at her like she had sprouted another head was Wesley. He was too busy sucking his fist.

"How do you know of him, dear?" Reed asked.

"When I took the stage to Helena, I shared the bench with a man named Marcus Whitcomb," Amber explained. "I ended up seeing him again in Montana City, along with that smelly guy who just walked out of here."

"Again?" Josh asked, eyeing the marshal.

"Yeah." She nodded. "Remember, I went for a walk when you were chatting with Marshal Kane? Anyway, I bumped into Whitcomb on the street. He noticed me first and came over to say hello before going to talk with that cowboy."

Reed eyed Josh, and then moved behind his desk. He shuffled through some papers. "Amber, would you be able to identify Whitcomb if you ever saw him again?"

She nodded. "I sure would."

"Good." Reed grabbed a stack of unorganized papers off the counter against the wall and plopped it on his desk. He spread out the oversized sheets, shuffling wanted posters around. "Are any of these men Whitcomb?"

Amber sorted through the descriptions, some featuring mugshots and with the subheading "wanted dead or alive." Most of the men were outlaws wanted for crimes such as bank robberies, forgery, horse thieving, and murder. Unfortunately, none were of Whitcomb. She shook her head. "No. Sorry."

Reed tapped his desk, pondering something. "When the new batch of posters comes in from Helena, I'll bring them over to your place," he told Josh. "You're not leaving right away, anyway. Next stage to Helena isn't for a few days. You'll have the entire town out to bid you all farewell."

"The entire town!" Amber gasped. That would throw a wrench into their plans of vanishing through the portal. How were they ever going to fake a stagecoach departure now?

"That's fine," Josh said, taking both women by the elbow before either could protest. "We'll see you then, Marshal. C'mon, ladies." He escorted them outside and down the street. He was in a hurry to get back to the wagon.

Emma stopped, settling Wesley on her other hip. "Days, Josh? I had hoped we'd be out of here today."

"Yeah, and what do you mean we'll see him then?" Amber shot out. "Why can't we just leave now instead of faking some goodbye coach ride?"

"Because I don't want to bail on Reed until we figure out what Earl's business with Whitcomb is about," Josh replied. "And considering we wanted to make a plausible exit, it makes sense to wait for the next coach. It would be odd if we just disappeared now. A few more days won't hurt."

"Why?" Amber countered. "So all your friends and half the town can wave goodbye as our stagecoach rides off into the sunset, just so it seems plausible? First of all, if we did take the stage, we'd have to hijack it just to get back to the barn. I'm sure the marshal or someone would catch us for stealing it. Not only that, but we're also never going to see these people again. What does it matter?"

"For the time that we've been in this century, we've made a life here," Emma explained, touching her hand. "I, too, would feel bad if we left without an explanation."

"We already told your friends that we're going back to New York. It's the same story we're telling everyone. I realize you want to part on a good note, but that only leaves them with the hope of a reunion someday. You heard Anne. She's planning to visit us in New York with Jonas! How heartbroken is she going to be when she never hears from you or me ever again?"

Emma sighed. "You're right. This is just…harder than I thought it would be."

Amber pulled Emma in for a hug. "I know. I get it. Believe me."

No one spoke on the ride back to the house. Except for Wesley making his cute baby sounds, the journey was quiet.

When they pulled up in front of the barn, Wyatt came out of the house to greet them. His smile quickly turned into a scowl. "What happened?" he demanded, helping Emma and Wesley down from the wagon.

"There's been a slight delay in our departure," Josh replied, dismounting, and then explained in detail.

Wyatt cursed. The brothers held each other's gazes. There was a silent conversation going on with their eyes, one which Amber couldn't decipher.

Finally, Amber cleared her throat. "Hello, Earth to Josh and Wyatt."

Josh turned to Amber. "Reed gets new wanted posters every week. You two and Wesley are not to leave our sight until we see the next round of notices from Helena." He pulled her into his arms and kissed her forehead. "Everything will work out the way it should."

****

Josh stared at the barn wall. It taunted him. If all went as planned, by tomorrow, that same wall would be replaced with the time portal. And Josh and his family would be transported back to their own time, leaving the nineteenth century trailing in the proverbial dust. His life, as he once knew it, would resume…but this time, with Amber.

More than once, he had told her how he felt, but they never really discussed what their future would hold when they returned to their rightful time. Amber admitted she was afraid of her feelings, and he wasn't going to push her. They had only known each other for a couple of months, but in that time, they had grown close. Falling for her was easy. He had given her his heart, something he had only done once before. Only this time, he knew it would be forever.

"Don't tell me you're trying to head home without us?" Wyatt asked.

Josh turned around. "No chance of that happening."

Wyatt walked through the doorway. "Once Reed comes by with the wanted posters, hopefully, Amber can identify Whitcomb, and then we can get the hell out of Dodge. With all that's transpiring with Grey, I want to get the women and Wesley back to our time as soon as possible."

"Speaking of that," Josh said, moving to a bale of hale and kicking some of the strewn pieces around. "I know we've discussed this before, but I'm worried about Reed. Once we're gone from here, there's no telling what could happen to him."

Wyatt clamped a hand on his shoulder. "Charlie Reed is an experienced lawman. He knows how to handle himself." He paused. "Are you having second thoughts about leaving?"

Josh shook his head. "No way. Just…worried about

our friend."

"I am, too." Wyatt sat on the bale, a glint of tears in his eyes. "We had fun here, didn't we? It was a lot of hard work and survival skills, but it was fun and…interesting and…educational."

"Yeah, plus, this is where we both found the women we love."

"And I became a dad," Wyatt added.

Josh sat next to his brother. "If I didn't say this before…part of me is glad that we ended up here. This is one experience I will never forget."

Wyatt nudged him in the ribs. "I know the women are eager to get the hell out of here, especially Amber." He chuckled. "I'm surprised she came all this way."

"Her best friend's life was in danger. How could she not come?"

"That says a lot about her character." Wyatt twirled a piece of hay between his fingers. "Do you ever wonder why my and Emma's names were on those tombstones to begin with?"

"Every day," he told his brother. "When Amber arrived with the news and a photo, I thought maybe it had something to do with Grey. Even with him behind bars, I still didn't feel like the threat to our family was gone."

"The year on them is 1883," Wyatt reminded him. "It's only October. We still have two months to go in this year."

Josh cuffed him on the arm. "We'll be out of here tomorrow, so there's no chance of anything bad happening."

"Anything can happen in a day. We don't control fate."

Josh wished he hadn't said that. He stood up and paced, before facing his brother. "What if our abrupt departure is why the town erected your two tombstones?" he suggested. "That's why there's no exact date on them. Maybe Reed never got my letter or—"

Wyatt stood and held up his hand. "Hold on a minute. If that's the case, and if Reed thought for a moment that we had *all* disappeared or died, there would be five tombstones, not two."

His shoulders slumped. "I guess you're right."

"Let's stop looking for trouble. I, for one, am glad to be going home. But I sure as hell am not going to leave in these damn clothes. I'm wearing what I wore the day I ended up here. We have no idea who or what will be awaiting us on the other side. I'm hoping everything we knew before…will be the same."

"The house is still in both Emma's and your names," he said. "At least, that's what Amber says. And she would know since she's been staying there. The only one who could or should end up on the property is James."

Wyatt winced. "I can't believe we left him for as long as we did." He rubbed his eyes and cursed. "I hope he won't be too pissed off."

"James? Of course, he will."

"He'll forgive me, being his favorite baby brother," Wyatt teased. "You, I'm not so sure."

"Not funny. We're going to owe him big time."

Wyatt laughed. "Knowing James, he's going to hand you the office keys and disappear for about six months on a much-needed and well-overdue vacation."

"I wouldn't blame him."

Wyatt clapped him on the shoulder. "C'mon, dinner's ready. Emma sent me in here to tell you."

They left the barn, closed the doors, and washed up outside from a bucket of well water. A small flame remained in the grill, and the aroma of something delicious beckoned them into the house. The table had been set with a cloth Josh had never seen before along with some fine dinnerware. Amber placed a platter of chicken in the center of the table and turned around in time for Josh to pull her into his arms.

"What's all this?" he asked.

Amber smiled, slipping her arms around his neck. "Emma and I wanted to make a nice dinner for our last night here."

"Ah, the last supper," Wyatt joked, taking his seat at the head of the table.

"We did our best to make a barbecue sauce for the chicken," Emma explained. "Go easy on us with the foodie reviews, please."

Josh smiled at his brother, who looked happy and content. He had never seen Wyatt look that way at a woman until he met Emma. Amber sat down next to him, and he tugged her hand to his lips and kissed it. All that was missing was James, but soon, they would all be reunited.

He picked up a glass already filled with wine and said, "A toast." With glasses raised, he continued, "To the future…our future."

They clinked glasses and drank and ate…and drank some more. A few hours later, after imbibing several bottles of wine, everyone started yawning. Josh pulled Amber into his arms and kissed her.

"You two have a room," Wyatt growled. "Use it."

"Oh, I intend to," Josh said, swooping Amber up into his arms.

"Josh!" she cried. "What are you doing? I have to clear the table and put stuff away."

"I've got this," Emma said, shoving them through the doorway. "Go on, you two lovebirds."

"I've got plans for you tonight, Ms. Harrison." Josh walked into his bedroom and kicked the door closed with his heel. "And those plans include me loving every inch of you."

"Oooh, I like the sound of that."

He gently placed her on the bed and claimed her lips in what was the beginning of one endless night.

Chapter Nineteen

Amber stretched across the bed to Josh's side, but it was empty. She rolled over and opened her eyes. Morning sunlight streamed in through the open window. The sheer curtains danced as a gentle, cool breeze wafted into the room. They had spent most of the night in each other's arms, loving, laughing, and talking. It was hard to fathom that this trip back in time to save her best friend also introduced her to the love of her life, not to mention the best sex she'd ever had. That was probably because she truly loved him. Josh Matheson Kincaid was the real deal. She would never find anyone else with his qualities. Until she fell for him, Amber never understood what Emma felt for Wyatt. Her best friend had been torn between returning to her own time…and staying in the past with the love of her life.

Unlike Emma who remained in the nineteenth century for the man she loved, Amber wouldn't have to make that choice. Josh was ready and willing to return home—with her. All the details of their relationship didn't need to be worked out right now. They had plenty of time. After being with him every day these last two months, she had no desire to live one thousand miles away from Josh and do the long-distance relationship deal. That meant it would be goodbye, New York. Hello, Montana. She and Emma had already discussed moving the business to Montana, so that was a big plus.

The aroma of coffee and burning wood filtered in through the open window, and she smiled, hoping it was Josh who made a pot on the outdoor grill. After a quick bath, she slipped into her nineteenth-century clothing, selecting a matching dark green shawl on this chilly morning.

She walked into the kitchen, added some milk and sugar to a mug, and then ventured out the back door. The coffee pot sat on the grill, and she poured herself some. The morning sun was bright and warm, but the air had quickly turned cooler than in previous days. It wouldn't be long before wintery weather arrived. Thankfully, they would all be long gone by then.

Emma sat on a bench with Wesley in her lap. He was playing with a handmade wooden rattle. Her friend was watching Josh and Wyatt in deep conversation in the paddock.

Amber took the empty spot next to Emma. She canted her head toward the men. "What's going on?"

"They've been talking for at least a half hour," Emma replied, her gaze fixated. "I was going to interrupt, but judging by their faces, it appears to be quite serious."

"I wonder what they're discussing."

"I'm no genius, but my guess it has something to do with the portal. It's a topic those two always get riled up over."

"Really?"

Emma nodded. "When we tried the portal before Wesley was born, they couldn't agree on who should go first or if we should go together, what to wear, what tokens to use. I wanted to clobber them both with the heaviest frying pan I had," she said lightly. "For days, they argued. It was like watching two little kids stomping their feet and pointing fingers."

"So what did you try then?"

"Everything. I tried going by myself, then with Wyatt, and then all three of us. After a while, we decided to try the portal in the order that we were brought here. Wyatt, then Josh, and then me. Obviously, that didn't work either, because here we are."

"Yeah, but hopefully, not for much longer."

"I'm with you," Emma agreed. "Reed should be stopping by at some point. Today's the day the courier arrives from Helena with the newly printed wanted posters. I remember that from Wyatt's time as a deputy. I'm sure after he's sifted through them, he'll bring those right over."

"I hope it's sooner than later. I just want to sleep in my own bed, ride in normal transportation, and drink gourmet coffee." She sighed dramatically. "It's the little things."

Emma kissed the top of Wesley's head. "Speaking of coffee, how is yours?"

Amber took a sip. "It's not bad. Wait, it's better than not bad." And then she took two more sips just be sure. She squinted at Emma. "This isn't Josh's or Wyatt's brew. It tastes too good."

Emma smiled. "It's mine. The trick is to double grind the beans. Otherwise, it's way too acidic, strong, and gritty. Matilda at the general store taught me that trick. Plus, I invented my own filter."

"Here's to you and Matilda," Amber said, raising her mug. After a few sips, she glanced back at Josh and Wyatt. "I can't take the suspense." She shouted, "Hey, how's it going over there?"

The brothers glanced in her direction and offered up a wave but went back to their conversation.

"Rude," Amber said, rolling her eyes.

"Men," Emma mumbled.

"I'm going over there," she announced, rising to her feet.

The sound of pounding hooves thundering down the long dirt drive stopped her. Marshal Reed sat tall and commanding on his horse, as if he was one with the animal. It was the first time Amber had seen him on horseback. Impressive. The silver star pinned to his vest, a symbol of his chosen profession, gleamed in the sunlight. His black hat was perfectly perched on his head, not even the slightest threat of blowing off in the wind. There must be a trick to that. Amber's hat never stayed in place.

Reed pulled to a stop by the paddock, dismounted, and landed on both feet. For being in his early sixties-ish, he was quite dexterous. He grabbed his weathered saddlebag, tossed it over his shoulder, and then shook hands with Josh and Wyatt. They spoke for a moment, and then Wyatt led him to where she and Emma were sitting. Josh lingered in the corral.

Reed lifted his hat. "Mornin', ladies."

"Hello, marshal," Emma said, bouncing Wesley on her lap. The baby gurgled and waved his hands excitedly when Reed tweaked his cheek.

"Hey, there, little fella. Boy, he sure does look like you, Emma."

Emma beamed. "Thank you, Marshal, but Wyatt thinks Wesley looks just like him," she added, casting a glance at her husband.

Reed chuckled and elbowed Wyatt. "Chalk it up to

a father's pride."

"Marshal, would you like some coffee?" Amber offered, coming to her feet. "Emma made a fresh pot."

Reed grinned. "In that case, I would love some. Thank you. Lord, knows neither Josh nor I can make a decent brew."

"Follow me," Emma said, leading the way.

Amber tugged Wyatt's sleeve as they followed a few steps behind. "What's up with you two and all your whispering like Emma and I don't exist?" she whispered.

Wyatt spared his brother a quick glance, and then patted her hand. "Nothing to worry about. We were just discussing a few things."

"Things, such as…?"

"Life." Wyatt gently propelled her through the door. He turned and stuck his head out the door. "Josh! Come on."

Emma placed Wesley into the playpen, and then served coffee and muffins to the marshal. Reed accepted appreciatively and had eaten halfway through a muffin when Josh came in. Amber walked up to him, searching his emerald eyes.

"Is everything all right?" she asked.

"All good." Josh smiled and leaned close to whisper, "I'll give you a real kiss good morning later, sweets. I didn't have the heart to wake you earlier."

"I'm sure going to miss you all," Reed announced. "Working with you boys has been interesting to say the least. The sayings you come out with and the ideas…I still don't know how you two could figure out cold cases and follow leads that I never recognized." He turned to Josh. "I won't deny it's going to be hard to fill your shoes, Deputy."

Josh cleared his throat. And when he spoke, his voice was raspy. "Thank you, Marshal. It's been a privilege working with you. This has been the experience of a lifetime. And I-I can't thank you enough for taking me under your wing and trusting me."

Reed waved a hand. "I think you taught me more about law than I ever knew before. It's I who should be thanking you." He reached for his saddlebag and pulled out a roll of paper held closed with brown string. "These all just came in from Helena, so let's have a look. Shall we?"

He tugged the string away and spread out at least a dozen sheets. Amber sifted through all of them, but one in particular caught her eye. She studied the image. The man on the poster looked somewhat familiar. He had the same shape face as Whitcomb, but the man in the image was much more handsome and maybe a few years younger. It was hard to tell considering it wasn't an actual photo but more of a rendering.

Reed watched her closely. "Do you recognize this man?"

On each side of the headshot were details of the man's height, weight, and when and where he was last spotted. But none of those things interested her. It was the name that got Amber trembling.

Escaped Prisoner
$10,000 Reward
Will be paid for the capture of Griffin Grey
Wealthy banker and prison escapee wanted for arson, embezzlement, and attempted murder. Immediately contact the nearest U.S. Marshal's Office

She dropped the sheet. A lead ball dropped to the bottom of her stomach, threatening to slice her intestines in half. Vomit rose in her throat, and she swallowed it down.

Josh came to her side and squeezed her hand. "Amber, what is it?"

Disbelief and shock paralyzed her. "Grey…? I-I don't understand." She searched Josh's face. "H-he told me his name was Whitcomb. This is *him*. Grey is Marcus Whitcomb!"

"Are you certain?" Josh asked.

She nodded. "Positive."

Wyatt swiped the poster from her and held it up. "Are you saying that this man is the same man you rode the stage with to Helena?"

Her fingers turned into cold icicles, and her chest tightened. There was a chance she would puke at any given moment. All this time, she never knew that Whitcomb and Grey were the *same* man. Amber's voice returned, and she managed a whisper, "Yes."

"Hell," Reed muttered.

"Yesterday, I spotted Earl with someone," Josh explained. "I only saw the man from the back, so I didn't see his face. He wasn't a cowboy or garbed in a sloppy fashion. I'd stake my life on it that the man he met up with was Grey."

"I can't believe this," Amber whispered in a shaky voice. "Traveling through time sure comes with major anxiety and inner turmoil, but this…this takes the cake."

Emma squeezed her hand. "You had no idea what Grey looked like."

"But…but if I had known what he looked like, I could've done, I don't know, something!"

Josh placed his hands on her upper arms. "Listen to me. Even had you known who Grey was, there's nothing you could've done."

"You're wrong! Had I known, I could've told you his whereabouts."

"We are going to find this bastard," Wyatt added. "And we won't aim to maim."

Emma touched Wyatt's arm, and then whispered, "If you change history now, we'll never go back to the way it should be in our time…"

Amber met Josh's gaze. "Emma's right. We've come so far. You two can't risk it now."

"What are you whispering about over there?" Reed asked. "Whether Grey rots in prison or gets a bullet in a fight, I don't care. He just needs to be brought to justice. I'll ride back to town and wire the lawmen in neighboring towns to see if they've caught sight of Grey."

"And in the meantime," Josh said, "we'll get Sam out here to keep an eye on Amber and Emma and meet you back in town to discuss forming a posse or two."

Reed plunked his hat on and shoved the posters back in his bag. "That's a good idea about Sam. The women shouldn't be alone, not even for a second." He walked to the door. "Now that I think about it more, maybe it's a good thing you're all heading back east. I'll see you two in town shortly." With that, he turned on his heel and left.

****

Before he and Wyatt rode into town to meet with the marshal and the new deputies, Josh had asked Sam to guard Amber and Emma. Sam and his stableman, Fergus, were more than happy to oblige. Sam always appreciated Emma looking out for him. Since Millie died, he was lonely and didn't look after himself much. Emma treated him like family. Sam and Fergus took their posts outside, staying hidden, but within clear view of the front and back sides of the house. With his friends outside, and Amber and Emma armed inside, Josh felt better about leaving them for a few hours.

The recently deputized men of Whisper Creek gathered inside the church. It was the best place they could come up with for a meeting place at the last minute. The reverend gave his blessing to use the premises and left the lawmen to conduct business. Marshal Reed stood on the dais, pacing. Josh and Wyatt flanked him on either side of the pulpit. Several recently deputized men sat in the first pew. A handful of men sat behind them, waiting to be deputized should Reed need them.

Reed took the podium, and his gaze surveyed the small crowd. "Thank you for coming on short notice. I didn't want to create a stir in town, especially with the womenfolk. I want you men to know that Griffin Grey is out of jail, and we need your help. Most importantly, Grey has made it known to the Kincaid brothers that he's heading to Whisper Creek to exact his revenge on them."

The men shouted their outrage.

"Please," Reed said, raising his hands. "Let me finish." When the group quieted, he continued, "I don't have to tell you what a conniving, scheming man we are dealing with. Deputy Allen was killed in the first fire Grey started. Wanted posters are already being circulated in town and throughout the territory. He was most recently spotted here in Whisper Creek. Wyatt and Josh are here to tell you more."

Josh stepped forward. "Gentlemen, I can't tell you how much I appreciate your friendship since my brother, Wyatt, and I came to this town a couple years ago. You took us in and accepted us like we'd been here since the beginning of Whisper Creek, which wasn't all that long ago. Many of you are like family. Wyatt and I are grateful for all that you do for us, our great marshal here, and our booming town." He paused. "My brother may be a former deputy, but there was a time he, too, enforced the law, protecting the innocent, and coming to your aid when you needed it, as I have. We've never let you down. Have we?" The men shook their heads. "Now, it's our turn to ask for your help."

"Since Grey escaped jail, he has assumed a new identity," Wyatt announced. "He's now calling himself Marcus Whitcomb." He held up the wanted poster in front of the crowd, and then handed it out to the audience to be passed around. "My wife's best friend, Miss Amber Harrison, encountered him in Helena, and most recently in Montana City. Unfortunately, she didn't know Whitcomb and Grey were the same man."

"Grey has an accomplice," Josh added, pulling another poster from the marshal's pile. He held it up, and then passed it to the group. "Earl Lester. So far, he's wanted for horse thieving and bank robberies, but nothing else. If you find him, you find Grey. They both need to be brought to justice."

The crowd erupted in shouts and curses. A few men in the second row rose to their feet, waving their guns in the air. Others, stomped their heels against the wood floor, creating a thunderous tremble.

"We'll kill them both!" one shouted.

"He's a dead man!" another cried.

"Gentlemen!" Reed bellowed, raising his hands into the air. Once the crowd settled down, he spoke. "There will be no killing, not with deliberate intent. I don't want to arrest anyone for shooting a man in the back. You'd be considered a cold-blooded killer. I can't have that in my town." His gaze traveled over the men in the audience. "Do I make myself clear?"

The men remained quiet and nodded. Everyone in town had respect for Marshal Reed. If he asked you to do something, you did it.

"Good," Reed said. "Now, I'm going to re-deputize Wyatt Kincaid here, and then we're going to split up. I'd like to form at least four posses, each one taking a specific location either in town or the roads leading out of town. I'll be setting up a rotating schedule for the overnight hours outside the Kincaid house to make sure Grey doesn't surprise them. Who'd like to volunteer to take the first watch?"

"Where we come from," Wyatt added, "we call them stakeouts."

"All right, then," Reed amended. "Who'd like to volunteer for the first stakeout?"

Every hand in the crowd went up. Josh glanced at his brother, moved by the loyalty these men had to him and Wyatt. In the short time they had been in the Old West, they established themselves in the community. They planted roots. What Josh told everyone was true. Some of these men had become their friends, but others, like Marshal Reed and Sam, were more like family. Families stuck together. They were there for one another.

It hit him hard, just then. His own family had been torn apart due to his selfishness. All because he and Wyatt lingered in their current century so they could play cowboys in the Old West. They deserted their big brother, the man who always looked out for them, took care of them, had their best interests at heart. The brother who protected them in the school yard when they were kids and helped them as grown men soldier on through the clouds of grief when their parents died unexpectedly. James was always there for them. But where was Josh when James needed him? Stuck in the past.

Gazing around the room, gratitude pulsed through him for these men. He knew that once he stepped through the portal, he would never see them again.

At last, he was going home…where he belonged.

Chapter Twenty

Amber sighed. It had been a few hours since Josh and Wyatt left to meet with the marshal, and she was climbing the walls. Staying indoors all day of her own accord was one thing, but being told she had to remain inside was another. Emma didn't seem to mind, though. She cleaned the house while Wesley napped. Amber couldn't grasp her reasoning since they would be leaving soon. What difference did it make if the house was clean? Amber, on the other hand, studied the revolver Josh slapped into her hands before he walked out the door. It was smaller than his and similar to Emma's. She didn't like the idea of handling a weapon, but she would have no problems using it to defend her friends should it ever come to that. Hopefully, her brief lessons would pay off. If it wasn't for Grey, she wouldn't need to even learn how to use a gun.

When Amber met Grey as Whitcomb, he had told her his long-ago fiancée perished in a fire and most recently the woman he loved married another man. Wyatt and Josh have spoken often of Grey's obsession with Emma marrying Wyatt, and that was one of the reasons he wanted revenge. Maybe the story Whitcomb aka Grey told her was truly about himself. Whether it was or not, he was clearly a psycho case.

Two riders on horseback approached the property. From a distance, it was unclear who they were. Her heart lurched. It could be Grey and one of his men! Her hand instinctively tapped the gun she had shoved into the band of her skirt. Within seconds, Sam and Fergus charged around from the back of the house on horseback, guns aimed and ready to be fired.

The riders came into view, and she let out the breath she was holding. Josh and Wyatt rode directly over to Sam and Fergus. They were too far away for her to hear what they were saying. Soon, the two men galloped away, and Josh and Wyatt led their horses into the paddock.

Amber bolted out of the kitchen and down the hallway. "They're back!" she shouted.

Emma emerged from the bedroom, tucking in strands of hair that came loose from her bun. "Thank goodness. I was getting worried."

They returned to the kitchen together and stepped outside the back door one at a time.

Wyatt palmed his gun, and they froze in their tracks. "I need you ladies to stay inside!" he bellowed.

"Come on." Emma yanked her arm, dragging her back into the kitchen. "He's being cautious. I doubt anyone's out there. If there was, I'm sure Sam and Fergus would've had them tied and gagged already."

Wyatt burst through the door with Josh in tow. He shoved his revolver back into the holster at his hip. "You two shouldn't have been outside."

"We've been inside the entire time until you rode in," Emma assured him in a calm voice.

"It's not like we don't have guns on us, you know," Amber retorted, pulling the revolver from the band of her skirt. "Besides, you were twenty feet away."

Josh kissed Amber's cheek. "It's all part of

protecting you and keeping you safe, sweets. When we're not here, we want you inside the house at all times."

Wyatt glanced out the window, pulled the curtain closed, and then did the same with the rest of the windows in the room. Trouble was coming. Maybe they were about to experience a real live shootout. Amber blew out a series of short breaths, hoping her anxiety would calm the hell down.

"Tell us what happened with the marshal and the townsmen," Emma said.

Wyatt pulled Emma into his arms, hugging her close. "Reed deputized a handful of good men…including me."

"What?" Emma cried, pushing away. "Wyatt, we're supposed to be going through the portal today! Why would you let him do this? You resigned ages ago. Now, this gives Reed the false hope that we'll be in town longer."

"It was a formality. I couldn't very well tell him the truth, could I?"

"I understand, but…I just want to go home."

"Me too," Amber added, wrapping her arms around Josh's waist. "You've done your duty in town. And you've told all your friends we're going away. Let's just try the portal now. Please?"

"I don't want to leave Reed like this," Josh argued, his gaze focused elsewhere.

"You're not leaving him like anything," Wyatt said. "Reed's a lawman. He knows what's at stake. Besides, we can't live our lives for others here. We have to try."

"All right," Josh conceded. "Let's give it a shot before the marshal sends anyone over for the first watch.

With any luck, it'll work, and we can be home in a few minutes. If not…"

He pulled open a drawer in the counter and removed a folded piece of paper. The letter K was imprinted in the wax seal, and the name Reed was scribbled across the front of it. He placed it on the center of the table. "Grab the safe with all our stuff," he said to Wyatt, but his brother was already on his way to get the small leather trunk.

"Got it," Wyatt said, tucking the chest under his arm.

"Let's roll," Josh announced, not glancing back at the letter.

Amber was so excited; she was doing cartwheels in her head. Emma swooped Wesley up from the playpen, perching him on her hip. Josh and Wyatt led the way, scanning the perimeter first. Guns drawn and sensing no imminent threat, they led the women and Wesley out of the house and into the barn.

Josh pulled the two large doors closed behind them. Inside, the air was cool and smelled of hay and horses. Gone was the summer dankness. Straw crunched beneath their shoes. Josh took hold of Amber's hand, and Wyatt draped an arm around Emma's waist. Wesley rested his tired head on his mom's shoulder. All four of them walked with tentative steps to the other side of the barn.

Wyatt canted his head toward the wall where the portal was located. "It's been a while since I've done this."

"Well, don't chicken out now," Josh teased.

"No chance of that, big brother."

"Maybe we should all hold hands," Amber suggested. "You know in case something goes wrong with the portal. No matter what, we'll end up landing together…if it doesn't vaporize us first."

"Thanks for that," Emma said. "Now I can't get that image out of my head."

Amber and Josh were already holding hands, so Amber linked her hand with Emma's. And Emma held onto Wyatt.

"On the count of three," Josh said, though his voice sounded anything but certain. "We start with the left foot and walk toward the portal. One…two…*three*."

Each of them stepped forward, one foot at a time, until they stood inches from the wall.

"I'm no time travel expert," Amber began, sarcasm dripping in her tone, "but shouldn't it, I don't know, do something, like zap us through to the twenty-first century?"

"Before I was transported both times," Emma said, "I walked around the barn first."

"Me, too!"

"Not me," Wyatt said. "One minute I was reaching for a tool, and the next, I ended up in a dilapidated barn, here."

"I wonder why it was different for you?" Josh mused.

Wyatt shrugged. "What did your buddy from the future say about this?"

Josh scratched his jaw. "Malachi didn't say anything about the actual physics of how the portal works."

Amber bit down on her lip and glanced at Josh. "What if it's still broken?"

"Dammit." Josh pounded on the wall. "Malachi, get back here! We want to go home!"

"Malachi!" Amber struck the wall, too.

Wyatt joined them and did the same. After several minutes of thumping away with no response, they stopped.

"I don't believe this!" she fumed. "We can't be stuck here."

"We're not," Josh said. "We have until New Year's Eve."

"Hell-o, it's not New Year's Eve," Emma said, rocking Wesley who was drifting off to sleep. "What if Malachi meant December thirty-first is the exact date that we all have to travel on, not have to complete our travel by?"

The ground suddenly trembled. Amber clutched Josh's arm to keep from falling. That tremor indicated only one thing. Beginning as a slight rumble, the earthquake grew to a full-blown roar. A blue-white light flashed, and the barn wall shimmered. All four of them stepped back several feet. Josh squeezed her hand tighter.

The metallic whoosh synonymous with a heavy steel pocket door sliding open filled the barn. Malachi emerged from the shimmering light. He was much taller than Amber remembered. And there was something familiar about him, more specifically, the shape of his eyes and jaw. He had an uncanny resemblance to someone, but she couldn't quite put her finger on who. Malachi's suit was similar to the one he wore last time, but this one was a darker blue. A light gray emblem with a triangle and star in the middle with some unrecognizable letters was sewn into the material on the left side of his chest. He turned his head to glance behind him, and Amber noted a small disc-like button fastened to his right temple. She wondered what it was.

Wyatt jerked a thumb toward Malachi. "This is the dude you were talking about?"

"Hello, Wyatt," Malachi said in that ethereal voice that gave Amber the chills. "Yes, I'm Malachi. I'm the one responsible for you being in this century. And before you ask, there are many reasons why the portal has been sealed off to you. I will disclose all the details. However, I must begin by telling you, I bring bad news."

"Of course, you do," Wyatt muttered.

"I think your news can wait," Josh said. "You told us when we were together, we could go through the portal. Well, as you can see, we're all here, and we're ready to go home."

Depending on how Malachi moved his head, his hair glittered with different colors, some of which Amber didn't recognize. They were unique and not from the color wheel she had been accustomed with. His facial expression was tense, and he clenched his jaw. "I'm afraid I can't let you do that yet."

"Why the hell not?" Wyatt shouted. "We've been stuck here long enough, thanks to you."

"You can't leave yet…because I need your help. It has to do with a time paradox that Grey created."

"What time paradox? What the hell are you talking about?"

"Griffin Grey did something here that affected his timeline in the future, and not just his timeline either," Malachi explained, glancing at the monitor on the armband gadget sewn into his sleeve. "Unless we undo or fix the chain of events he has triggered, circumstances will be dire, I assure you. First, can you confirm Grey is no longer an inmate at Deer Lodge?"

"That's correct," Amber replied. "He recently

escaped."

"Wherever he is, you must find him."

"That won't be too hard. He was last seen here in Whisper Creek yesterday."

"Hang on," Josh said, holding up a hand. "Grey's not *our* responsibility. He's done nothing but cause everyone grief. Why do we have to find him? You're in charge of the portal and who comes and goes, shouldn't that be your job?"

Malachi glanced at each of them, his gaze softening on Wesley. "In the original history of your universe, Griffin Grey spent the remainder of his life in a nineteenth-century prison. He died there at the age of sixty. However, since he is no longer an inmate, the future has now changed, and not for the better." The gadget on his armband beeped, and he glanced at it. "In conclusion, I cannot allow him access to the portal."

"What are you suggesting we do?" Amber asked.

Malachi hesitated before responding. "Grey needs to be stopped at all costs. I will leave it to your discretion as to how you want to handle that."

"Whoa, hold on," Josh said, taking a step toward him. "The last time you showed up here, you told us we had until the end of the year to go back. Has that changed?"

"As I stated, everything has changed now that Grey is no longer in prison," Malachi said. "The portal will permanently close on December thirty-first; however, to remedy the situation with Grey, you need to do this as soon as humanly possible, preferably by All Hallows' Eve."

"Halloween? That's only two weeks away!" Amber cried.

"It is," Malachi said with curt nod.

"Then what?" Josh demanded. "We do your dirty work and you let us go through the portal? That makes us no better than Grey."

"Grey was a criminal. I, however, am enlisting your help to save the future…and your future lineages." He tapped the disc on his temple, and then blinked a few times. "After December thirty-first, you four and the baby will be denied access through the portal. It will be shut down permanently. Unfortunately, at that time, there will be nothing I can do to change that. I wish I could, but it will be out of my control. If you want to return to your own time as it *should be*, you will need to assist me. Alas, I cannot go through the portal. If I do, it would be catastrophic for us all. I must remain in my own time." He paused. "Will you please help me, and help your future selves?"

Everyone exchanged glances and nodded.

"Good." He glanced over his shoulder. "The Inspectors are breathing down my back. I must go."

"Wait!" Josh reached out to grab Malachi's arm, but his hand went right through him. He jumped back. Malachi was a hologram. "Whoa…you're not even real. Is this some kind of trick?"

"This is far from any trick," Malachi told them. "I am quite real, I assure you. Nevertheless, at this time, it is best that I appear to you as a hologram. It is safer for me this way and prevents me from having to endure further unnecessary questioning from the Inspectors. And it is a protection for all of you, so that no one can slip through the portal unexpectedly, like Grey, should he be lingering in the shadows behind you."

"What if we can't catch Grey?" Amber asked,

sparing a glance over her shoulder. "Will you still give us access to the portal?"

"Of course." Malachi inched his way backward toward the portal. "However, should you fail to secure Grey's permanence in this century, you would return to a parallel world with different people in your lives. That is why I am asking for your help. I trust you will do the right thing."

He tapped the disc on his temple, and then stepped backward into the shimmering doorway. The light flashed, the door disappeared, and the wooden barn wall returned. Malachi was gone.

The four of them stood in complete silence. The only sound was Wesley's soft snoring against his mother's neck. He had slept through everything.

Amber understood the full extent of what Malachi told them. Uneasiness skated down her spine, quickly snowballing into an avalanche of fear. "This is insanity," she managed. "And now, our futures hinge entirely around Griffin Grey. How the hell did this happen?"

Josh pulled her close, hugging her tight. "I don't know, but it's time we do what we should've done in the first place."

"What's that?" Amber asked.

"We take care of Grey once and for all," Wyatt stated.

If things didn't go well, they just might find out if Grey was the one truly responsible for Wyatt and Emma's names on those tombstones after all.

Chapter Twenty-One

Josh stood at the back door that faced the barn, silently cursing the portal within. Ironically, getting it to work was never up to them, and Malachi wasn't about to let them gain access until they secured their own future. But shit, it involved Grey. Malachi was either a mastermind or a madman. For as much as Josh hated Grey, he could never shoot a man in the back. He didn't intend to, either. However, self-defense was another thing. If it ever came down to it, Josh would do anything and everything to protect his family and Amber. With Grey, nothing was predictable. They needed options. Josh hated to ask others in town put their lives on the line to keep him and his family safe. If any of them were injured or killed…he would never be able to forgive himself.

"Incoming," Emma announced, stopping in front of him with a heavy platter piled high with chicken and vegetables fresh off the outside grill. He took the tray from her and set it on the counter. She wiped her hands off on a nearby towel. "I'm so glad you boys made that outdoor grill, but I'm even more excited we won't be here for indoor winter cooking." Tossing the towel aside, she added, "I hope you're hungry. I don't know how you men can eat in times like these. I can't even look at food when I'm this anxious."

"I'm sorry about all this," he said.

Emma squeezed his hand. "Please, don't even go there. No one could've foreseen this. Besides, we had the experience of a lifetime. Who else could say they traveled to another century?"

"True, but it's the returning to our real century that has me worried. If we don't nail Grey by our deadline…everything could change."

"Then we better come up with a solution as soon as possible," she said, and looked over his shoulder. "Where's Amber?"

"She's probably still napping."

Emma patted his arm. "Why don't you go wake her? We can discuss everything over dinner, which is ready now."

Josh smiled his thanks, and then walked down the hallway to his room, which had become his and Amber's room. He smiled. There she was, snuggled up in the center of his bed, hugging his pillow. In just a few short months, this woman had quickly woven her way into his heart. He had been captivated by her from their initial meeting when he held her at gunpoint. Never in a million years did he think a woman from his own time would be the one he ended up falling for in this century. Strange how life had a way of working itself out. One thing was for certain; he would always be damn grateful to Wyatt and maybe even Malachi for his and Amber's chance meeting. After all, if he and Wyatt hadn't gone through the portal, and Emma never came out to Whisper Creek to meet with James about her inheritance last year, he and Amber would've never met.

He sat down at the edge of the bed, leaned over, and pressed a soft kiss to her cheek. Amber stirred, and her eyes fluttered open. A slow, sensual smile spread across her lips; one he would never tire of seeing. God, she was beautiful, with her flushed cheeks and auburn mane. That sexy sleepy look in her eyes tempted him, but there would be plenty of time for that once they returned home.

"Hey there, sleepyhead," he said, gently pushing a lock of hair off her face to tuck it behind her ear.

"Did I really fall asleep?" she asked, sitting up.

"Yep, for about an hour."

"I'm sorry. I just wanted five minutes to myself. Everything is so...overwhelming. What Malachi said—"

He cut her off by planting a long, slow kiss on her lips. She tasted like honey. "We'll come up with something. I promise you. Nothing is going to prevent us from going back to our lives and how they should be." He took her hand in his. "I, for one, am going to do everything humanly possible to make sure we live out our lives happily in the future, the future we're meant to have...our future."

She quirked an eyebrow. "Our future?"

"I know it's only been a few months, but I want to be with you. And I want us to figure out our future together. When we get home, we should find a place and make a home of our own. Maybe even get a dog."

"Our home. I like the sound of that. And I love dogs. Lap dogs. Little ones." She linked her fingers behind his neck and pulled him to her for another kiss. "Just promise me we won't ever end up living like this."

"Like what?" he teased, lowering his head to nibble on her neck.

"Like anything that resembles this 1883 lifestyle," she said, giggling when he tickled her.

"What?" He feigned horror. "You mean you don't like cold baths and bitter, gritty coffee and tight corsets and bruises on your sexy ass from riding a horse too long?"

She laughed. "Exactly."

"Okay, then. We'll have none of that in our future." He kissed her thoroughly and wanted to do much more than that, but now wasn't the time. Reluctantly, he stood up. "Come on, it's time to eat. Emma made enough food to feed an army."

Amber swung her legs to the floor and got up. She ran both hands through her hair and expertly tied it back in a low, loose knot using a thick strand of her own hair. "Do you think…Will we really be able to apprehend Grey without killing him in the process? This all seems so surreal and like some nightmare from hell that we can't escape. How much worse can it get?"

Josh let out a deep breath and clasped her hands in his. "I'm hoping no one will have to lose their lives, including Grey. Malachi was unclear on what he wanted us to do. With any luck, we'll be able to apprehend him and throw him back into prison where he'll stay this time." He pulled her closer. "Cadmus and one of the other new deputies arrived a few minutes ago to take the next watch. Wyatt and I agreed to let them stay for a few hours, but after that, we'll discharge them. They should be out with the posse, not in our backyard protecting the house. Wyatt and I can handle that."

"Okay, but, um…what about Grey?"

He wrapped his arms around her waist. "Grey wants to go home, sweets, to his real time. We all know that. Of course, he's going to show up here. The question is…when?"

****

Counting sheep? That didn't work. Meditation? No luck there either. Closing her eyes and thinking of her mental go-to place did nothing to create the inner serenity it usually did. No matter what Amber tried, it was impossible to fall back to sleep. Her mind raced like a thoroughbred on its way to winning the Triple Crown. Maybe it was because she couldn't stop worrying about the situation with Grey. Soon, the financier-turned-criminal would make an appearance to gain access to the portal. And when he arrived on the property, Josh and Wyatt would be waiting for him. It didn't help ease her worry that a little before midnight, Josh and Wyatt relieved the two deputies.

Josh. To her, he was invincible. He was her protector, her shelter, her world. *Dammit, nothing bad can happen to him*! Not that it would, but still. She hated Griffin Grey for walking this earth and threatening to harm the man she loved and her best friend and family.

Over dinner, their group had discussed a dozen scenarios, including setting traps on the property. While that was a help, Amber wasn't about to remain idle, twiddling her thumbs, waiting for Grey, anticipating his moves. It was bad enough her anxiety was ramped up to the nth degree. Something had to be done.

Amber got up and glanced at the clock on the mantle. There was enough moonlight for her to see the time. Four a.m. She paced, letting her mind run through different scenarios. The door creaked open, and she gasped. "You scared me!"

"I'm sorry," Josh whispered, closing the door behind him. He stripped out of his clothes. "What are you doing up?"

"I couldn't sleep."

He walked over and placed his holster next to his side of the bed, and then pulled her into his arms. "Come back to bed with me, so I can hold you close. I sleep better when you're beside me, and I need some shuteye. It's been a long night. Wyatt said he'd stay up for a couple more hours until daylight."

She slid beneath the covers, curling up against his warm body. "You and Wyatt must be exhausted. It doesn't seem fair that you two are out there most of the night."

"We would rather be out there, especially when Grey could be arriving at any second."

"I know." She paused. "Did you ever wonder why a wealthy guy in our rightful time would traipse across the country to some small town in Montana, get sucked through the portal, and cheat people in a past century?"

"It doesn't really matter to me anymore. The man needs to be stopped. I'm hoping we can apprehend him and throw him back in jail by our deadline."

"I know, but I just can't bear the thought of anything bad happening to you or Wyatt or any of us. Not that it would, but, well, you know what I mean."

His arm tightened around her shoulder, pulled her even closer. "Ditto, sweets. I want us all to be safe so we can return home and not have to wonder if anyone is breathing down our backs."

She draped an arm across his chest and leaned up on an elbow. "Aren't you worried that he'll show up here and take us by surprise? You and Wyatt can't be everywhere at every minute."

"We are doing everything we can to make sure that doesn't happen. Wyatt and I set up those booby traps we had discussed. But…yes, I'm worried. It's like being prepared for battle but unwilling to admit that the enemy could have some tricks of his own up his sleeve."

"Are you trying to freak me out on purpose?"

"Sorry, sweets." He kissed her. "Wyatt and I plan to head into town early to meet with the marshal again. Sam and Fergus will come out and keep an eye on you both."

"I'm getting pretty good at wielding a gun if I do say so myself. If and when I see Grey coming, I'm gonna blow his balls off."

"That's my girl." Josh yawned, and she put her head on his chest. "You should also keep the derringer in your pocket or boot just in case. It's in the drawer over there."

"Okay," she said. "Now, please, get some sleep." Her mind was already racing through fresh scenarios of how to eliminate Grey…for good.

Chapter Twenty-Two

Josh and Wyatt rode toward town. They opted for the road on the hill that looped around closer to the marshal's office. It would keep them behind the line of trees as they entered the town limits. Josh's gaze darted everywhere, homing in on the smallest movements and sounds from tree branches swaying and rustling to the billowing grass dancing to and fro.

His mind should be on Grey and their upcoming meeting with the marshal, but he couldn't get this morning's image of Amber out of his mind. Before leaving the bedroom, he had pressed a soft kiss against her luscious lips, careful not to wake her. He had watched her chest rise and fall with her gentle breaths as she lay snuggled up in the center of his bed. Her thick auburn mane fanned her face like a silk curtain. His heart tightened now, and he smiled, thinking of what their mornings might look like when they returned to their rightful time. One thing was for certain, he would never tire of watching her, admiring her, and wanting her.

"Are you ignoring me on purpose?" Wyatt asked.

Josh glanced over at his brother. "What?"

Wyatt gave him a wide grin. He waggled a finger at Josh. "I've seen you infatuated before, big brother, but never lovesick like this. You got it bad."

His attempt at hiding a smile was unsuccessful. "I know. The truth is I've never felt this way before.

It's…uncharacteristically me."

"Nah, you just didn't find the right woman until now. Believe me, I get it."

"I know you do," Josh agreed. "You're a lucky man. Emma is the best."

"And so is Amber. Although I haven't known her too long, with all the stories Emma has been telling us, I feel like she's always been around, part of the gang, part of you, you know what I mean?"

"Yep, I do."

"Will you get a bigger place when we get back to our time?"

Josh couldn't stop smiling. "I've been thinking a lot about that. Yeah, I want to start fresh with Amber. I want her to move in with me when we get back, but we need to find our new home together. After all, I do plan for us to grow old in the home we choose."

"You do, huh?" Wyatt's smile widened even further. "Well, just don't wait too long to start a family. I'm sure Emma will want Wesley to have cousins close to his own age. She's probably already nagging Amber about it as we speak."

Josh chuckled. "Let's get back home first before I start thinking about all that. Besides, I don't want us to have kids until we're married."

Wyatt stared at him. "Which will be…?"

"You and your questions." He waved Wyatt off. "You're cruising, bro."

"Fine, I'll let you off the hook…for now."

Josh rolled his eyes. "It's about time."

"I don't know about you," Wyatt began, "but since we've been here, every once in a while, I wonder if James ever considered selling Mom and Dad's place."

"He may have considered it, but there's nothing he can do without all three of our signatures."

"True." Wyatt sighed. "Still, it has crossed my mind. That place was like a mansion in the middle of nowhere. It was wonderful growing up with such space and the hills and quietness. I have the best memories…"

"Me too."

"I just don't want to see it go to waste."

"And it won't, knowing James," Josh assured him. "He's probably still got the staff in there for everything you could possibly think of like property management, house cleaning, auto maintenance, and all that. You know how anal he is. He's just like Mom. I'm sure the house is in tip-top shape." He glanced at his brother. "Why are you bringing all this up now?"

Wyatt chuckled. "I was thinking that maybe…you and Amber might want to move in there?"

Josh sat up straighter. "I don't know. I hadn't even considered that. It might be too weird, too many memories, you know?"

"Good, because I have a better idea. I'll build you two a house."

Josh laughed. "Now, why didn't I think of that?"

Two gunshots rang out. Josh cursed himself for getting distracted. His horse reared up on his hind legs, and he scrambled to grasp the reins. He gave a whistle that would normally calm his horse. Instead, he got tossed backward and landed on the ground with a hard thud.

Wyatt's horse whinnied, taking off at a gallop until his brother could get him back under control with a sharp whistle and a verbal command.

Josh lay on the ground, unable to catch his breath. It

felt like he was breathing through concrete. His brother came to his side, dragging him into the nearby bushes.

"Don't talk." Wyatt put his hand on Josh's chest, his gaze darting everywhere, gun drawn. "Slow, shallow breaths."

After a few seconds, the shock left his body and his breath returned to normal. Josh groaned and sat up. "What the hell happened? Who shot at us?"

Wyatt scanned the perimeter. Two more shots rang out. He ducked, throwing himself protectively over Josh while shooting off a round.

"I'm okay," Josh managed to say, nudging Wyatt, and palming his gun. He listened to their surroundings, waiting for the right moment to shoot.

All was silent, and then…

Wyatt's jaw clenched. "Shit."

"What…?" Josh craned his neck and followed his brother's gaze. "No!" Rage flowed through his veins. His treasured horse had been shot in the heart, crimson blood flowing onto the ground. Delorean lay lifeless. He had planned to leave his horse with Sam when they went back to their own time. Whoever killed him would pay, Josh would see to that.

He sat up straighter and swallowed down the rising anger. *Shit*. His dead horse wasn't their only worry. Two men approached on horseback, each with a gun in hand.

"Deputy," Earl Lester sneered, pushing his hat back. He had a revolver in one hand, another in the holster at his hip, and a rifle strapped to his saddle. The second man had the same number of weapons. Josh was about to get up, but Earl pulled the hammer back on the gun. "Sit down and drop your guns. Now."

They were outgunned, and Josh didn't want to put

him or his brother in any further danger. Surrendering was their only option…for now.

He glanced at Wyatt and gave a curt nod. He and his brother lowered their guns, placing them on the ground but still within reaching distance should they get the opportunity. "What do you want?" Josh demanded.

Earl grinned, and tobacco-colored saliva slid out the side of his mouth and down his chin. He wiped it away with his sleeve. "Aint' it funny now that I'm the one pointin' the gun?" He laughed. His accomplice, another village's idiot, chuckled along.

Simple minded men like these two could be just as dangerous and calculating as someone like Grey. They were the type that enjoyed hurting or killing for money or even just for amusement. "Are you here to do Grey's dirty work?" Josh asked.

Earl's eyebrows shot up. He turned to his friend who had just dismounted and was walking over to Wyatt. "Tie them up."

His accomplice, a young sap with a wiry beard that was too long, removed the second gun from his holster, and now each of his weapons was aimed at him and Wyatt. "Either of you move, the other gets it," the young punk said. "And I'm a pretty good shot, fellas."

"What's your plan, Earl?" Wyatt asked, ignoring the kid. "Remember, Josh and I are lawmen. That makes killing us a big problem for you."

"You ain't no lawman," Earl scoffed. He waved his gun at Josh. "Just this Kincaid is law."

"That's where you're wrong, genius." Wyatt grinned. "I was recently re-deputized. Maybe you should've thought about that first. After all, kidnapping a deputy is nothing like kidnapping a regular citizen.

You'll rot in jail for the rest of your miserable life for kidnapping *and* assaulting two lawmen. Those are some hefty charges."

"*If* you make it to jail, that is," Josh pointed out. "Our kind, other lawmen, won't take what you've done lightly. You're going to have to pay…one way or another."

Earl waved the gun around. "You talk too much, 'specially for a lawman." He glared at his cohort. "What's taking you so long, Bart? Tie them up!"

"Don't say my name, fool," Bart shot back. He stooped behind Wyatt and tied his hands behind his back.

"Bart, is it?" Wyatt asked over his shoulder.

"Shut up!" Bart shouted.

He moved to Josh, yanked his arms behind him and tied his hands tight. The rope cut into his flesh like it was made of razor blades, and he winced.

"What is it you two clowns want?" Josh demanded. He spared his brother a quick glance, encouraging him to play along. "How much is Grey paying you for capturing us?"

Earl's face scrunched up, and he rubbed the back of his neck. "What do you care?"

"Because I know how you can get more money than he offered you to capture us."

"What's that supposed to mean?"

Josh gave a shrug and glanced around, as if he hadn't a care in the world. "Nothing."

"Don't give me no shit, Kincaid," Earl shouted, marching over to him. "My boss wants you alive; but I don't have to oblige."

Josh grinned. "You do, if you want Grey's money." He paused, thinking of the best way to taunt this piece of

275

shit. "I know where he keeps it. The money, that is. And there's a lot of it, too."

"Yeah," Wyatt chimed in. "More than you'll ever see, even if you lived ten lifetimes."

Earl cocked the gun and pressed it to Josh's temple. "How do I even know you're telling me the truth?"

"We have no reason to lie, especially when you're the one with the gun." Josh angled his head away from the revolver. Even though his heart pounded, he wouldn't let this creep see his fear. "If you kill me or my brother, you'll never find out where Grey keeps his money stashed. And that would be a real shame."

"How do you know where it is?" Earl demanded.

"We followed him once. It's in a place you'd never expect it to be."

"You better not be lyin' to me."

"I guess you'll never know."

Earl spit out a wad of tobacco. It landed next to Josh's boot. "Just hush up, fool, and maybe we'll let you live another hour." He nodded to his partner who was still behind them.

Josh craned his neck. The kid removed a small brown medicine bottle from the band of his pants and yanked the cork out with his teeth. He then dumped some of the liquid on a filthy handkerchief. "Oh, shit!" Bart jumped back. "I think I poured too much."

"Just do it!" Earl demanded.

Bart grabbed Wyatt by the hair, jerking his head back. He shoved the cloth over his nose and mouth. Wyatt struggled a good fight, but within seconds, his body buckled, and he lay unconscious.

"I think I killed him, Earl!" Bart yelled, panic in his voice.

"Shut up, idiot," Earl said. "The deputy's next. Hurry up!"

Josh dug his heels into the ground, ready to jump to his feet. Earl pulled the hammer back on his second gun, aimed both at Wyatt, and said, "Go ahead. Watch what happens to him."

Anger swelled in his gut. He glanced at his brother, motionless, next to him. His chest moved in time with his breathing. Thankfully, Wyatt was still alive. "You hurt him, and I'll—"

Josh didn't get to finish that sentence. From behind, Bart clamped the cloth over his face. It smelled like chloroform. He barely had time to give it a thought when darkness overcame him.

****

Amber checked her disguise one last time in the mirror. A pair of men's loose pants and shirt, both Josh's, would be much more comfortable riding Emma's horse into town. One of her hats would do nicely, too. It wasn't too big or feminine by any stretch of the means, and she could tuck her thick braid inside it. By dressing like a man, Amber would appear less conspicuous. No one would give her a second glance, at least that was part of her plan. After Josh drifted off to sleep this morning, she had come up with an idea.

"Where do you think you're going dressed like that?" Emma demanded, walking into Amber's room with Wesley perched on her hip. Her eyebrows pitched downward, and her mouth was set in a grim line.

Amber swiped the small derringer Josh had given her from the drawer and tucked it into her right boot. She threw her hands up. "I've got to do something. Sitting here and waiting is driving my anxiety through the roof.

Fear not, girlfriend, I've got this," she added over her shoulder, breezing through the door.

Emma chased her down the hallway. "Anything that involves you leaving the property is a bad idea. You know it, and I know it." They reached the kitchen, and she grabbed Amber's arm. "What are you doing?"

Amber straightened her hat and backed up toward the door. "I can't lose anyone else in my life. I have to try something."

"What are you going to do?"

"I'm going to ask Caroline for help."

"Are you crazy?" Emma shrieked. She lowered her voice, swaying Wesley on her hip. "You can't ask anyone for help outside our circle. It's too dangerous. The guys don't even want anyone else guarding our property."

"She won't be involved directly, I assure you."

Emma blocked her exit. "Then tell me or I don't let you go. Don't forget, I'm packing heat."

"All right." Amber huffed. "If we tell Caroline that we are trying to lure Grey to the property, maybe she can ask questions to any strangers looking for medical attention. Even the guys at the saloon get drunk and knock each other around. She might overhear something or someone in a drunken stupor could just divulge something."

"Divulge what? Grey is a calculating, evil man. He's not going to take any chances by having a few too many drinks."

"I don't mean Grey. The goons he has working for him."

Emma's glare was unwavering. "I don't like this plan. It's stupid. And you're risking your safety."

Amber squeezed her friend's arm. "I know, but I have to do *something*. Please."

Emma nodded slowly. "Promise me you'll be careful."

"Of course." She kissed Emma and Wesley on the cheek, and then headed for the barn.

"Miss Amber!" Sam emerged from the bushes in lightning speed, gun in hand and rifle slung over his shoulder. "You shouldn't be out of the house."

Amber touched his arm. "It's all right, Sam. Josh and Wyatt know. I'm, um, meeting them at the marshal's office. I'll see you later."

With that, she marched into the barn, saddled up Winnie, and took off as fast as she could.

Chapter Twenty-Three

Amber was impressed with her riding skills and gave herself a mental pat on the back. Maybe when they returned to their own time, she and Josh could go horseback riding every so often. Riding was different when it was a fun excursion, but as a main mode of transportation, well, that was a whole different bowl of cherries. If she was going to ride a horse anywhere, it should be Montana, the beautiful, scenic place that brought her to Josh.

Thankfully, her arrival into town went without incident. She was careful to keep watch of her surroundings like Josh had taught her and was even more vigilant to keep Winnie out of sight. So far, luck was on her side. She tied the mare to the hitching post outside the back door of the doctor's office, and then went around to the front, keeping her hat pulled low like she had seen Wyatt do before.

The door opened and out walked a man with a thick bandage on his hand. He nodded a greeting, and then continued walking, without giving her another glance. She went into the office and closed the door. "Anybody home?" she called out.

Caroline emerged from the exam room, wiping her hands on her apron, stained with dried splotches of blood. "Amber, it's wonderful to see you. Anne and I were planning to come for a visit before…you…all…leave." Her smile quickly faded as she took in Amber's attire. "Why are you dressed like a man? What has happened?"

Amber removed her hat and her braid tumbled out. "I need your help."

"Of course," Caroline replied, waving her into the room. She closed the door and stood next to Amber. "What can I do?"

Amber swallowed. "This all sounded so much better in my head, but now that I think about it, I'm not so sure."

"Tell me."

"It's about…Griffin Grey."

"What about him? I've heard he's highly dangerous. Amber, I'm concerned for your safety. You're living under Wyatt and Josh's roof, and it's well known how much he hates the Kincaid brothers."

"I know, but as long as Grey doesn't get wind of our true plans, we should be okay," Amber assured her, meaning their true plans about the portal, which she couldn't reveal. "The marshal, Josh, and Wyatt think the best way to catch Grey is to send a posse in every direction leading in and out of town. But we need to lure Grey to the property. We're going to set a trap for him."

Caroline gasped. "Why on earth would you want to do that? That makes no sense. If Josh or Marshal Reed were to catch him with a posse, he'll go back to prison and be out of your lives. Isn't that what you want?"

Amber couldn't tell Caroline the entire truth, so she made up something that was close enough. "Yes, but most of the men in this town want to see him dead, hanging by the end of a rope. Josh wants to arrest Grey in a secure location without anyone attempting to lynch him in the process."

"Oh, yes, I completely understand."

"Plus," Amber added, "I, uh, we, have something Grey wants."

She frowned. "What's that?"

Amber bit her bottom lip, thinking of a reply. "He thinks…we owe him money, but we don't. It's a long story. Anyway, it's best I don't go into details. What I can tell you is that I have a plan to lure him to us, and this is where I need your help. Grey and his seedy sidekick won't suspect you, the local doctor, if you were to nose around."

Caroline's eyebrows shot up. "Nose around? How so?"

"You get a lot of patients in here, mostly men, right?"

"Mostly."

"Well, in my opinion, men are crybabies when they're sick or injured. I'm sure you could pry information out of some of the more seriously injured. Some of these men, with the right questioning, could divulge details without realizing it. You know, maybe they saw someone fitting Grey's description riding into town or shacking up with one of the women in the saloon. I know how risky this is, considering the kind of men Grey hires, but it's worth a shot. That is, if you agree."

A smile tugged the corner of Caroline's mouth. "You'd make a wonderful Pinkerton detective, my friend. I like your way of thinking."

Amber grinned. "Does that mean you'll help me?"

"Of course, I will."

"Thank you. You're the best." Amber hugged her,

and then rushed to the door. "If you find out anything, anything at all, send a messenger to the house with a note."

"All right," she agreed. "I'll do that."

"I've got to run before Josh spots my horse. I hitched her out back, and I'm hoping he's still inside the marshal's."

"He doesn't know you're here?"

Amber shook her head. "Nope, only you and Emma. Mums the word."

****

Josh opened his eyes to darkness. He shifted his jaw left to right and back again. No pain there, thankfully. A glimmer of light appeared with his movements. A tight band was wrapped around his head. He was blindfolded. His hands were tied behind his back. The rope nearly cut off his circulation; his hands were numb and tingly, like he'd slept on them the wrong way for hours on end. On top of that, every inch of his body ached from head to toe.

He racked his foggy brain. The last thing he remembered was taunting Earl, and then it was lights out. *Earl Lester*. That piece of shit would pay for killing his beloved horse. Right now, though, he had to figure out where the hell he was and if Wyatt was all right.

He shifted from his back to his left side. Wiggling his ass across the flat surface a few inches, he discovered a seam in the flooring. Something nicked the material of his pants. Apparently, he wasn't on solid ground. If the floor was made of wood, which felt that way from where his fingers could touch, perhaps he was being held in a building somewhere or an old barn. But where, and most importantly, why? He closed his eyes, tuning into his surroundings, hoping it might give him a clue as to his whereabouts. Birds chirped. Trees rustled. A breeze wafted over him.

Someone groaned. Wyatt, he hoped. He moved closer until his left shoulder touched someone. "Wyatt?" he whispered. "Is that you?"

"Yeah," Wyatt croaked out. "Ah, shit."

"Are you okay?"

"Fan-fucking-tastic, big brother. Never better. You?" At least, Wyatt could still joke.

"I feel like I got run over by a truck," Josh replied.

"Yeah, I agree with you there." Wyatt's voice was raspy. "I'm blindfolded, and my hands are tied behind my back."

"Same here," Josh replied.

"Where are we?"

"No clue, but if you can sit up, we can press our backs together, and we might be able to untie each other's bindings. Want to give it a try?"

"Let's do it."

Josh wiggled his way into a seated position, inching his back toward his brother. "First, I'll try getting this blindfold off so I can see where we are. I'll need to press my head against your back. Maybe the movement will loosen it or slip it off."

"Go for it."

He scooted lower, leaned his head against Wyatt's shoulder, and slid his head up against Wyatt's back. The blindfold lifted off and fell into his lap. The sun was bright. He blinked, adjusting to the sunlight, and checked out their surroundings. They were in an old, dilapidated uncovered buckboard parked under a tall, shady tree. Hills sat in the distance. Nothing was recognizable.

"I can't tell where we are," Josh said, "except that we're in a wagon. Now, come closer. Hurry before anyone discovers us."

Wyatt scooted lower and skidded his head against Josh's shoulder. After several attempts, his blindfold came loose. He sat up and gazed around. "Where the hell did they take us?"

"No clue," Josh replied. "But let's get the hell out of here. Move this way so I can get your bindings."

Wyatt scooted closer. With all their fidgeting, a bottle in the corner of the wagon rolled over. It looked like the same one Bart had used. He couldn't quite read the label on it, but it had to be ether or chloroform.

Josh ran his fingers over his brother's bindings, tugging and pinching to loosen them. It took a few minutes. "Got 'em," he said.

Wyatt yanked his hands free and then turned around to grab Josh's bindings. He slipped one knot out and continued working the other. A twig snapped in the distance, and he tipped his head toward the sound. "Oh, fuck, it's you," Wyatt sneered.

Earl approached the wagon, one gun drawn with a finger on the trigger, and two rifles slung over each shoulder. "I wouldn't try escapin'. It won't end good for either of you." He turned to Josh. "Damn shame about your horse, Deputy, but these things happen." Brown juice slid down from the corner of his lips, dripping onto his shirt. He spit out a wad of tobacco onto Josh's boot and watched it slide down the side.

Josh clenched his jaw. His bindings were off, but the ones at his feet weren't. It took every ounce of strength not to lunge at Earl and beat the shit out of him. From where he sat, it was impossible to tell if Bart was nearby or not. He didn't want to make a half-assed attempt and get shot in the process. "I see you're racking up the charges," he bit out instead.

Earl frowned. "What are you talkin' about?"

Josh indicated the little brown bottle in the corner. "Stealing medicine from the doctor's office is a criminal offense. That, plus kidnapping two lawmen, well, I'd say, you're going to be in jail for the rest of your life."

"Not if you're dead, and they don't catch me."

"No one's going to die," Wyatt said.

Earl glowered at him. "I wouldn't be too sure about that."

"Hold on now," Wyatt added. "I think we can all come to some sort of agreement. You know Grey can't be trusted. He's only looking out for himself."

"The only agreement I'm comin' to is the one I made with Grey. Now, shut up before I shut you up."

Josh was about to argue with a wiseass comeback; however, there was no time. The back of his head exploded. There was a bright light before darkness descended once more.

Chapter Twenty-Four

Amber steered the mare down the back streets of town, slipping in and out of alleyways, keeping her hat low over her eyes. She did her best to stay off Main Street and out of sight. Grey and his accomplices could be somewhere nearby, and her anxiety ramped up to DEFCON one. She was also on the lookout for Josh and Wyatt, worried they might take her by surprise. If he caught her, Josh would be pissed off to the extreme.

Her strongest hope now was that Caroline would uncover information leading to Grey's whereabouts so they could lure the bastard to the property. That way, they would have a heads-up and could trap him. Then again, he could make an appearance at any time. After all, Grey wanted access to the portal and would probably try anything to gain it. What was stopping him from going there now?

Tugging the reins, she stopped the horse in front of the church at the end of town. The whitewashed wood building was nearly the same as the old church once upon a time in the future. Presently, the church was only a few years old. Even though Amber had been in the nineteenth century for a short time, she took great care not to venture anywhere near the church or that part of town. The place was a blatant reminder of the exact moment she came across Emma and Wyatt's tombstones in her own time and the panic it elicited. Now, however, something compelled her to explore the small cemetery behind the church.

Amber tethered Winnie to the fence and stepped through the narrow, creaky gate and into the cemetery. Cold, icy shivers ran up and down her spine, collecting at the base of her neck. Even her feet tingled with a frosty sensation.

There hadn't been a thunderstorm in days but judging by the dark, cumulonimbus clouds heading toward the town, one was on its way. She gazed across the small cemetery and pondered the last time she had visited the same spot in her rightful time. It was much larger then with hundreds of tombstones. Now, though, only a handful of gravestones sprang out of the ground. Her feet kept moving until she came to the exact location where Emma and Wyatt's tombstones were in her own time.

Heart pounding, she closed her eyes and drew in a slow, deep breath, letting it out even slower. That did nothing to slow her racing pulse. She opened her eyes. Her shoulders relaxed. Not that she thought the tombstones in the future would be there, seeing as Emma and Wyatt were still very much alive, but she had no clue what to expect. She was dealing with time travel, and it was unpredictable to say the least.

Turning to go, she tripped, falling face first into the overgrown grass. She pushed herself to her knees, glaring at the culprit, a thick tree root. Rising to her feet, she dusted off her dirt-smudged trousers and shirt, and then swiped up her hat that had fallen in her mishap. "Awesome."

"Hello?" a masculine voice called out.

Amber spun around, surprised, and a little annoyed

that she was caught off guard. The unkempt young man staring back at her couldn't have been more than his mid-twenties. It was hard to tell with all that gross facial hair. Bits of a previous meal or two were caught within the wiry mass. Gross. His hat was pushed back, revealing a sweaty forehead with stringy hair. He had two holsters strapped around his waist, and his hand was on the hilt of one of the guns. That wasn't a good sign.

"Hello," she said, warily.

He gave her a creepy stare. His lip curled up as his eyes roamed over her. Caution bells rang in her head.

"What do you want?" she asked when he didn't say anything else.

They were the only two in the churchyard. Her mare tied to the post by the gate was at least a hundred feet away. There was no one walking by on the street. She donned her hat, tying the knot below her chin, ready to bolt.

He stepped toward her; his brows furrowed. "Ain't you…Miss Harrison?"

"Me?" Fear twisted in her stomach. She wasn't about to admit anything until she knew who this creep was. "No, why?"

The idiot frowned and scratched his beard. "Oh. Do you know where she might be?"

Amber took a few slow steps backward. From the corner of her eye, Winnie remained outside the gate, munching on some grass. Too bad she didn't know any whistle commands like the guys did. That would come in handy about now. "No, I don't know where she is."

"You sure?" He thrust both hands on his hips and glanced at the sky before gazing back at her.

"Look, pal, I don't have time for this," she said. "I

gotta go." Turning on her heel, she hoped to make it to Winnie in time to gallop off toward the house.

The scruffy man grabbed her by the arm and palmed his gun. He pressed it against her temple. "You ain't going nowhere, ma'am."

****

Josh's head pounded more than the worst migraine he'd ever experienced. He opened his eyes, but darkness surrounded him. The material of the blindfold pinched his eye sockets. The back of his head throbbed, vibrating down to his shoulders. Bart had clobbered him good, too good, dammit. And when he was able to, Josh would see to it that both Bart and Earl paid, not only for what they did to him and Wyatt, but for killing his horse.

The wagon bounced over a road oblivious to any oncoming potholes. Shit, his head throbbed and spun at the same time. His stomach churned. That feeling of impending nausea indicated he could hurl at any given moment. He must have a concussion. The sound of the wheels trouncing and the rickety wagon didn't help.

"Josh, you awake?" Wyatt whispered loud enough for him to hear over the din.

He groaned. "Yeah."

Wyatt scooted closer. "I've been counting the minutes since I came-to. It feels like we've been riding for about fifteen minutes or so."

"Any idea where?"

"The wagon keeps pitching in the same direction. My guess is we've been riding in circles. For all I know, we could be in the same spot as before."

"They're trying to confuse us." Josh groaned. "My head is killing me."

"Yeah, you got a nasty bump. Bart got you bad. I

know what *that* feels like." His brother was referring to last year when someone had clocked him over the head, rendering him unconscious and leaving him with a concussion.

Josh's hands were tied in front of him this time, which was lucky for him. He scooted himself to a seated position and pushed the blindfold up his forehead. It was difficult to see anything over the sides of the wagon, but he recognized the tree line. They were nearing their property.

He lifted Wyatt's blindfold just enough so he could see and tipped his head toward the property. Wyatt inched himself up for a better look. Josh used his teeth to loosen the knots around his wrists, and then loosen Wyatt's ties which were secured behind his back. He wanted to take Earl by surprise, but the timing had to be right. And if Earl was the one steering the wagon, his attention was still on the road.

Josh leaned closer to Wyatt, and whispered, "Wait for my signal. Our bindings are loose, just don't drop yours or they'll know."

The wagon came to an abrupt stop. Josh tugged his blindfold back down over his eyes, keeping his hands in his lap. Within seconds, the rear gate of the conveyance dropped down with a bang. Earl, he assumed, grabbed Josh by the feet and dragged him across the wagon bed until his legs hung over the edge. And he fought the urge to kick the bastard.

"Keep your mouth shut, and don't try nothin'," Earl warned. He removed Josh's ankle bindings and shoved him to the ground.

Josh landed on his knees and arms. At least it kept his face from slamming into the ground. His knees took the hit bad, though. Luckily, Earl hadn't picked up on the fact that his bindings were loose.

"Either of you tries anything," Earl said, "you get a bullet."

"Whatever you say," Wyatt replied.

Earl shoved both men forward. Being blindfolded didn't help. Wyatt stumbled, ramming into Josh. A door creaked open. Josh drew a deep breath, reveling in the familiar scents of the barn. *Their* barn. Grey had to be inside, why else would Earl bring them there? Now, Grey was on their turf. He would soon be at their mercy.

That is, as soon as they freed themselves from Earl's clutches.

Chapter Twenty-Five

Amber mentally counted to ten. She needed a few seconds to think through a plan, one where she wouldn't get shot. Now was not the time to react. If she did, the scumbag might shoot her. If she made any attempt to reach for her gun now, it might cost her life.

Her captor glanced back over each of his shoulders, and then retreated a step. With one hand, he pulled out a short piece of rope from the band of his pants. "Time for us to take a little ride, missy," he said.

"Where to?" she demanded.

"That's none of your concern." He aimed the gun at her temple again and said, "Kneel down and put your hands out in front of you."

Adrenaline flowed, igniting a response she couldn't ignore. When her captor holstered his gun to tie her hands, she put all the force she could muster into her leg and kicked him in the face. A crunching sound was her reward. *Yes!*

The man stumbled backward, clutching his nose. "You bwoke my nowse," he cried, blooding oozing through his fingers and over his hands. "Shit, woman! I'll kill you befowe I tuwn you ovah to Grey."

He reached for one of the guns at his hip, but Amber was faster. She kicked him again, this time in the groin. He went down like a cement block, crumpling to the ground and crying like a baby. His hand shot out, and he grabbed her ankle, knocking her off her feet. She fell backward onto the thick grass and quickly rolled to her side to kick the bastard in the stomach. He clutched his groin with a bloodied hand but with his other reached out to grab her again. She responded by crashing her knee into his face. Jumping to her feet, she expected him to come for her again. This time, he didn't budge.

Thank you, Master Tee, for your years of self-defense classes.

She was super thankful it all came back to her when she needed it, just as Master Tee assured the class it would.

Instead of making a run for it, Amber removed the man's guns and tucked one into the front of her pants and the other one tucked at her back. Swiping up the rope he had dropped when she kicked him, she tied the thug's feet first, then secured his hands behind his back. She snatched the two bandanas from around his neck and blindfolded him with one and stuffed the other into his mouth so he couldn't cry for help. *Scumbag.* A part of her wanted to know his name so she could curse him to a thousand fiery hells every day. Scumbag would do for now.

Amber took one last look at him lying in the tall grass, and then ran straight for her mare. She climbed into the saddle and glanced down the street. No one was around. It was oddly quiet. Without another thought, she kicked the mare's sides and rode as fast as the horse would take her toward the house. Every few seconds, though, she glanced over her shoulder to make sure no one was following.

Riding toward the property, she recalled Scumbag had mentioned Grey by name. He must be one of his underlings. Maybe Grey was already at the property. *No*! Emma and Wesley were there *alone*! Well, not entirely alone. Sam and Fergus were there on the property.

She urged the horse faster. Anxiety rung at her heart, pounding in her ears. When she neared the property, she tugged the reins and pulled Winnie into a copse of trees. From her angle on the far side of the hill, the roof of the barn was visible in the distance. She tethered the horse to a nearby tree and quietly made her way toward the barn. Opting for the gun tucked into the front of her pants, she pulled it out and weighed it in her hand. This one was heavier than the small derringer in her boot and much heavier than any of Emma's. She just hoped she wouldn't have to use it.

Her heart banged against her chest. The usual breathing exercises did nothing to steady its erratic rhythm. The barn came into full view, and she didn't recognize the rickety old wagon next to it. She crouched down and quietly observed, but after a few minutes, she didn't see or hear anything unusual.

Stealthily, Amber snuck away from her hiding spot to the rear of the barn. There were no windows to peek through, so she tiptoed until she found a small door. She wasn't even sure it would open. It could be locked from the inside. Voices came from within. She pressed her ear to the wall and listened. Her blood froze. Grey was in there! His chilling voice was one she would remember for as long as she lived. Unfortunately, the responding voices were muffled, and she couldn't make out who else was with him. Only a word or two here and there by Grey were audible.

She checked the door again, but there was no handle. The doorjamb was wide enough to slip her fingers in between. Slowly, she ran her hand up the side and through some sticky spiderwebs and even a crawly critter or two. It took a lot of mental strength to keep her screams inside her head instead of verbalizing them at the mere contact. Bugs were just as creepy to her as snakes. She probed for a lever but couldn't locate one.

Frustrated, she searched for a stick. A thin, wiry branch might do the trick. She grabbed one off the ground and ran it up the length of the doorjamb, starting at the bottom. Halfway up it got caught and broke. Dammit. Now what?

Stepping back, she gave the door a more thorough examination. She kneeled and ran her hands along the lowermost part of the door. At the very bottom, hidden under the grass, hay, and some dirt pressed up against it, was a sliding latch lock. Bingo! She slid the latch away and reached her hand between the door and the jamb to inch it open. Thankfully, it didn't creak or make a sound. She opened it just enough to slip through and then pulled it closed behind her.

Inside, Amber stood at the end of the aisle near the tack room and stalls at the far rear of the barn. The main area was up ahead and out of sight. The sounds of rustling hay and a man's low voice drew her forward. She had never been so nervous in her life. Her veins pumped blood at record speed, pounding uncontrollably in her ears. Considering she snuck in and was armed with two guns, she had the element of surprise.

"Earl!" Grey shouted. "Get in here!"

Thankfully, Amber was out of their sight. Instead, she listened. The large barn door creaked open.

"Where's the Kincaid woman?" Grey demanded.

Amber inched her way from the rear of the barn to

the front end of the aisle, keeping her back to the wall.

"I don't know," Earl responded. "She ain't in the house."

"Then find her. Don't come back until you do. And where's that asshole, Bart? Did he get the Harrison woman yet?"

Amber gasped.

"He should be back soon with her."

If it was just Grey in the barn, there was a chance she could take him. After all, she had two guns on her. But with Earl there, and whoever else he was talking to before, she couldn't chance anything yet. She had to be strategic.

Inching closer, she reached the open archway at the front end of the aisle that led into the main area. Josh and Wyatt were both tied and blindfolded, lying in a heap of hay. Grey walked over to them and yanked their blindfolds off. Wyatt's eyes focused on Josh before quickly assessing the room.

"Gentlemen," Grey said.

An explosion of fear erupted in her stomach. Now was not the time for a panic attack. Shit!

Josh blinked a few times, glanced around, and then returned his gaze to Grey. "If you kill either of us, I promise, you'll never get through the portal."

Amber couldn't see Grey's face because he had his back to her. He stepped closer to Josh and Wyatt, hands clasped behind his back. If he had a gun, it could be tucked into his pants, hidden beneath his jacket. There was no way to be sure.

"Oh, I will get through the portal, I assure you," Grey said in his usual chilling tone. "And we're going to do it in style when the rest of the party arrives. As soon as the lovely ladies make an appearance, we'll have ourselves a little…negotiation."

"We sent the women away," Wyatt said.

"Earl will find them."

Grey walked out of Amber's sight, toward the door. With him out of her view, she waved her arms frantically, trying to grab Josh's attention. Wyatt saw her first and nudged Josh. Sparing Grey a quick glance, Josh then gestured to his tied hands. He made a facial expression she couldn't decipher.

She threw her hands up with a "what?" shrug. He replied by mouthing something she couldn't make out. He waved at her, with that "go away" glare.

"Ah, Miss Harrison," Grey said, appearing in front of her. He leaned against the doorframe casually. His eyes swept over her, and he grinned. "So glad you could join us."

Chapter Twenty-Six

Josh swallowed down the rage. He forced himself to bite his tongue and keep quiet. With his bindings loose, unbeknownst to Grey or his minion, he had an idea on how to take Grey by surprise. Of course, that was before Amber showed up. Now, Grey had turned his attention in her direction. He tried to signal her, but clearly, she was useless when it came to charades. That would be one game they would not play as a team when things returned to normal.

Grey grabbed Amber's hand, tugging her toward him. He glanced down the aisle behind her. "Is anyone else with you?"

"Why should I tell you?" she retorted.

He gripped her face in his hands and growled, "Don't get smart with me. I asked you a question."

"No." She pulled her head back and rubbed her jaw with her free hand. "I'm alone."

"That's too bad." Grey's grip must've tightened around her wrist because Amber winced. The man's gaze ran up and down her body, stopping at the gun tucked into the band of her pants. He yanked it out, admired it, and then pointed it at her head. He pulled back the hammer, smiling as he did so. "Over there," he said, canting his head. "Move."

Over there happened to be where he and Wyatt were lumped together on the hay. Josh kept his attention focused on Grey, but occasionally glanced at Amber. She was a strong woman; she would be able to handle this. Hands raised, taking small steps, she walked, keeping her back to Josh. *That's my girl.* Amber had another pistol tucked into the back of her pants that Grey missed.

Grey pulled out a short string of rope from his jacket pocket and said to Amber, "Put out your arms, hands clasped, and don't try anything."

Amber did as she was told and extended her arms. Grey tucked the gun under his arm, his gaze darting to Josh and Wyatt, while he tied her wrists. He tugged it so tightly that she gave off a grunt. That done, he held his gun mere inches from her head. "Now, sit down like a good girl, and keep your mouth shut."

Slowly, she walked two steps backward, and her eyes widened. Sam and Fergus lay in a heap by the front door, slowly coming to from whatever knocked them out. They were bound and gagged. Her head snapped around to Josh before glaring at Grey. "What did you do to them?" Amber demanded.

"*I* didn't do anything," Grey said, sparing a quick glance in their direction. "Now, sit down, and keep quiet. Once the lovely Mrs. Kincaid joins us, we can have a going away party…in style."

"What are you talking about?" Amber kneeled when Grey shoved the gun closer to her face. She was careful to keep him from seeing her back

"Unless you want to know what it's like to have a gag shoved into your mouth, I suggest you stop talking."

Josh's jaw clenched. It took every ounce of inner strength not to react. He and Wyatt had to wait for the precise moment to make their move. His bindings were no longer an issue, but Grey was too close, holding a gun on the woman he loved. And Josh wasn't about to take any chances yet. He just hoped they would be able to do something before Earl and the other asshole returned.

"As I was saying, when my associate returns with Mrs. Kincaid, we can get this show on the road." Grey stepped back a few feet, his gun still trained on Amber. "Until then, do keep quiet. I don't like incessant chatter."

"What does my wife have to do with any of this?" Wyatt demanded. "If you want to go through the portal, just go."

"Oh, I will, but not without her. Since the tokens don't work for me, I'll use her as my token. I'll guarantee Emma's safe travel through the portal and once we arrive in our own time. In return, you will not kill me before I walk through the damn thing, holding the woman you love in my arms. It's that simple."

Josh squeezed his hands between his bent knees, slowly working the bindings around his ankles. He loosened them to the point they would come off quickly, same as the ones around his wrists. Until Amber showed up with the gun tucked into her pants, Grey's was the only weapon he could get his hands on.

"She's not going anywhere with you," Wyatt bit out.

"And I assure you otherwise." Grey paced before them, a twisted smile curling his lips. "If only you had left Emma alone, her life would've been so different. I was building a financial empire that she could've been part of. Instead, she chose this ridiculous hillbilly lifestyle…and you…something I'll never understand." Wyatt shifted, and Grey swung his gun hand toward him. "Careful, Kincaid. This little beauty is loaded."

"What does Emma have to do with any of this?" Amber prodded, turning his attention back toward her.

"How did your obsession with this all begin?"

Josh would give her a big thank you kiss for that later. He knew she was trying to stall so he and Wyatt could figure out a way to disarm Grey without any of them getting hurt in the process.

Grey quirked an eyebrow. "I wouldn't consider building a financial empire an obsession but more of a necessity. I wanted to secure my future for years to come."

"Yes, I get that, but what does that have to do with the portal?" Amber pressed.

"The portal was the link to my success, and it was supposed to be mine. I discovered it on the Kincaid property in the future." He glowered at Wyatt, and his face tightened. The tone of his voice was lethal and edgy. "And it would've been mine too, if only you would've sold it to me. I knew what the property was worth. You didn't. That portal alone had the answers to everything, to my financial future, to the control of countless companies, and so much more. It's why I kept coming and going and hired my own men from my own time. Contrary to what you might think, I didn't want to marry Emma." He laughed, an evil sound. "No, I wanted her fucking property. It's why I want her to return with me now. Once she is safely on the other side of the portal, she will sign over the deed to me."

"Son of a bitch!" Wyatt shouted and lunged for Grey, but the bastard was faster and pulled the trigger. Wyatt went down like a rock, clutching his left side and groaning.

During that quick exchange, Josh jumped up, swiped the pistol from the back of Amber's pants and shouted, "Duck!"

Amber hit the ground, covering her head with her hands. Josh didn't hesitate. He pulled the trigger three times, each bullet hitting Grey. The bastard stumbled backward, gripping his stomach. Dark blood seeped through his shirt and jacket, soaking his hand. Judging by the amount and color of blood, he wouldn't survive.

Josh advanced on him. Grey turned back and cocked his pistol. A gunshot rang out from behind Josh, and he dropped to his knees. Grey's eyes widened, he stilled, and then collapsed onto the floor. He'd been hit. Blood seeped out from his leg, spreading down his thighs, staining his pants crimson.

Josh whirled around. Amber lay flat on her stomach, a smoking derringer in her hands, her gaze fixated on Grey. "So I missed his balls," she said, coming to her feet.

He pulled her into his arms, and her body trembled against him. "I'm so sorry you were involved in this nightmare," he told her. "I'm just glad you're all right."

She hugged him back. "Please go check on your brother, make sure he's okay."

Josh kissed her, and then tended to Wyatt. Thankfully, his brother had no more than a flesh wound. By the looks of it, the bullet went straight through his side. Another few inches toward his lungs, and he probably wouldn't have been so lucky.

"Aww, shit, this hurts," Wyatt complained, his face contorted with pain.

"Be still," Josh said, putting pressure on the wound. "We've got to stop the bleeding."

Wyatt groaned and bit down on his lower lip, gazing at Josh. "Grey's dead, right? It's finally over."

"Indeed, it is."

Amber joined them, kneeling beside Wyatt. She checked his wound. "I'm not a doctor, and I hate the sight of blood," she said. "But it really doesn't look too bad."

"You're of no help," Wyatt joked, wincing at the pain. Amber pulled the bottom of his shirt out from the band of his pants and pressed it over the wound. She placed Wyatt's hand on top. "Keep pressure on it."

"What, now you're suddenly a doctor?"

"Work with me here. I've seen this a bazillion times on TV."

"Glad you can joke as I lay here bleeding to death," he shot back with a slight attempt at a chuckle.

"Just trying to distract you," she teased. "And I don't think you're bleeding to death, so chillax."

Josh gave his brother a reassuring smile, and then went to examine Grey. Kneeling beside him, he rolled the body over and lifted his wrist, checking for a pulse. The guy was dead, all right. Josh pried the gun out of Grey's cold fingers.

Suddenly, the main doors swung open, and a breeze swept into the barn. Josh whirled around, Grey's gun in his hand. "Stay where you are," he commanded.

Earl stumbled through the doorway, wincing with each step. His arms were half raised. "Don't…shoot."

Emma walked in behind Earl, armed. She shoved him forward.

Josh lowered his gun. Well, damn if the women in his life didn't know how to take care of themselves.

Chapter Twenty-Seven

The barn door creaked open. Earl limped inside, his torn right pant leg soaked with blood. He raised his hands and winced with each gimpy step. Amber jumped to her feet, her senses still on full alert, and anxiety hiked sky-high to cruising altitude. She turned to Josh. He lowered the gun in his hand. *What*? Then she saw why.

Emma appeared from behind Earl, her gun pointed at the back of his head. For a petite woman, she shoved the creep forward with great strength. "Move, asshole," she commanded. "One wrong step, and I'll blow your damn head off. Do you hear me?"

Earl nodded, his gaze darting warily from Josh to Amber. He stopped, and pain twisted his face, deepening the lines around his eyes into rigid edges. Emma shoved him again. "Move it!"

Josh grabbed one of Earl's hands, twisted it behind him, and then shoved the outlaw onto the floor. He kneeled and pressed his other knee to Earl's back, preventing any attempt at getting up. "Tie him up," Josh said to whoever was listening. He glanced at Earl's bloodied leg. "It looks like you met with one of our little booby traps. Nice."

Amber picked up Josh's discarded bindings and handed them to him. He tied Earl's hands behind his back and then pushed his face into the hay. "You make a move or say one word, and you're dead. You got that?"

The only response was a nod.

"Emma...?" Wyatt called out.

Emma gasped. "Wyatt!" She ran to her husband, checked his wound, kissed his face, and then checked his wound again. Tugging at the hem of her skirt, she tore off a section, balled up the material, and placed it against his wound. "You'll be all right. It doesn't look too bad or bloody."

"Where's Wesley?"

Amber joined them and added, "Is Wesley all right?"

"Wesley's safe." Emma nodded and turned to Amber. "After you left to speak with Caroline, I snuck into town and left him with Anne and Mattie. Marshal Reed should be on his way any minute. I told him about your plan—"

"What plan?" Josh asked, joining them. His gaze volleying from her to Emma.

Amber slid her arms around his waist, basking in his sandalwood scent, tinged with the smell of hay, the outdoors, and a little sweat. "I had the dumb idea to have Caroline listen in town for any details on Grey's whereabouts so we would know when he'd head our way. That way, we could trap him."

"You put yourself and the rest of us in danger," Josh told her.

"I'm sorry, but I couldn't sit here and not do anything. I'm not good at that. Besides, I couldn't take the chance on losing another person in my life."

He squeezed her against him. "You're thinking of your mom and grandpa."

She nodded. "And...Caitlin. My...twin. She drowned when we were kids, two years after my mom and grandpa died. I couldn't save her…I watched her drown. That's why I had to try…"

"Oh, Christ, Amber. I didn't know."

Josh hugged her tight, and she clung to him. Amber never talked about her sister to anyone, outside of Emma and her therapist. But with all the crazy emotions zipping through her system, especially now that Wyatt was shot and Grey had bled to death, it just tumbled out. She had to admit, it felt good not to keep it all bottled up inside.

"That's a whole other nightmare I'll need to fill you in on," Amber told him.

"I'm a good listener, sweets," he assured her. "And I'm ready to listen whenever you're ready to share."

She nodded against him, clutching tighter.

"What's that sound?" Emma asked.

Amber pulled away from Josh. That something was the thundering of hooves galloping toward the barn. Judging by the vibration, the marshal must've brought an entire posse with him.

Outside, Marshal Reed shouted, and then seconds later, he, Doc Wilson, Caroline, and a handful of the newly deputized men from town rushed into the barn, all spreading out in different direction.

Doc Wilson went directly to Wyatt. He kneeled beside him and removed what looked like an ancient stethoscope from his medical bag. After checking Wyatt's heart and breathing, Doc announced, "You'll live, my friend."

"It sure doesn't feel like it," Wyatt grumbled. "I've got a fireball in my side."

Doc gave further inspection to the wound, pushing Wyatt onto one side, probably to check for an exit wound. He sat back and nodded. "As I thought, the bullet went right through. With a little medicine and a dash of some gentle tending to by your beautiful wife, I'd say you'll be feeling better in no time."

Caroline kneeled between Sam and Fergus, still in a drowsy state. She removed their gags and bindings, and then tended to Sam first. She lifted his eyelids, checked his pulse, and then turned to Fergus to examine him.

"What happened?" Fergus asked in a groggy voice, trying to sit up.

"Lie still." Caroline pressed a gentle a hand on his chest. "I discovered a bottle of chloroform missing from my exam room. I'm guessing it's that same bottle that Grey and his accomplices used on you and Sam. You gentlemen are lucky he didn't give you more, otherwise, you wouldn't be talking to me now. I assure you'll be fine but will experience some lingering effects. Judging by the looks of things, I'd say you two had quite a day."

Reed circled the barn, taking in Grey's body bathed in blood, Wyatt's bullet wound, and the current state of Sam and Fergus. "Will someone please explain what in tarnation happened here?"

"Earl and another lowlife, Bart, were on Grey's payroll," Josh replied.

Reed frowned. "Who's Bart?"

"If I had to guess," Amber began, "he's probably the creep that tried to knock me out in the cemetery."

Josh turned to her; his brows furrowed. "You didn't tell me about that."

"When was there time?" She turned back to Reed. "Marshal, you'll find a young man tied and blindfolded in the churchyard. The fool didn't know what hit him. He thought he was going to mess with some country girl. Well, I showed him what us city girls can do, thanks to my training with Master Tee."

"That's my girl," Josh said, and pulled her close to kiss her.

Reed chuckled. "Well, that explains it. One of the new deputies found a man right there in the middle of the cemetery, just as you described, rantin' and ravin' that someone attacked him." He turned to one of his deputies. "Find him and arrest him." He spared a glance in Grey's direction. "As for him…?"

"Hey, at least, I didn't shoot him in the back," Josh told him.

Reed nodded. "I never thought you were the type, my friend."

Josh draped his arm around Amber's shoulders. "But you'll be happy to know my beloved here got a bullet into him, too."

"Is that so?" Reed smiled at Amber. "You've got sand, Miss Amber. Sand, indeed."

Amber wasn't sure what that meant, but considering the marshal smiled when he said it, she assumed it was a compliment. "Thanks, Marshal. I'm just glad this whole nightmare is over."

Reed nodded. "Now you can all go back east without ever having to look over your shoulder again."

Amen to that.

Chapter Twenty-Eight

Two days later, after all the interviews with Reed and the judge, Amber and the Kincaids were finally able to put their nightmare with Grey to rest. He was gone for good, dead, never to return or take advantage of another unsuspecting homeowner or have anyone else killed again. It was the first time Amber had ever witnessed a cremation. All she wanted to do was watch the bastard burn for all the misery he had caused them and the town.

Amber, for one, was beyond ecstatic that they were finally ready to go back to their own time. She hated to admit it, but there was a teeny tiny part of her that would miss this place, this century…because it's where she met Josh. It wasn't enough to ever keep her or make her want to stay, though.

After one last walk around the paddock and perimeter of the property, and locking the beautiful, peaceful scenery into her memory, Amber strolled into the barn. Josh was there, standing near the back wall and staring at what would soon be the portal once it was activated.

She slipped her arms around his waist. "Are you impatient…or having regrets about leaving?"

He turned around and hugged her tight. "Impatient is more like it. I'm sure so much has changed since I've been gone. I miss my brother, James. Most importantly, I can't wait to get home and start our life together."

She leaned back to gaze into those green eyes she loved so much. "And why is that, cowboy?"

His smile reached his eyes, sending sparkling emeralds shining back at her. "Because before you, I thought I knew what I wanted. Even if the portal had worked, I could've stayed here forever. I would've been happy being a deputy and riding off into the proverbial sunset. But since you came into my life, things have changed. I've changed. My desires and my wants are different and have a new meaning…because of you. And now, I want to begin a life with you in our own time, in our own home. What we started here has brought us closer together. I can't imagine a single day without you."

He stepped back and handed her a small blue box. She cast him a questioning look but took it and removed the lid. An elegant sapphire ring set in yellow gold sat in a tuft of royal velvet. Her throat tightened. The ring was one of Emma's designs.

"It's beautiful," she gushed, tears burning her eyes.

"And it's yours, if you accept me." He removed the ring from the box and slipped it on her ring finger. It fit perfectly. "You're the best thing that's ever happened to me, Amber. And I want you with me forever and then some. Marry me?"

"Holy shit!" she cried, tears brimming in her eyes. "Really?"

"Really. How 'bout it?"

"Yes, yes, yesssss!" She threw her arms around his neck and kissed him. The world around her faded away, leaving only the two of them, and she squeezed him tight. Tears streamed down her cheeks. Love and joy overflowed in her heart. *This must be what Emma felt for*

Wyatt when she decided to return to the nineteenth century. Now, she got it. Totally. "I love you, Josh."

"I love you more."

She drew him in for another tongue-wielding kiss that ignited her body into a blazing inferno. What did she ever do to get so lucky? She would be kissing this man for the rest of her life…and she loved that thought.

"For cryin' out loud," Wyatt shouted from the doorway. "Would you two quit acting like a couple of horny teenagers for once?"

Amber broke into laughter. Wyatt stood framed by the large doorway, holding the leather trunk and grinning like a fool. His wife came up next to him with Wesley in her arms.

"We thought you'd be ready by now," Emma said, shielding Wesley's eyes from their PDA. Like he would know what that was at seven months old. "It's time to go!"

"But first, let's check out that gorgeous rock on Amber's left hand," Wyatt said, nudging his wife, like he didn't know a thing. He winked at Amber, walked over to her, and then pulled her in for a big brotherly bear hug. "Congratulations! Josh told me his plans the other day. Welcome to the family, sis."

After Wyatt's hug ended, Emma threw her arms around Amber's neck, and cried. "Finally, we'll officially be sisters! Forget the in-law crap."

Hugs went around, happy tears were shed, and then, all four of them faced each other, bracing themselves for their next big step.

The portal.

But no one moved.

Amber had been the last one to join them on their

time travel journey, and now that she was in love with Josh, looking back, she wouldn't have changed a thing. She risked her life traveling to an unknown time to save her best friend, but it was her best friend who had saved her. Amber had so much loss in her life, but she found love and life here with Josh all because of her quest to save Emma. And now they were about embark on their new life…together.

"So," Josh began at last, "if the tokens never worked like Malachi said, how do we go through?"

"Shouting his name seemed to work last time," Emma said, rolling her eyes. "I say, we try that first."

All four of them shouted Malachi's name over and over.

There was no response. No light. No shimmer. Nothing.

Then…

The ground rumbled. The barn wall shimmered with blue-white light. And that heavy metallic noise blasted so loud this time, Amber covered her ears.

When all sights and sounds ceased, Malachi appeared. He was wearing another tight-fitting suit, but this one was black. "Hello again," he said, and a hint of a smile teased his mouth.

"If I didn't know better," Amber said, "I'd say you're trying *not* to smile."

"Let me say, I am relieved that a potential threat has been eliminated," he told them. "And I am even more relieved that all our lives will go on as they should. If you are ready to return home, I would be happy to lead you there."

"It's about time," Emma grumbled, hugging Wesley close. He was leaning forward, reaching for Malachi.

The gizmo sewn into Malachi's armband turned into a crazy light show of twinkling lights and unusual beeps. He spread an arm wide toward what looked like a doorway. "Shall we?"

"Yes," Josh and Wyatt said at the same time.

"This way, then." Malachi turned, disappearing into the shimmering light.

Wyatt took Emma's hand and wrapped an arm around her waist, tucking her and Wesley close as they walked through the time doorway and back into their rightful time. In a blink, they too, had vanished.

"I guess it's our turn," Amber said, slipping her arms around Josh's waist. "There's no turning back, cowboy. Now that I've said yes, you're officially stuck with me."

"There's no one else I'd rather be stuck with, sweets," Josh told her. "You're my heart's desire."

Epilogue

Whisper Creek, Montana—Present Day

James propped his feet up on the porch railing and took another swig of beer. He surveyed his brother's empty property, his gaze automatically shifting to the garage at the side of the house. He thought of his family stuck in 1883. Had they given up on him? Did he ever cross their mind? As if on cue, a low rumble shook the ground. James jumped to his feet, his heart thundering in his chest. Call him crazy, but this felt a hell of a lot like the day Amber went through the portal. Could it be that she came back?

He descended the steps and walked over to the garage. The rumble grew louder and closer, and then it quickly subsided. A blue-white light flashed from around the gaps in the doors. He stopped in his tracks, a tightness wrapped around his chest. What if it wasn't Amber that had returned?

One of the garage doors slid open. Wiping his ice-cold palms on his back pockets, he swallowed, hoping to steady his pounding heart. One by one, his brothers and Emma, along with Amber, emerged from the garage.

This was the first time he'd seen Wyatt and Josh in nearly three years. They certainly looked like men from the 1880s garbed in linen shirts, weathered leather vests, and pants tucked into knee-high boots with spurs. And the women were clad in long skirts and high-neck blouses stylish in that era.

"Surprise!" Josh shouted, running toward him, arms wide. There was a deputy badge pinned to his vest. Deputy? He pulled James into a bear hug. "We're back!"

"I c-can't believe it," James replied, hugging his brother tight. "You're really here! Holy shit."

"We've missed you more than you know," Josh said, pushing out of James's arms. "We didn't mean to be gone for so long, big brother. I hope you can forgive us. It was out of our control. We'll fill you in on everything."

"Yeah, I'd say we have a lot to catch up on."

"That's an understatement," Wyatt added, shoving his way between them. "Come here, Jamesy," he said in a raspy voice, embracing him in a bear hug. It was the nickname Wyatt had given him when they were kids.

James stepped back and shoved a hand through his hair, shaking his head. His mind was a jumble of emotions. "I…shit, I've missed you both. When I felt the ground shake, I wasn't expecting…Hell, I don't know what I was expecting."

"Let me at this guy, will ya?" Amber squeezed herself between him and Wyatt and threw her arms around his waist. "You have no idea how good it is to see you and to be back in the real world." She laughed. "Mama sure does need a cocktail after that trip."

"I second that," Emma chimed in, joining them. "I'm sick of nineteenth century whiskey. How about a frozen margarita?"

"Excellent choice."

Emma hugged James with one arm, while her other held the most precious baby he had ever seen. "Uncle James, there's someone very important I'd like for you to meet. This is your nephew, Wesley."

Tears burned James's eyes; he blinked them away. He swept his nephew from her arms and held him high, spinning around and around. Wesley responded with baby drool and giggles that melted his heart. He had a nephew! Hell, he was going to spoil Wesley, and there'd be nothing Wyatt and Emma could do to prevent that. "He certainly looks like you, Emma," he told her. "Of course, he's gorgeous, but I see he's got Wyatt's blue eyes."

"What are you talking about?" Wyatt argued, chuckling, and draping his arm around Emma's shoulders. "He looks just like me."

"He has your eyes," Emma stated, planting a kiss on her husband's cheek. Wyatt swung her around, kissed her, and then planted her on the ground. "It's so good to be home!" she cried, wiping the tears away.

James agreed with that statement. It was good to be home…now that his family had returned safely.

"Hey, we know you've been watching the place all this time," Wyatt said, nudging him. "Technically, it's still mine and Emma's, but how about inviting us in? We could sure use a hot shower, cold beer, and some good conversation."

"A real shower!" Amber cried. "Yesssss! Shower first, margarita second! I hope James kept the bar stocked." She grabbed Emma's hand, and they dashed inside the house, laughing the entire way.

James settled Wesley on his hip, letting the baby play with his shirt collar. He wasn't the type of guy to get all emotional and weepy, but shit, his family was back, finally. And while he had a million questions he wanted to ask, he basked in this moment. The Kincaid brothers, side by side, were finally reunited.

His family was home. And God willing, they would stay together, and the damn time portal would cease to exist.

****

Whisper Creek, Late October 1883

Caroline tugged Winnie's reins, and the mare came to a stop outside the Kincaid's barn. Emma had left her beloved horse to her since they couldn't take her with them to New York City. While the house and property still looked the same as they did when her friends left last week, the atmosphere was…different. Empty. It was as if all the love and joy associated with Amber and Josh and Wyatt and Emma had vanished along with their presence.

"Howdy, Doc," Sam called from the porch with a wave. He descended the steps, tapping a letter in his hands. "Thanks for meeting me here."

"When I saw you in town earlier, you made it sound like I had no choice," she commented, dismounting. She tethered Winnie to the post and walked over to Sam. "What can I do for you?"

"Well," he said, a tinge of red staining his cheeks, "it's about this letter. It's for you."

He handed her a letter with her name written across the front. The unusual penmanship looked like Emma's. Her friend's handwriting was bubblier in nature with lots of circles and hearts, she'd know it anywhere. "Oh? What's all this about?"

"You'll see."

"Did you read this?"

His shoulders slumped. "Of course not, Doc. Miss Emma and Wyatt asked me to deliver it to you."

She broke the seal and read the letter. It was only a few sentences, but it got right to the point. Her hand flew to her chest. "Oh my!" she cried. "The house…Sam, they want me to stay here."

No one had ever been this generous before. She hadn't known Emma and Wyatt all that long; but in the short time, she'd come to know they were good, genuine people with kind hearts and always looking to help others.

"I know." He looked over her shoulder to glance at the letter, and then handed her a key. "They asked me to look after the place while they're gone. Wyatt thought maybe you'd want to stay here instead of living at the doc's place in town."

Wyatt and his brother treated her like she was their equal, not just a pretty face who wasn't squeamish at the sight of blood and assisted in medical procedures. If only all the doctors back in Boston would see her that way, too.

"Whatdya say, Doc?" Sam prodded. "Will you stay? I know it's a few miles from town and all. Maybe take some time to think about it."

"Yes, it is a few miles away, but I'd have my own place again." She missed her home in Boston. After her father had passed away, living there hadn't been the same. It's one of the reasons why she accepted Doc Wilson's plea to join his practice out here. That and he was a friend of her father's.

"I hope you stay," he added, shifting his hat from one hand to the other. "I miss having the Kincaids and Miss Amber nearby. It sure would be nice to have you for a neighbor."

She smiled. "Thank you, Sam. You'll be the first to

know. I'd like to take a look around now."

"Yes, ma'am." Sam nodded. "I'll have Fergus bring the wagon over for you to collect your things in town. That is, once you decide on staying. Wyatt and Emma left that at my place."

"Oh, I thought it would be here in the barn."

He scratched the back of his neck. "If I were you, I would keep out of the barn."

"And why is that?"

"Wyatt told me…he thinks it's haunted."

Caroline nearly laughed. "Haunted? Oh, that's just nonsense." Sam's face said otherwise. "Do…do you think it's haunted?"

"I can't rightly say, but I have seen a strange light coming from this direction." Even though no one else was around, he added in a conspiratorial whisper, "The day they left on the stage, a little while later, there was an odd…flash of light…and then it was gone. Saw it from my paddock." He nodded. "Could just be my imagination. In any case, Wyatt doesn't want us going in."

She spared the barn a glance. "I'll stay out of there, then. Thanks for the warning."

Sam donned his hat, walked over to his horse tethered to the post, and then swung himself into the saddle. "Even though Grey's long dead, I'd still lock the doors at night if I were you. And don't forget I'm down the road a spell. If you're in a bind, just stand on the hill out back and blow that whistle that Miss Emma keeps inside the back door. I'll hear it clear across the lake. Afternoon, Doc." He touched his hat before riding off.

Haunted, eh? Thankfully, she didn't believe in ghosts.

After waving farewell, she climbed the steps and unlocked the door. She walked inside and stopped. The atmosphere was different there, too. Everything about the place felt hollow, like it was waiting to be loved again. Maybe it was just her, and she missed her friends. Life as a doctor in a remote town certainly came with challenges. Acquiring and maintaining lifelong friendships was apparently one of them.

Emma did a thorough job of cleaning. The house was spotless, and a hint of lye soap and verbena lingered in the air. It was a bit chilly inside, even with the windows closed. Walking through the house, she came to one of the bedrooms at the end of the hall. If she decided to accept their offer and live there, she would choose that one for herself. The windows overlooked the back of the property. It was much better than staring out at Main Street.

Outside, Winnie neighed, jarring Caroline away from her musings. She hurried through the house and out to the porch. The horse was prancing, snorting, and tossing her head back. Looking around, she didn't see anything that could've spooked her. She reached for the reins, gently gliding a hand down the mare's neck. "Shh, girl. It's all right. What's got you so spooked? There's nothing to worry about."

An eerie sensation prickled at the back of her neck. She scanned her surroundings first, half expecting to see Emma or Amber. That was silly; they were two thousand miles away.

She walked toward the barn but stopped and sucked in a breath. A bright, blueish white light flashed from within, visible in the cracks surrounding the double doors. She knew that electric lights were being used in some bigger cities and had even seen some back East. However, this light was unlike anything she had ever seen before. Perhaps it was that same light Sam had mentioned.

A cold sensation quickly coiled around her neck, and she shrugged it away. Thrusting her hands on her hips, she glared at the doors before her. "Haunted," she scoffed, shaking her head. "That's such drivel. I'm a doctor. I know better than to believe such nonsense."

The doors were secured with a rope tied around the handles, warding off trespassers. She returned to the horse and grabbed a scalpel from her medical bag.

"There are no such things as ghosts," Caroline stated, firmly, quickly sawing through the rope.

When it severed, she pulled it off and tossed it to the ground. She reached out but hesitated before slowly pulling the doors open.

"Oh…my!"

A word about the author...

Heather Alexander began writing as a child, inspired by her mom who loved to write fiction and poetry. Putting pen to paper—or rather fingers to keyboard—she began writing in the genres she loves—romance and time travel. When she's not writing, Heather enjoys spending time with her family, sipping a good cup of tea while cozying up with a great book, and traveling.

http://booksbyha.com

Thank you for purchasing
this publication of The Wild Rose Press, Inc.

For questions or more information
contact us at
info@thewildrosepress.com.

The Wild Rose Press, Inc.
www.thewildrosepress.com